The Thief of Moments

T.R. Hull

ISBN: 979-8-9889853-2-7

Second edition 2023

To Linda

Evil is unspectacular and always human, and shares our bed and eats at our own table. **Herman Melville**

Chapter One

The new helper told the skinny girl that this is his first day working on the ward. I think he's nervous about being around people who have lost their minds. He approaches me as if I might bite him or do some other hideous thing. But I'm a peaceful man.

"He's big," the new helper says.

The skinny girl nods. "Yeah, he's a big boy."

"You sure it's okay?"

"Don't worry. Virgil's a sweetie."

The new helper runs the razor around my jaw like this is a race. I reach to grab his hand and direct it to a missed spot, but he jerks his arm away and gasps. So I have named him the nervous helper.

I'll spend another day rubbing chin stubble against my chest. My frustration used to get the better of me, and I'd yell at the workers, but I don't do that anymore. My yelling is gibberish to their ears since my stroke. At least, I think it was a stroke. I don't recall anyone actually calling it a stroke, but that's what it must have been. Whatever it was, it hit my head like a sledgehammer. The pain was incredible, as I recall. When I recall anything.

The nervous helper sets the razor on the counter and looks over his shoulder at the skinny girl.

She nods. "That looks fine."

The nervous helper pats me on the shoulder. "There you go, Virgil." His hand shakes.

I can't decide who's more relieved, him or me. He plops the razor back into the drawer and heads for the door. I stand and follow him into the hall.

The smell of oatmeal— the daily God of Morning in this place—mixes with the fecal smell that wafted down the corridor earlier. There's a musty rankness under the odor of eggs and oatmeal, as if the patients' bowels have gone the way of their brains and no longer turn out a healthy product. It's sort of a shit and piss odor like I used to find in my kids' rooms back when Joshua and Mia were babies. But that was a different smell—a healthy, living fragrance.

When I'm in the bathroom these days, I turn around and check before I flush. My stool looks healthy to me, and that's a comfort. At least I seem to be okay physically. But everyone here treats me like I've lost my mind. Maybe some of my brain went away when the pain hit my head, but most of me is here.

Losing your mind might be awful, but who knows? If your mind is gone, aren't you gone too? I mean, the part of you that counts? It's like a rock trying to think about how awful it is to be a rock down there in the earth's crust for eons. It doesn't make sense to me. Why should it necessarily be a problem? I'm no rock, even though I feel stuck way down underground sometimes, a long way from what I was.

Like he does every morning, gray guy blocks my path. He creeps along the hallway with fragile deliberation as if he's stepping onto a frozen pond. Each foot shuffles forward and stops to test the squares of beige tile like sections of thin ice. Finally, he clears the doorway, and I scoot around him and into the dayroom.

The television is tuned to the same unchanging blah, blah news channel. A steady wind of information pours out, but all that stuff about the world outside must be shooting across the room and through the windows. The wheelchair people fan out around the television in perfect alignment, like a perimeter of weathervanes.

Some of the wheelchair people stare into the light like they're soaking up at least some of that information. But most of the light bounces right off their pasty white foreheads and keeps traveling. Their intent stares used to fool me until I discovered you can park one of these guys facing a blank wall and see the same look on their face.

The wheelchair people are big oatmeal eaters. The kitchen people probably try to change the menu around, but the helpers mix just about anything that shows up on the trays with oatmeal, perhaps because it's easier to spoon it into the wheelchair people. You can't blame the helpers. They've probably arrived at this process through trial and error. And the wheelchair people don't seem to mind.

Over near the window, I sit with the table people where there's a view of the grass and lake beyond the building. Most of the table people still talk a little, but none of them say much. They aren't like the wheelchair people, who have almost all lost their minds. The table people are well on their way to losing their minds, though, so the conversation can be spotty most days.

Not that I'm doing any conversing myself. It took me a while to realize I wasn't making any sense when I talked. The words are okay in my head, and they sound fine to me when I speak, but I figured out that nobody was hearing what I heard. One of the table people, an old guy who's since passed on, said to me, "Son, you talk like you got a mouthful of marbles." Once in a while, I get the urge to say stuff, just not as often anymore.

Why is it that when you have one defect, people automatically assume you have all kinds of other problems? My hearing is perfect, but people talk loud to me like I'm deaf—loud and slow, with that deliberate enunciation they'd use when giving directions to a foreigner.

Over at the table, I sit in my usual spot facing the food cart and with my back to the big window. The trays come up by the kitchen. After a lot of fussing, they finally stopped trying to make me eat what they sent on my tray. Most mornings, the helper sets a bowl of oatmeal in front of me, maybe with a poached egg or a side of yogurt. The thought of choking scares me, although I don't usually have any trouble swallowing. Perhaps it's my imagination. Since the pain hit my head, it's harder to trust the information coming to me. For instance, I can piss all over myself and feel as dry as toast. It's hard to decide if that is a plus or a minus.

Gray guy makes it to the table and settles into the chair across from me. He lowers into the seat with all the care of a rodeo cowboy settling onto a bull. I don't know his name, and I don't know how long he's been on the ward. Maybe as long as me.

Names escape me most of the time. Oh, I can recognize people like my wife when she visits or my kids. I know gray guy is gray guy, and I don't mistake him for someone else. But most people flow through my life as nameless characters with recognized faces. If I ever knew the gray guy's name, it's long gone. Maybe I've been around gray guys for a long time or a day. It can feel like a long time or no time at all.

Sometimes I blink my eyes, and the scene outside the big window in the dayroom goes from winter to summer. The nearby lake goes from frozen and colorless to a deep warm blue. But no matter how many times I blink, the dayroom stays the same—the smells, the glowing television, the oatmeal, the eggs, and the row of wheelchairs.

Gray guy sits scrunched down in his chair with his elbows poking into his skinny thighs and his arms crossed. His shoulders slump inward, and his bone-thin body gets even narrower. He always wears a shapeless gray shirt and weathered ash-colored pants. Pale, big-knuckled hands stick out well beyond his shirt cuffs.

He must've had the same nervous helper shaving him this morning. His chin sprouts a scattered crop of white whiskers. Above his chin, his purple lips hang slack, and his cheeks sag as if his face muscles are frozen. Big knobby nose–something most old men wind up with eventually. Ears and noses must be like pumpkins or squash, getting their size in the last days of a life's seasons, winding up big and plump just when the rest of the body is closing down like a garden in October.

Gray guy has deep, rich, walnut-brown eyes. The kind of brown the pupils can disappear into, so you can't tell if they're little pinpoints or widened up to take over the whole center of the eye. His eyelids should be tired and drooping like the rest of his face, but his scraggly eyebrows pull them up into round, brown aggies instead of little half-moons. Maybe he's surprised to find himself safely planted in his seat. He must've caught me looking at him because he turns and looks across the table at me.

I don't see any surprises down there. Not at all. My look gets sucked down deeper into his eyes, and I start to get sort of panicky. Deep inside his eyes—way down at the bottom of those black pupils—I see terror so powerful the wind gets sucked right out of my lungs. I choke on a bite of egg and cough, and get so dizzy it bends me over. I don't want to look again, but I do. This time, his eyes turn away, and I can't see clearly down to the bottom of them. But I'm sure of what I saw that first time.

I stand and go out into the hallway by the nursing station. Most mornings, I sit in the chair closest to the desk. It's the best spot for watching people. But today, I sit out of the traffic in the chair by the storage closet. I want to think about what I've seen way down inside the gray guy's head.

There's plenty of agitation in the people on this ward, at least in the ones who arrive here still moving around. By the time they wind up in the wheelchairs, though, they're as quiet and worn down as a crowd of folks waiting for a bus at the end of a hard workday. But the walking, talking people come in hitting, cussing, crying, pacing, and generally raising hell, at least for a while. I did my share of raising hell when I got here, probably. Gray guy probably did his share too. Now he's given all that up; only he's not one of the wheelchair people yet.

I was in a nightclub one time when a fire broke out. People panicked, running for the exits and screaming—me included. They say time slows down in situations like that, and you can focus on the damnedest things. Like the fear on people's faces when they're scared witless. Gray guy had that kind of look in his eyes in the dayroom. Those of us in the nightclub eventually got out the door and away from the fire. When we were safe, our panic eased off to a giddy excitement. So as bad as it was, the gut-twisting fear didn't last long. I hope gray guy's fear is like that—maybe as bad as I thought, but blessedly short. What would it do to a person if that hung on for a while?

I blink a couple of times, and day turns to night. The light from the television still glows in the dayroom. Did I miss lunch and dinner? The helpers must've taken me to eat because I'm not hungry. I get up and walk down the empty hallway to the gray guy's room. The helpers are all in the dayroom in front of the television.

Gray guy is in bed, covered up to his neck, and awake. I kneel next to the bed and look down into his eyes again. Even in the dark, I can see way down deep, just like this morning. He's still stuck down there with the agony blazing away. His suffering isn't letting go. Not one bit.

I saw a horse break a leg once in a rodeo. That horse shied up and tried to walk around with the broken leg flopping from side to side until someone came and put the poor thing down. That horse never made a sound. Most people in the stands that day turned away and couldn't watch–me included. If I'd jumped out of my seat right then and gone down and looked in that horse's eye, would I have seen the suffering cooking away, trying to get out?

I stare at the gray guy, and he stares right back at me, and we stay that way for a time—is it two minutes? An hour? The agony down in there burns like a steady flame.

The dresser drawer next to the gray guy's bed is open. The drawer holds his socks—the thin, dark kind. I grab a pair and peel one away from the other, wad it up at the toe, and push it down into the gray guy's throat. His teeth are sitting in a glass on the nightstand, so he can't bite my finger. He thrashes around on the bed a little, but he's a little guy compared to me, so it doesn't take much effort to hold him still.

When I'm sure the sock is going to stay down in his throat, I reach and pinch his big bulby nose shut with my fingers. We stay like that for what seems like a long time. When I finally look down into his open eyes, the terror is gone, so I let go of his nose and pull the sock out of his mouth. Then I put the two socks together and back in the drawer, give the gray guy a little pat on his skinny thigh, and walk back to my room.

In the morning, I start to wonder if there are more people on the ward, like gray guy. I look into a lot of eyes. The wheelchair people are mostly gone already—gone down deep. Most of the table people have a lot of fire, just like that rodeo horse. I think I'll need to sort the people into two groups. Rocks and horses.

Chapter Two

Kester Grayson slid his key into the lock and opened the door. The janitor kneeling beside the door picked up a toolbox and stood.

"Careful when you put that key in your pocket, Doc. That graphite I just put in the lock'll get all over your pants."

"Thanks, Gordy." Kester pulled the key from the lock and wiped it against his palm. "How are things?"

"Can't complain," Gordy said. He stood and handed Kester a rag. "Somebody peed in the dayroom again. Probably that Mr. Fisher. But hey, it's great weather outside, and I won't let a little cleanup job ruin my mood."

"Great attitude, Gordy." Kester swiped the rag across his palm and handed it back to the janitor. "Thanks for this little clean-up of mine too." Kester walked in, closing the door behind him, and turned down the short hall toward the C Ward nursing station.

Urine, feces, bad breath, and the ubiquitous odor of sweat on old skin mixed with the aroma of food and the scent of medicine and cleaning supplies assaulted Kester's nose, just like it did every morning on the ward. He hardly noticed it anymore.

The television chattered in the dayroom across the central atrium. A wheelchair banged against a wall. The phone in the nursing station rang and sat ignored by the busy staff. Murmured conversations and sudden laughter from the aides and nurses drifted out of patient rooms.

Kester walked to the end of the curved desk separating the nursing station from the atrium. He reached across the top of a wooden half-door and pushed a hidden button to open the latch.

The middle-aged woman at the front desk stopped typing and glanced over her shoulder. "Make sure that gate latches," she said. She turned back to the typewriter. "Arlene Stoutmeyer got in here a little while ago and dumped the chart rack over before Lonny got her back out." She nodded toward an open door on the wall behind the desk. "There's donuts in the break room. I saved you a maple bar."

"Thanks, Jen," Kester said. He closed the gate and tested the latch. "A little sugar for energy and a cup of crappy coffee to get my heart started." Jen swung around in her chair while Kester walked toward the break room.

"Why you stay so skinny with all the junk you stick in your mouth is a mystery, Doc. What's your dinner routine at home, a crust of bread and a cup of water?"

"Nope," Kester said. He filled a Styrofoam coffee cup with the dregs from the pot near the breakroom door. "I eat all my meals out of the can, directly over the sink. I call it Doctor Grayson's Bachelor Physician's Diet. Out in hardback next month."

He brought his coffee and pastry and sat next to Jen.

"If you found another wife, maybe you'd get a little meat back on your bones," Jen said. "You're still a good catch for a skinny, balding, middle-aged guy. My daughter is still available, you know."

"Jessica is what—twenty-eight now?" Kester said. "I'm sure she's looking for a forty-one-year-old skinny, bald guy, Jen. What kind of mother are you?" He bit into the maple bar and checked the computer screen on the desk.

"I'm the kind of mother who's tired of having her twenty-eight-year-old daughter living at home," Jen said. "She needs a rich doctor, and I need a rich son-in-law. Give it some thought. I'm not too demanding these days."

"If she needs a rich doctor, she should look elsewhere. I'm one broke physician." He picked up the daily tally sheet and read through the patient reports. "Mr. Tyler died last night?"

"Yeah. Sometime on mid shift. Died in his sleep," Jen said, her attention still on the computer screen before her. "I'll have the death certificate for you by morning rounds. Doc Ronson was on call last night and came over to pronounce him."

"Okay." Kester finished the maple bar and stood. "I'll be in the back working on charts until rounds." He wiped his hands on his white coat. " Thanks for saving the maple bar for me." He tossed the coffee cup into the trash. "I'll give some consideration to your proposal about Jessica. I may need a mother-in-law with a basement I can live in."

Kester walked to the chart rack and found the medical record for Ivan Tyler. Then he sat in a chair beside the rack and leafed through the pages to the last entry. Doctor Ronson's distinctive, scrawling penmanship covered barely half the page.

Called to ward to see the patient after staff reported finding him unresponsive in bed. Patient was pale, with skin cool to the touch. No detectable pulse or respirations. Pupils fixed and dilated. 'No Code' order present in chart. Pronounced dead at 12:55 AM. Family and funeral home notified.

Kester flipped back to the admission note at the front of the chart. Three months before, Ivan Tyler arrived at Foothills, diagnosed with advanced Alzheimer's dementia and a history of deteriorating behavior over the past year. Kester ran his finger down the medical problem list. It mentioned several conditions, including mild coronary artery disease, chronic obstructive pulmonary disease, arthritis, and colon cancer in Mr. Tyler's early fifties. He'd turned seventy-five just three weeks before his death. Ivan, a carpenter for more than forty years, smoked cigarettes for most of his life, according to the social history in the chart.

An image of a young, tanned Ivan pounding nails on a half-framed roof, a Lucky Strike hanging from his lip, formed in Kester's mind. He put the chart back on the rack. *Maybe the smokes finally caught up with poor Ivan. Better that than a few more months on the ward.*

At nine o'clock, Kester finished his morning notes and left the nursing station for the conference room at the end of the hall. Aides moved about the ward, gathering breakfast trays and mopping floors. In the dayroom, patients sat in a half-circle of wheelchairs watching a morning news show or wandered back in to sit at the tables and wait for visitors or lunch.

Kester entered the conference room and sat in a swivel chair beside a long wooden table. The room's beige walls muffled the din out on the ward. Scrawled notes from a previous day's meeting covered a nearby whiteboard.

The conference room door opened, and a petite blonde in jeans, a sweater, and a white lab coat pushed the wheeled chart rack into the room. She hurried over to Kester and bent and kissed his cheek. Kester smiled and stroked her cheek.

"I just love doing that," she said. She planted a kiss on his lips, looked down at his white coat, and frowned. "You've got graphite all over your pocket again."

Kester studied a smear of gray along the top of his pocket. "Dammit!" he said. "I've done that twice this week!" He dabbed at the smear. "I think I'm losing it."

"Quick!" Clare said. "Tell me your bank account number and password before you get too senile." She sat next to him. "Seriously, Kes, I don't think you're losing it. You're in your prime." She grinned. " And I intend to spend a few more years using you up." She stole a glance at the door, then whispered. "We going to tell everyone we're seeing each other?"

"Sure." Kester wiped graphite from his hand onto the desk. " I think we should announce to all our friends and colleagues on C Ward that Doctor Grayson is officially boinking Head Nurse Clare Williams." He leaned forward, imitating her whisper. "Then the administration will move you to another ward and a different shift, and Doctor Grayson can boink Nurse Williams only on alternate Tuesdays when their schedules coincide. So you will be using me up at a very slow pace." He smiled.

"Okay," she said. "I see your point. But I won't wear a fake nose or a trench coat when I sneak over to your place after work. Well, maybe the trench coat—with nothing underneath." She leaned toward him again, a seductive smile on her face.

"We'll figure something out," Kester said, stroking her cheek. " But for now, we'd better keep them guessing."

The door opened a crack, and Nathan Mallory's chronically hoarse voice echoed down the hall. "Okay, okay! I'll quit stealing the toast! Wouldn't want Foothills State Hospital's budget blowing up over a couple pieces of bread and some jelly!"

Nathan pushed his butt against the door and backed into the room. A cup of coffee and a paper plate jostled precariously atop the notebook in his hand. He placed the notebook on the table, straddled one of the chairs, and slathered jelly across the toast.

"Mandy thinks her job as ward dietician is to keep an exact count of the jelly packets," He jabbed at the toast with the flimsy plastic knife. "Maybe she should spend some time finding a substitute for that crappy meatloaf they serve on Wednesdays." Half the toast disappeared into his mouth beneath a bushy mustache. He chewed, ignoring Kester and Clare until he'd swallowed.

"Okay, let's get going," Nathan said. "I'm not waiting for Mandy. Or the others." He stuffed the last bit of toast into his mouth and plucked a stack of index cards from his coat pocket.

A trim young woman in a lab coat entered and sat opposite Nathan. She slammed a pile of papers down. "Doctor Mallory, I really don't mind if you steal a little toast now and then, but every day isn't 'now and then.' Don't you have a kitchen at home?"

"Never use it," Nathan said. He wiped a smear of jelly from his chin with a paper napkin. "As they say, I wouldn't have one, but it came with the house." He tapped the cards against the tabletop. "Let's get going."

Kester slumped back in his chair and twirled his pen. Clare picked up the daily report sheet and read. "The census is twenty-eight today. Mr. Blanco is still in the emergency room being evaluated, and we had one death overnight—Mr. Tyler. We're keeping one bed open for a transfer from B Ward later today."

Mandy glanced up from her notes, a look of surprise on her face. "Ivan died? He seemed to be doing pretty well lately." She looked around the table. "What happened there?"

Nathan leaned forward across the table toward the dietician. "Death by meatloaf, Mandy."

Mandy threw her pen across the table at him. "You're such a jerk sometimes."

Kester leaned forward and placed his elbows on the table, avoiding the smear of graphite. "I reviewed Ivan's chart before rounds. He wasn't acute, but he had some chronic stuff that could've got him. Maybe a heart attack or stroke. He was a heavy smoker for years." He turned to Nathan. "Think we need a post?"

"Only if you want to stick his family with a bill for about eleven hundred bucks," Nathan said. "I don't think the administration will pop for a freebie. He was DNR anyway, wasn't he?"

"Yeah," Kester said. "He's been no-code for a few months." He twirled his pen and shrugged. "Maybe we should skip the autopsy. I know his family doesn't have that kind of money. And he's already at the funeral home."

Nathan shook his head and scribbled a note on one of the index cards. "Let's let it go. I don't think there's much to learn from one anyway. He was pretty typical Alzheimer's."

Nathan placed the stack of cards on the table. "Okay, let's move on."

Clare continued. "Margery Anderson had a good day. She ate well at dinner. A large bowel movement later, and slept. Frank Ballinger was off the ward with his family and, in the afternoon, saw the podiatrist and was a little sundowny in the evening but slept through the night. Mr. Brondos is still having some big episodes of agitation. He took a swing at Roger in the afternoon, and they had a heck of a time getting him to stay in the dayroom during dinner." She turned to Nathan. "Staff would like you to consider upping his meds."

"I'll look at his chart after rounds," Nathan said. He removed a card from the pile before him and penned a note.

Clare worked through the alphabet of patients. Kester sat with his eyes closed, half-listening while he twirled his pen. Most of the people on the list were well-known to the staff at the table. The ward was the destination—often the final destination—for dementia patients too challenging to handle in traditional nursing homes. Most were in the late stages of their dementia. Once admitted, few patients ever left the ward. Some stayed on the ward for months or even years. But death came for one patient or another at least weekly, keeping turnover high.

Clare finished her report. "Virgil Washington ate all three meals yesterday but slept by the nursing station most of the afternoon, so he was restless on mid shift. Walking the halls a lot. Doug, the new aide, said Virgil slapped his hand yesterday morning when he was shaving him. But most of the time, he's not a problem."

She tucked the report sheet in her pocket. "And that's it Doctor Mallory, you have a meeting with Mr. Jensen's wife and daughter at ten and Kes—uh, Doctor Grayson, you have the transfer patient from A Ward to see after lunch."

Kester stood and stretched. He turned toward the dietician. "I don't know. Maybe the meatloaf did Ivan in after all. You poisoning the patients, Mandy?"

Mandy grabbed her papers and headed for the door. "You guys are such idiots."

Kester followed her out. In the hall, Virgil Washington sat in his usual place by the nursing station. His broad shoulders and solid arms looked like they belonged to a football player. A four-year all-conference guard for the University of Colorado, Virgil spent the next thirty years sitting at a desk with little exercise. Even with the extra pounds and sagging gut, his body retained some of its earlier bulk and power. Virgil's affliction became apparent only when he opened his eyes and tried to speak.

Chapter Three

I think I was a classy dresser at one time, but now I wear the same clothes every day. My gut swells out in front of me like a tumor, with white slip-on tennis shoes peeking out underneath. I was in good shape once, with a board-flat stomach. And I remember crisp, white dress shirts, high-end slacks, and a black leather belt. And soft, polished leather shoes. Now, that gut pushes against a black and gold sweatshirt with a few dabs of dried egg sticking to it.

This place is noisy, especially during the day. I don't have much trouble sleeping anywhere. Sometimes I wake up if someone slams the nursing station gate too hard, or if a worker laughs right next to me, or calls out across the desk.

And when the screamer gets going. She's across the hall from me right now—in the washroom—getting cleaned up. The door is propped open, and the white and green tile shows through the steam. A shower curtain divides the washroom in two. The screamer's scrawny chicken feet and the bottom of her wheelchair are visible under the curtain. Her feet and the wheels drip water and suds onto the tile floor. The screamer tugs her feet up and curls her toes like she's pulling away from hot metal. And each time her feet go up, she screams.

The sound isn't what I'd call a "blood-curdling" scream. I never knew what that meant until I heard a mountain lion call out one night up in Wyoming. That scream made the hair on my neck stand up. The screamer is sort of screaming in slow motion. It starts low, builds up louder and higher, then holds steady for a while before it fades down. Like I said, not blood-curdling, but she can keep at it night and day, like a marathon runner.

The curtain swishes on its ceiling track, scrunches up against the wall, and out rolls the screamer in her wheelchair. A couple of damp white towels cover her from neck to knees. Her white hair sticks to her skull like wet toilet paper.

Dickweed's drying the screamer with a third towel. He attacks her hair as if he's slapping at bees, pushing her head from side to side. The screamer pulls her feet up and away from the floor and starts another round of wailing.

I've named dickweed in honor of Leonard, my brother. That isn't a made-up name—Leonard. That is my brother's real name. I remember some names. Mostly people close to me sometime in my life.

Leonard had a knack for smelling out jerks and assholes. He'd give them interesting names—names like fuck-face, fecal head, or dickweed. Leonard would've taken one look at the dickweed over there roughing up the screamer and said, "That dickweed ain't worth a pinch of shit." And Leonard would've been right. Dickweed looks ordinary enough. Late twenties, maybe. A little on the tall side, a little on the heavy side, and a little on the pale side, but not someone you'd focus on in a crowd. But Leonard would've seen past all that, down to dickweed's rotten little core.

The screamer lifts a skeletal, white claw from under the towels and bats dickweed's hand away from her head. He checks to see if anybody's watching, then thumps her with a knuckle behind her right ear. She grabs her ear while he scoots her out of the washroom and down the hall. Her scream fades off into the general hum of the ward.

I've tried to make sense of this whole rock and horse thing since I helped gray guy. The rocks don't make me ponder too much. Once you hit rock level, I suppose you're ninety percent out of here anyway. Have those folks already passed on, and their bodies are just a little slow to catch up? They say you see that light and tunnel when you're dying and then run into a bunch of people you were close to in your life—people who passed on before you. There was a sense of that light and tunnel when the pain hit my head. Maybe all the rocks have already gone through that.

There are a few lucky folks here stuck in some middle place. They aren't wild and scared, and they haven't turned into rocks. They're more like—misinformed. Travel guy was like that. He thought he was on a cruise ship, and the helpers were crew members. Travel guy always had a dopey smile and acted as if he was having a lovely time. How he mistook the food for cruise ship cuisine is a mystery. He got transferred out of here, so I don't know if his mind still has him somewhere down in the Caribbean.

The horses, though, are all about suffering. I used to have dreams where I'd be traveling somewhere, and things would go from normal to spooky and get darker, and more forbidding, and finally terrifying. And I had no control, no matter what I tried in my dream. I think the horses are on that kind of journey. They're not traveling down a tunnel toward some light, and definitely not on a cruise ship.

The helpers here are good folks—most of them. At least they mean well and probably have a fair amount of pity for those of us in here. But how must all this feel to the horses? They have no idea what's happening.

One day, you wake up in a strange place that's nothing like your home. It doesn't matter how many pretty pictures they hang on the walls or how bright and cheerful they try to make the rooms; you're in a place with all the charm of a bus station. You lie down on a single bed—maybe with some strange man or woman muttering in the bed across the room. Maybe for fifty years, you rested next to a spouse each night, and now you share a room with some stranger. You've spent a lifetime sitting down to breakfast at your own table in your own kitchen, and now you eat in a big room full of half-people, and you stare out at some damn lake and try not to hear the moaning and coughing and forlorn muttering all around you.

When I was drafted and went off to boot camp right out of high school, I remember how scary it was even to go to the bathroom or shower. But I got over that. The horses here don't get over it, at least not until they dwindle away to rocks. But while they're still horses, someone like dickweed runs them into a room and sprays water all over them every couple of days, and it's bewildering and terrifying. Every time.

Dickweed makes it a hundred times worse. Popping the screamer behind the ear is nothing compared to what he does to other folks in this place. I've seen it. Another thing that happens after you get here is that people don't notice you as much, or they act like you're far away. Maybe that's why they talk loud. Stay quiet, and you blend right into the background. It's like being invisible. So I get to see a lot of things, like how dickweed treats the people he's supposed to take care of.

I've seen him steal things out of people's rooms. Not big things. Nobody in here has anything of much value. Just little things, like clothes. He steals a lot of food. Maybe that's why he needs to lose a few pounds. The other day, he snatched some ice cream right off the tray before he set it down in front of one lady. The nurses are supposed to give out pills from a little cart and mark down what they give. But sometimes dickweed will offer to take the pills to a patient but slips them into his pocket when he thinks nobody is watching.

Dickweed wheels his next victim into the washroom. The shower curtain hisses across to block him from view. I leave my chair and walk down the hall, away from the washroom and the nursing station.

It's not hard to tell where the screamer is. I follow her siren wail and find her sitting by the window at the end of the hallway. She's tucked back into a little alcove, away from the activity and noise. Sunlight cascades over her. She's slumped down low in her chair, with her butt off to the side. Her shoulders are narrowed down like gray guy's used to be, except she's even thinner across than he was.

Dickweed has tucked her arms under the wheelchair tray, pinning her elbows against her thighs. Her body is tiny, and the tray has her squeezed together into an even smaller, narrower space. She's wearing cotton sweats, sort of like mine.

I turn her wheelchair away from the window and study her face. Her head perches above her shoulders, thin and delicate as an eggshell. She has a pinched, pained expression, with little spidery red lines of blood vessels on her cheeks and throbby blue veins at her temples.

Even though her eyes sit in deep, ash-colored sockets, they still shine as blue and clear as glacier ice. But under the ice, that agonizing flame blazes, just like it did with gray guy. The screamer goes silent. Her eyebrows arch upward as if she's just seen someone she recognizes.

I turn her wheelchair back to face the window. The hum of the ward continues, but it's quiet here at the end of the hall.

I kneel behind the wheelchair, and we watch the clouds for a few minutes. My arms encircle her chest until my fingers meet and clasp. Just a little squeeze and the back of her wheelchair sucks up against my gut. Her heart thumps against my left wrist, and her chest is so thin. I squeeze some more, and the air whooshes from her mouth in a soft moan. The hard tile floor sets my knees to aching, so I have to squirm around a little, but otherwise, we stay quiet and unmoving.

We stay like that for a few minutes until the thump of her heart against my arm finally stops. I stand and move around until I'm between her and the window. Her eyes are open. Sunlight sparkles on her pupils. But the fire down deep is gone. I leave her there, staring at the light, and head back to the dayroom for lunch.

Chapter Four

Kester turned into the parking lot, the car rolling to a stop with a squeal of worn brake pads. Clare fumbled with her seatbelt.

"Good Lord, Kes," she said. "Why don't you get rid of this thing?"

"Gotta drive it until the wheels fall off, babe," Kester said. "You thinking maybe you should look for a rich cardiologist?"

"They're too stuffy." She checked the parking lot, leaned across the console, and kissed him on the cheek. "You're poor but fun."

Kester touched her cheek. "Are you worried someone won't buy our carpool story?"

Clare blushed. Her smile brought out small wrinkles around her blue eyes. She turned and rechecked the parking lot.

"You know, they won't buy our story forever. Somebody'll figure it out or see us together in town," she said.

"Yeah, I know," Kester said. "I'll sort of ease into the subject with Reggie and see what he thinks."

"Thanks, hon." Clare opened the door and stepped out of the car.

Kester raised the handle on his side and slammed his shoulder against the door. It popped open with a loud groan. He stepped out and slammed the door twice before it latched. *One more year,* he thought. *If it will just last one more year.* He patted the faded metal hood.

Foothills State Hospital sat on a gentle slope along the east side of a valley. The green hills to the west of the buildings lapped up against the taller, dark-blue mountains beyond. The brick-and-sandstone administration building faced east, with five low-slung ward buildings radiating westward like a half-set sun.

Dixon Lake filled the bottom of the little valley below the hills. Farther west, the three dams holding back Horsetooth Reservoir broke up the line of hills stretching north and south.

The psychiatric hospital, originally built to hold over five hundred patients, now housed less than half that many. All general psychiatric patients were now sent to other places. These days, Foothills admitted only geriatric cases with advanced dementia or psychiatric problems too severe for traditional nursing homes.

Kester arrived at Foothills three years ago after a brief and unsatisfying career in family practice and a semi-brief and unsuccessful marriage. Foothills was not his first choice, but he loved the location. Initially isolated and rural, now the hospital sat tight up against the city limits of Fort Collins. His mother, his brother, and many of his childhood friends lived close by. And now there was Clare.

It was a short walk from the parking lot to the administration building entrance.

"See you after the M and M," he said, squeezing Clare's hand. Kester swung open the door of the Admin building and entered. At the end of the tiled hallway, he turned and entered a stately, wood-trimmed conference room. In the center of the room, two men sat at a large wooden table.

One of the men glanced up and smiled. "Ah, Doctor Grayson!" he said. "I knew it was you by the banshee wail of your worn brake pads."

Kester sat in one of the oversized wooden chairs. "At least it's paid for. How much do you still owe on the Mercedes, Mikey?"

Mike Flores raised his hands in surrender. "Touché'."

The white-haired man beside Mike removed his glasses and closed the chart on the table before him. "Congratulations, Kes. It looks like you didn't kill too many of our patients this month." Reggie Wilson was twenty years older than Kester and Mike and was by far the most imposing figure in the room at two hundred and forty pounds. He'd been at Foothills for twenty-five years, serving as medical director for fifteen years.

Kester grinned. "Morning, Reg."

A plump, dark-haired woman entered, sat next to Kester, and placed a yellow legal pad on the table.

"Take good notes, Janet, Kester said. " You know how forgetful the boss can be."

Janet ignored him and turned to Reggie. "Doctor Martin won't be here today. He's ill".

"Okay," Reggie said. "Let's get this Morbidity and Mortality meeting going." He opened the top chart on the stack before him and read the cover sheet.

"First case—Ivan Tyler, age seventy-five. Died on C Ward on June 16th. End-stage Alzheimer's, some COPD, an old colon adenocarcinoma, and some coronary artery disease. Chad Ronson pronounced him on night shift. No acute illness at the time. Was a no-code. No autopsy."

Reggie lowered the chart and peered over his glasses at Doctor Flores. "What the hell, Mike? Don't we post anybody anymore?"

"Hey, talk to CDHS the next time you go to Denver," Mike said. He leaned back in his chair. "If they don't meet the criteria for unusual circumstances, the state says the family's got to pay. Not many relatives want to fork out a thousand bucks to find out Grandpa died of old age."

"We used to autopsy at least fifty percent of our patients years ago," Reggie said. He turned toward the secretary. "We're getting old, Janet." He shook his balding head from side to side. "And when we finally die on the job, the damn state probably won't even investigate unless we're sprawled out in the parking lot with tire tracks across our asses."

Janet smiled and continued writing.

Kester sat forward. "Ivan was only here for a few months, but he was deteriorating quickly," he said. "He was found in bed with no signs of distress. Maybe a stroke or MI, or maybe aspiration. He needed more and more meds."

They discussed Ivan's medications for several minutes, and then Reggie turned to Doctor Flores. "Any further thoughts, Mike?"

"Nope."

Reggie turned to Kester. "You satisfied, Kes?" Kester nodded.

Reggie set the chart to the side and picked up the next one. "Marion Pettigrew, eighty-three. Died on C Ward on June 19th." He picked up another piece of paper. "And on her, at least, we have an autopsy report. Cause of death: probable respiratory arrest."

Kester pulled a sheet of paper from his pocket and placed it on the table. "Could be a problem with this one," he said. "This is an incident report from Marion's ward. She was found dead in the hallway after a shower. The activity tray on her wheelchair was snugged up tight, and her arms were trapped under the tray. It didn't look at the time like the tray was tight enough to cut off her chest expansion. But I don't have any good explanation for her cause of death."

He slid the paper across to Mike. "She was pretty frail, and we were watching her med dosages, but she was getting more agitated and vocal. In fact, she screamed most of the time, so it's hard for me to believe she died from over-sedation."

Mike scanned the report. "I talked to Pettigrew's daughter. She's aware of the tray incident. This autopsy finding will only upset her more."

Reggie tapped his pen against the chart and turned to Kester. "Kes, I'd like you to take another look at this and give us more detail." He pointed his pen at the secretary. "Janet? Let's schedule a short M and M for next Tuesday to discuss this again."

The committee reviewed two more deaths, both of them due to pneumonia, and both expected. Finally, Reggie adjourned the meeting.

Kester waited until Mike and Janet left the room. "Got a second?" he said. Reggie looked over his glasses. "Sure."

Kester cleared his throat. "How aggressive is state policy regarding employees working with a spouse or significant other?"

"Well," Reggie said, "if you're asking if your little deal with Clare Williams will get your butt transferred, it all depends."

"So you know about this?" Kester said.

"Sure." Reggie laughed and leaned back in his chair. "I heard it from Diane at the switchboard, right before I heard it from Gordy in Housekeeping, and right after it was the general topic of conversation in the lunchroom last week. Ain't no secrets around here, slick." He winked at Kester and stood.

"What do you mean by 'it depends'?" Kester asked.

Reggie picked up the stack of charts and started for the door. "It depends on what I decide to do about it."

Chapter Five

Lloyd Simpson leered as Clare walked toward the nursing station. His eyes traced the faint panty line visible through her white slacks and the curve of her buttocks.

A little old, but I'd do her. He pressed his groin harder into the back of the wheelchair and pushed it down the hall. The woman in the chair hunched forward, frowned, and sat back against the pressure. Lloyd laughed.

Muscular and trim in his teens, Lloyd now carried an extra forty pounds, mostly around his middle. Although approaching thirty, he'd never moved beyond a gawky, self-conscious social ineptness. A wispy mustache struggled for survival above his chapped lips, and pimples flourished on his pale, full cheeks. His eyes, a nondescript brown, nestled deep in their sockets beneath thick lids.

Thickness defined him, from his blocky frame to his heavy thighs and leaden thoughts. A lustrous growth of thick, black hair swept back across his scalp. Even this one good feature suffered from a thinning across the top of his head.

Uniforms hadn't been required at Foothills for years, but Lloyd wore his own uniform daily—black Converse tennis shoes, tight jeans around his broad thighs, a red t-shirt stretched across his protruding belly, and a white lab coat. He claimed he wore the coat to avoid getting crap and drool on his clothes. His co-workers smirked behind his back, amused by his transparent vanity.

He pushed the wheelchair into the dayroom and returned to the nursing station. The ward door opened, and Kester Grayson slipped through and locked it.

"Lloyd. Got a minute?"

"Uh, sure, Doc."

Lloyd followed Kester down the hall into the empty break room. Kester threw the incident report on the table. "What happened on this deal with Pettigrew?"

Lloyd stood in the doorway and crossed his arms. His head slumped forward. He stared at the tiled floor. One hip tilted to the side and came to rest against the doorframe. A frown turned the corners of his mustache downward.

"They said I trapped her arms under the tray, and it cut off her air." He looked up for a second and then back down again. "But I didn't do it. She was always flailing around like a fuckin' windmill."

His eyes remained riveted on the tiled floor. "Maybe she got her arms down under the tray and got 'em stuck." One shoulder rose in a shrug. "Some of these people do a lot of weird shit."

"Nobody's saying you're responsible for Marion's death, Lloyd." Kester tapped the incident report. "But her arms were trapped, and you were the last to see her. We got the autopsy report today. She died because she couldn't breathe." He paused. "And she had a little bit of bruising along her ribs."

"Like I said, she was always flailing around." Lloyd shrugged again. "Maybe she banged her ribs against the arms of her wheelchair when I was washing her."

"Did you notice any bruising while you bathed her?"

"No." Lloyd cleared his throat. *Should've said 'yes'.*

"So," Kester said, "the bruising must've happened after her shower."

"I guess so, Doc. All I know is she was screaming her head off the whole time. I parked her down the hall because of the screaming. Nothin' wrong with her then. She was fine. Just screaming, like she always did."

Kester nodded. "Yeah, she could get going sometimes. I know that must get on your nerves—listening to that all day long. I know it does me." He shook his head. "But that's no reason to abuse someone, of course."

The sounds of the ward came in through the doorway. Neither man spoke. Lloyd fidgeted, his face wrinkled with anger or maybe with distress.

"Okay." Kester folded the incident report and stuck it in his pocket. "I just wanted to see if you had any information that might help prevent this sort of thing in the future."

That's a crock of shit. Lloyd's face remained passive. *You want to burn my ass.*

"No problem, Doc," Lloyd said. He smiled. "Sorry I couldn't be more help."

Kester gave the young man a tight-lipped smile and left the break room. Lloyd collapsed onto the couch next to the coffee stand, ran his hand through his hair, stared at the wall, and thought about old lady Pettigrew in the washroom.

He'd rubbed soap over her shrunken, wrinkled breasts and rib cage. Even now, it brought on a little rush of excitement. There'd been no bruises on her pale skin. As for slapping the old lady on the head, no big deal. They thrashed around and screamed even louder if you didn't pin their arms under the tray. The hospital didn't allow restraints, but assholes like Grayson never dealt with all the shit Lloyd endured every day.

He sagged lower on the couch and fiddled with a button on his coat. "Fuckin' doctors." They were great at prancing around giving out orders, like some kind of fucking royalty. And then the underlings were supposed to deal with all the bullshit. Let that fucking Grayson wash a few wrinkled bodies and change a few shitty diapers, shovel food into an endless line of toothless pieholes, and see how damn easy he thought it was.

Clare entered the break room. "Lloyd, Viola Larson needs changing and put down for a nap."

Lloyd's gaze settled on Clare's slender waist and the curve of her hips. "Sure," he said. He stood and slouched toward the door.

In Viola's room, Lloyd paused and listened to the hum of the ward. No sound of footsteps or voices nearby. He closed the door and turned back to Viola. She sprawled in the chair, plump, and drowsy, with her arms draped slack across the armrests. He unbuckled the belt holding her to the chair and bent to slide his hands under her shoulders and across her back. His hands clasped, and he hoisted her up and pivoted to deposit her onto the bed. She gave a faint grunt and fell sideways onto the pillow.

Lloyd squatted, pulled her heavy legs onto the bed, and glanced at the door. Still no nearby sound. Viola grunted again as Lloyd unzipped his pants and guided her hand inside. He thrust forward, jerking her hand back and forth. Within seconds his body shuddered. His eyes shut tight and then opened as his body relaxed. Viola's hand dropped back onto the bed. Lloyd zipped up his pants and thought about the curve of Clare's hips.

Chapter Six

Looks are deceiving. I sit on the ward every day and observe the truth of this. Invisible, sitting here next to the nursing station, I discover hidden aspects of people. Stuff they don't want others to see. Sometimes it's a simple thing like Doctor K and the cute nurse not wanting anyone to see how much they care for each other. They stand close but stiff, their eyes casting around to see if anyone notices their little touches and smiles. Or how the chubby nurse sneaks back to the break room and comes out with her cheeks bulging and her mouth chewing. She peeks over the top of the counter to see if anyone might be looking, but her eyes pass right through me. Or how dickweed licks his lips and stares at all the women—from the skinny girl to the cute nurse and even the chubby nurse—when he thinks he won't get caught.

Once, when the staff was meeting about me, someone said this place is a "long-term care facility." Like I said before, I don't handle time too well, so I don't know how long-term they're talking about. But I know that thing about "care" is deceiving.

When my kids were small, they each won a goldfish at a school fair. We brought the fish home in little plastic bags full of water and put them in one of those round fishbowls with some colored rocks in the bottom and filled the bowls up with fresh water.

Joshua's fish died right off. Maureen found the thing floating on top of the water one day, and we scooped it up and buried it in the yard behind the fence. Mia's fish held on, and it was too big for the little round bowl after a while. We bought a bigger tank with a pump and filter, and Mia fed the fish and cleaned the filter daily. The fish grew bigger, and Mia began to neglect it after a couple of years. I'd walk by her room and find the fish almost lost in the murky water. So I started cleaning the tank—hauling it out to the yard, hosing off the slimy gravel, and scrubbing the glass clean. I'd stick the fish in the old round fish bowl while I cleaned the big tank and then put him back into it after filling it with water. I did this for about a year.

That fish grew bigger and uglier. There was some kind of white fungus on its tail. Its eyes got big and bulgy. And it got rounder and rounder. It didn't even swim around in the tank much anymore and spent most of its time hanging motionless in one spot.

One day, when Mia was away at camp, I found the tank filthy again. So I netted the fish and began to lift the tank off the dresser to take it outside. I looked at the fish drifting motionless—all bloated and ugly and a far cry from the little goldfish Mia carried home from the fair.

I was tired of taking care of it, so I went to the kitchen, got some paper towels, and returned to Mia's room. The fish barely fit in the little net anymore. I lifted it out of the bowl, laid it on the paper towels and wrapped it up, and left it there on the dresser for about half an hour while I went out and cleaned the fish tank. Then I slipped the fish back into the clear, fresh water.

It floated with its swollen belly sticking up above the surface. Mia would return from camp later that afternoon and find the fish floating. I imagined we would decide it died of old age and bury it in the yard.

While the fish floated motionless, I went on to other chores. Two hours later, as I passed Mia's room, the fish hung in its usual spot in the tank. Its gills moved as it breathed, and its bulgy eyes were clear and alive. I don't know how it survived all that time wrapped in paper towels, but life can be pretty tenacious sometimes.

I scooped the fish up in my hand and carried it to the garage. Then I put him in a plastic bag, laid the bag on my workbench, and smacked him with the flat side of an axe. Something inside the round, ugly body popped, and his head busted open. There was no way I could put him back in the tank looking like that. So I threw him and the plastic bag into the trashcan.

When Mia came home that night, I told her I'd found the fish floating dead in the tank and had flushed him down the toilet. She took it well, but I felt terrible about what I'd done. But I just couldn't take care of it anymore.

I think the fish was partly responsible, though. He grew ugly and old, and worthless. I'm not saying it's right to feel like I did, but it isn't all that unusual. That's why I say looks are deceiving. They take care of us in this place, but time has scraped away most of what we were, and all of us on this ward hang suspended in a murky place, all of us as old and ugly and as worthless as Mia's fish. These people feeding us, dressing us, and changing our pants can talk all they want about how much they care, but I bet sometimes they'd like to stick us in a plastic bag, lay us down, and give us a good whack with the flat side of an axe.

The picture lady is over by the window in the dayroom. She's showing picture cards to one of the new people. I haven't looked into the new patient's eyes, but he must still be one of the horses. He looks scared. I see Doctor K watching him, too, from the hallway. Other than his deal with the cute nurse, I think Doctor K stays the same whether people are watching him or not. He looks out at the folks in the dayroom and smiles. It's a sad smile, but it doesn't look like he wants to start whacking them with an axe.

The picture lady keeps holding up her cards and mouthing some words to the new patient. She showed me the picture cards a few times, and I knew everything on them, but there was no way I could speak up and tell her what I was looking at. She worked and worked at that but gave up in the end. I don't think she wants to whack me or whack anyone else. But I can tell when she gets frustrated because her mouth shrivels up into a tight little circle. She's doing that now.

Doctor K turns and heads down the hall. I call him Doctor K because his name begins with that letter. I just can't remember the whole name. Something different—not Kevin or Keith. He's getting skinnier lately, and I don't know if he's happy.

Dickweed stands beside me and watches Doctor K disappear into the conference room. A smile spreads across Dickweed's pimply face, but I don't think it's a happy smile.

Chapter Seven

Kester glanced into the dayroom. The staff speech therapist, Katie Lattimer, sat by the window with one of the newer patients. The old man's eyes followed the movement of the therapist's lips and chin and then slipped to the side to take in the room. Then he turned back and fixed her with a stunned expression. Katie pointed to the card in her hand and said something. The man glanced down at the card and back at Katie. His mouth hung loose with bewilderment. Katie pointed to the card again, the old man glanced at it again, and the cycle repeated.

The usual line of wheelchairs surrounds the television. Eight chairs in all. Eight faces turned upward with closed eyes and slack jaws. Each body is clothed in nondescript shirts and trousers or dresses. Slippers or tennis shoes cover every foot. Hospital policy said all residents should be up and dressed during the day unless the doctors ordered bed rest. Except for brief sessions with counselors or therapists, or doctors and occasional diaper changes, the wheelchair-bound patients were deposited before the television, where they stayed throughout the day. They wore their street clothes as if they might rise from their chairs any minute and hurry away to their former lives. They were fed three times a day. They were changed when necessary and washed every second day. The staff undressed them, fitted them with hospital gowns, and tucked them into bed each night.

Kester monitored their medicines and treated their colds, constipation, rashes and agitation, frequent bladder infections, pneumonia, and occasional bedsores. He guessed about the causes of their discomfort. Rarely did he have an opportunity to question a patient about what troubled them. He relied on subtle cues, intuition, and the reports of the staff. Patients with pain that would leave a strong man crawling and gasping sat stone quiet sometimes. Even a broken bone or a ruptured appendix might give no sign except a vague fussiness. Maybe their pain stayed muted inside them, like an annoying sound or a hunger pang. Perhaps they didn't suffer like ordinary folk.

If his patients often remained mute and enigmatic, the same couldn't be said for their families. Spouses, sons, and daughters weren't spared their share of suffering. But unlike Kester's patients, family members were seldom silent. Kester turned down the hall for his meeting with Marion Pettigrew's daughter.

Amanda Pettigrew was tiny and frail, like her mother. Her mouth held a permanent frown from years of worry. Her pale forehead pinched in parallel furrows of concern beneath a frame of thin, gray-blond hair. She leaned across the table in the C Ward conference room and spoke in a low, accusing tone.

"It's not right—those bruises on Mother. You--all the staff people—were supposed to be watching after her."

She pointed at Kester to make it clear that she included him in her accusation. He leaned back in his chair and crossed his arms. "I know, Amanda. Believe me. We try to watch for these things."

Amanda's lip quivered. Kester cleared his throat and let the moment settle. It was so hard for families. They always entered the strange world of the dementia ward with either relief or wariness. Those who'd witnessed a loved one's mind blow away like an explosion came with stunned distrust. Those who brought a spouse or parent to Foothills after a long hopeless, and exhausting battle at home radiated shame-filled, apologetic gratitude.

Kester leaned forward and clasped his hands on the tabletop. "I can't explain your mother's bruises. But you saw how agitated she could get."

Amanda picked at the wadded Kleenex in her hand and nodded. "I know—the screaming. So many months of that. Not like her at all." She raised her head and wiped at her nose. "She was a happy person."

"I see that kind of change a lot," Kester said. "Sometimes they just get stuck in a scary place, mentally."

"Yes, I think she was scared much of the time there at the end," Amanda said. She wiped the balled Kleenex across her cheek. "Like she knew something wasn't right but couldn't figure out why."

"Alzheimer's can do that," Kester said. "I see it over and over."

"Do you think the--the Alzheimer's thing--is what killed Mother?" Amanda said.

Kester hesitated. "I honestly don't know, Amanda," he said. "We've got the autopsy report showing she wasn't getting enough oxygen, and we have the bruising on her ribs. I talked to the staff member who was last with her, and he assured me she was fine when he left her by the window."

Amanda thrust her chin forward and frowned. "But her arms were trapped under the tray."

Kester nodded. "Yes, that's true," he said, "but she could've done that herself."

"Was it her medicine?" Amanda said.

"She wasn't on memory medicines," he said. "The Namenda quit helping last month if you remember. We stopped it then."

"What about the other ones?"

"The Seroquel?" Kester said. "Yes, she was still on that. It can be sedating, we know. But she'd been on it for a while without bad effects."

Amanda sat rigid in the chair, her hands twisting the tissue. "I don't think it helped," Her voice was soft but definite. She picked at the wad of Kleenex, slowly shredding it. "I don't think any of it helped."

"We try," Kester said. He reached across the table and patted her hand.

Amanda stared at the tattered Kleenex. "No, you don't."

Kester tensed. "We do what we can."

"No, I think you all do what you're supposed to. But you don't do what you should."

Amanda's face flushed in embarrassment, but her voice held steady, and her eyes flashed with indignation.

Kester tensed. "What do you mean?"

"I mean, you don't see it. You don't see it like it really is. I even got used to it, a little, visiting Mother every day."

"See what?" The words caught in Kester's throat.

Amanda's face tilted toward the ceiling, and she sniffed. Tears covered her cheeks. "Mother screamed every day for months." Amanda's voice choked. "For months—every day. Sometimes all day. The only other time I saw her carry on like that was when my brother, David, was in a car accident, and they told Mother he probably wouldn't live through the night. She said afterward it was the worst thing she'd ever been through. She screamed for about ten minutes." Amanda's eyes squinted in anguish. "Ten minutes."

Kester sat forward and tapped his finger against the table. "We can't be sure this is anything like that," he said. "We simply don't know."

"But what if it is? What if it's exactly like that?" Amanda said.

Kester stared at his hands, avoiding her eyes.

Amanda continued. "I think you get used to it. I felt that happening to me after I'd visited a few times. You get used to it because none of these people are running up to you and yelling, 'Help me!'" Her eyes widened briefly, then she dropped her head and stared at the table. "You get used to it because you have to. But you shouldn't."

Amanda sniffed again and reached across the table. She grasped Kester's hand, and her eyes locked onto his. "It's not right," she said. She stood and shuffled toward the door. "Mother's at peace now," she said as she passed Kester. "However that happened, it's what should've happened." She opened the door. The clamor of the ward drifted into the room. Amanda listened for a moment, then wiped her eyes. "My god." The door clicked shut, and the room was silent.

Kester placed his elbows on the table and his head in his hands and stared at the soggy clump of Kleenex across from him.

Chapter Eight

Clare slipped out of bed and crouched to pick up her panties. The glow of the muted television outlined her with a pale light. One lovely breast stood out, silhouetted against the screen. Kester chuckled.

Clare stood and held her arms across her bare chest. "What?"

"Nothing," Kester said. "Just admiring your boobs."

"Well, quit it," Clare said. She slapped her panties against his foot. He turned on his side

and propped his head on his hand.

Clare laughed. "You've been admiring them way too much tonight," she said, turning toward the bathroom. "And if you ever act like one of those jerks who refers to the female bosom as 'fun bags,' you'll be admiring them from afar."

She flounced toward the bathroom. "And now, if you have no objection, Doctor, I will use your potty." She closed the door with a flourish.

Kester caught a brief second of her laughter. He smiled and smoothed the crumpled sheet, then pulled it up to the level of his navel. The light from the television revealed work clothes scattered across the bedroom—flung off in haste earlier that evening. One of his socks had become entangled with the sheet at the foot of the bed.

He and Clare had been dating for over three months. Kester took it for granted that even boiling passion eventually settles down to a mild simmer. So far, he'd been proved wrong. Clare brought joy to his life and was genuinely concerned for his happiness. And he was happy. But Amanda Pettigrew's accusation earlier that day rattled him.

The toilet flushed, and the sound of water running in the sink drifted through the door. Clare emerged wearing her panties and one of Kester's old blue shirts. Her hair was freshly brushed. The soft shirt hung to her knees. She struck a pose, her arms outstretched and her feet planted apart.

"Tah dah!" she said. "All back together." She took two small, skipping steps to the edge of the bed and pulled the sheet back. "Why, Doctor Grayson! You have no clothes on!" she said. Her eyes opened in mock alarm.

Kester laughed, rolled off the bed, and knelt on the floor. He found his boxer shorts and stood to pull them on. Clare climbed into bed and patted the pillow beside her. "Hop back in here, Kes," she said. "I'm not through with you yet." She laughed and patted the pillow once more.

"Oh, not again," he said, rolling his eyes. He smiled, got back in bed, and pulled the sheet up as she snuggled against him.

"You tired, hon?" Clare said.

"Not yet," Kester said. "I'm thinking."

"And what deep thoughts are keeping you awake?"

"Just thinking about what Marion Pettigrew's daughter was saying today," he said. "She

was really upset."

Clare stroked his arm. "Well, it is a puzzle. I was sure Marion had a heart attack or something. Do you think the tray on the wheelchair made her suffocate?".

"No, not really," Kester said. "She was a skinny little thing. I don't think there's any way that tray could've been on there tight enough to restrict her breathing. And the bruises on her chest were fairly wide. If the tray had been up against her chest, I'd think the bruises would be narrow." He frowned. "But I can't find any other good explanation."

"There's going to be another meeting about it?" Clare said.

"Yeah, on Tuesday," Kester adjusted the pillow behind his back.

They stared at the muted television.

"Something else Amanda Pettigrew brought up got me thinking," Kester said.

Clare turned and kissed his bare arm. "What's got you thinking?"

"She thinks we let her mom suffer," Kester said. "She thinks we follow some mindless formula that lets us off the hook—that we don't do the right thing for our patients."

Clare sat up and leaned back against the headboard. "Well, what does she think we should do?" she said. "Kill them outright?"

"No." Kester shook his head. "I don't think that's what she was saying. But she thinks we ignore their suffering."

"I think we do a great job of treating them when they're sick. We don't let them sit around in pain—not at all," Clare said. She folded her arms across her chest and furrowed her brow. "We do a good job—*you* do a good job, Kes."

"I thought so, too," Kester said. "But I think she meant we don't understand some other way they suffer. I guess kind of a 'psychic' suffering—because of their dementia."

Clare brought her knees up and wrapped her arms around them. She rested her chin on her forearms. "What the hell is 'psychic' suffering?"

He rolled to face her. "Think about it this way. You know those dreams where you're in a horrible, terrifying place and feel helpless, and it gets so bad you wake up?"

"Sure."

"What if you couldn't wake up, and you didn't realize it was a dream, and it kept going on and on?"

"Well—"

"Would you call that suffering?"

"Of course it is," Clare said. "But it's not like pain. It s not like breaking a bone or

something."

"Maybe not." He stared at the ceiling for a few moments. "But if you break a bone, it eventually heals, and you go on with your life. What if it never healed and it kept you in agony for the rest of your life? And—and everyone acted like you were fine, and meanwhile, you're limping around on a broken bone?" He shook his head. "But I'm talking about something much worse. I'm talking about living in terror for the rest of your life. Like you're stuck in that bad dream."

Clare pondered for a moment. "Okay, so let's assume what you're saying is true, and some of those people are terrified and suffering. That's why we give them medicine—to help that."

"Like Marion Pettigrew?" Kester sat upright. "I gave her everything in the book, and she never settled down. And eventually, we sort of accepted her screaming like it was part of her nature—like it was okay."

Clare turned and studied his face. "Kester, I don't think for a minute you wanted that woman—or any of your patients—to suffer. You did what you could for her."

"I wonder, sometimes," Kester said. "Amanda said we do what we're supposed to, not what we should. It made me think of that thing about the Nazi concentration camp guards just following orders."

"Oh, stop it," Clare reached out and punched him playfully on the shoulder. "You want some water?" She jumped out of bed and headed for the kitchen.

"Sure," he said. She disappeared out the bedroom door, her hips shifting under the thin blue cloth. He loved her playfulness away from work and her professionalism and compassion at the hospital. At thirty-five, she was five years younger than him, but sometimes she made him feel like a twelve-year-old. She babied, scolded, and rolled her eyes at some of his offbeat humor, but she'd already developed a fierce, protective attitude toward anyone who criticized him.

The refrigerator slammed shut, and Clare returned and handed him a bottle of water, then climbed back into bed and rested her head against his chest. "I still don't think Amanda is right about that pain thing," she said.

Kester twisted the cap off the water bottle and drank before answering. "I don't know, Clare. It's easy to get complacent in our line of work. Sometimes I can't help but wonder if we do the right thing for those people. I sometimes wonder if we should even be trying to keep them alive." His voice hardened, and he pointed at her with the water bottle. "Would you want to be stuck in that place? And I'm not even talking about the worst patients—the really demented ones. Would you want to live like that even if you were still pretty together? Away from your home? Away from everything that explained your life? That has to feel like the ultimate last stop."

Clare snorted. "So what do you think we should do with them? Run them off a cliff or something?"

Kester smiled. "Hmm—no, I don't think there'd be much running left in that crowd." He raised the water bottle to his mouth and drank, then wiped his lips. "No, I don't know. Do you remember Bernie Halbers?"

"Sure," Clare said. "Nice man."

Kester capped his water bottle and set it on the nightstand. "I remember one day I was pushing his wheelchair down the hall. It was one of those times when he was pretty lucid, and he said—' Why do you do this?' I said—' What do you mean?' And Bernie said, "I'm sitting in this goddamn chair. If I need to take a leak, I have to do it in this chair, in this goddamn diaper. Everyone I ever knew or ever loved is dead. I'm no goddamn good to me or anyone else. Why do you keep us alive?'

"I told him—' Because they won't let us kill you, Bernie.' "

Clare frowned. "Jeez. That's harsh."

"I think that was maybe the most truthful conversation I've ever had with a patient," Kester said. He waited for her reaction. Clare lay silent, staring hard at his face.

Chapter Nine

Maureen came to visit today. Perhaps she's a better wife than I deserve, but I don't know if that's the case. Maybe she was the original bitch from hell before the stroke. Not that she isn't a good woman now—better than a lot I've seen around here. But maybe she was only average—you know, before. It's not as if I have any comparisons to base that on.

I don't think there's only one woman you can live with. Probably many of them would turn out to be excellent partners. I'm not talking about the love of your life because I have nothing to go on in that area, either. A lot of the old songs say only one love can complete your life. I wouldn't know based on Maureen. Maybe our life together was solid. If that description—solid—smacks too much of stodgy, unexciting, plodding, I guess that fits most folks. And a reliable pair of shoes can get you a lot farther down the road than a fancy pair of pumps.

I think Maureen has stuck with me through a shitload of anguish. I don't remember many details since the pain hit, but I get glimpses of a busy, hectic life. I think I was away on business quite a bit, and Maureen must've sometimes raised the kids alone. I get half-formed pictures of other women—brief hook-ups in hotel rooms—that kind of thing. Did I cheat on Maureen? I honestly don't remember. But those barely-glimpsed hotel scenes make me think so. Did she know? If so, as far as I remember, she's never mentioned it. I hope my memories of those things are from movies I saw and not from my own life.

However stodgy and cold our past relationship might have been, now Maureen is a trooper. I think she visits a lot. I don't know how long she's been coming to the ward, but probably since I arrived. She has an ease and familiarity with the routine in this place, just like the helpers.

We're in the dayroom, by the windows. I'm eating a chocolate chip cookie she brought me, and she's talking about the kids.

"Mia had her second date with David, that boy from Greeley," Maureen says. "I don't know if it will work out, but she seems excited about him." Maureen paws through her purse and pulls out a picture of Mia beside a tall, dark-haired man. How old my little girl looks! Maureen sticks the picture back in her purse. "He seems okay, but who can tell?"

Who indeed? Is this David fellow going to be the love of Mia's life, or do we place him in the "solid but stodgy" group? Or even in the "dickweed" category?

It's hard to raise kids, especially a daughter. Mia was a good kid. Joshua, too, most of the time. They gave us very little trouble compared to some. No, it was hard to raise kids because of those flashes of terror a parent feels when they realize how puny our defenses can be against an unpredictable world. You can love your kids to death, but you know in your heart that's a weak talisman against the evils they'll encounter.

Maureen goes on while I nibble on the cookie. "Josh had to put in extra hours at the golf course this week." Her lips quiver into a tiny smile. "Always short of money these days."

According to Maureen, Josh is halfway through college now and works at a golf course over the summer—the same one I used to belong to, so she says. I don't remember the name of it. My boy was a good guy, other than a short period of rebellion when he was in high school. I remember that all too clearly. Wrecked a couple of cars, did some heavy drinking a few times, and maybe even took some drugs. But he pulled up before he hit the ground and turned out fine, it sounds like.

"Mia is twenty-four and in graduate school, and Josh is twenty-two and working on his degree in business, just like you did, Virgil," Maureen says.

I nibble my cookie. How odd it is for Maureen to tell me this about my kids. The truth is, the information's new to me—fresh and interesting. But I'm sure this is one of the things my wife must tell me often during her visits. It doesn't stick in my memory, is the thing. Just some of the older memories ever come to mind.

I study the fleshy droop of her face. The skin sags around her nose, flowing down along the corners of her mouth like mud around a couple of boulders. She was a good-looking woman at one time. I catch glimpses of images—Maureen at a younger age with smooth, firm features and long, blond hair. She's dressed okay today—nice white blouse and dark slacks, short gray-blond hair neatly brushed, some makeup on that gravity-drawn face. I surely loved her at one time, although I don't feel that now. I'd need more memories than I'm left with to feel love for the neatly dressed woman who sits with me now. But gratitude? Definitely gratitude.

I think most people take it for granted—those images in your brain of times past. Even if most images get corrupted in our heads somewhere along the line, they give some context to the present. Sometimes living only in the moment can set you totally adrift. Life is all about context.

Maureen is still talking, but I've lost interest. I take a final bite of the cookie and check out the Mexican.

I've been keeping track of him because I think he might be one of the horses here. He isn't the tall, elegant, Spaniard type of Mexican. He's one of those short, stocky guys with nut-colored skin and ageless, black, shiny hair. I worked with a lot of guys like him when I was a kid, bucking hay bales, thinning sugar beets—hard physical stuff. Those guys were machines. Even the ones who were twice my age at the time and half my size outlasted me. Maybe the Mexican across the room was one of those guys who used to run my ass into the ground back then.

Despite the thick, jet-black hair, he's older than me, and he moves as if all those years of labor finally used up his fuel. He shuffles around the ward like he has no energy to spare.

I passed by his room the other day, and some of that mournful Spanish music was playing on his radio. Sad stuff, even if you don't understand the words. The Mexican was on the end of his bed, all slumped over like every load he'd ever carried was still perched on his back. He faced the wall, so I couldn't see into his eyes. I'll have to take a closer look.

Maureen reaches over, dabs at my face with a tissue, then leans in and gives me a kiss on the cheek. I stand and walk out of the dayroom. Maureen is still talking, but I'm not listening. I have to think some more about the Mexican.

I sit by the nursing station. Down the hall, the housekeeping lady mops the tiled floor. Either it's the usual time for cleaning there, or maybe someone pissed in the hallway, and she's cleaning up the evidence. They spray everything down with Clorox or something. The housekeeping lady is doing that now, spritzing liquid from a big plastic bottle like she's shooting bad guys. Then she runs the mop over that part of the floor before moving on.

Maureen is no longer in the dayroom, so she's probably gone home. I don't know where her home is these days. Maybe she still lives where we used to live, or perhaps she moved somewhere else. She's probably told me before, but it didn't stick.

I get a quick-flash vision of cooking hamburgers on a black patio grill. Mountains rise up to my left, off about five miles or so. The patio is flagstone. The odor of grilled hamburger mixes with that warm grass smell you only get at the end of certain summer afternoons when the day's been bright and hot. There's a wineglass in my left hand, and the dark purple wine smells wonderful. Then the vision is gone, and I'm staring at the housekeeping lady again as she mops around the corner and into one of the rooms.

At dinner, I make sure to sit across from the Mexican. He hunches over with his head down, eyes riveted on his tray of chopped-up spaghetti. Up close, his hair is blue-black. There's one small bald spot about the size of a quarter right where his cowlick should be. The skin there is as white as a fish belly. I wait for him to look up across the table, but he keeps his eyes on his food. Finally, I say a few words to get his attention. They probably sound like babbling to him, but it gets him to look up and over at me.

"Que'?" he says. His dark eyebrows thrust up in puzzlement. Down inside his pupils, the anguish is so deep and sad it makes my throat catch for a second.

"Caballo," I say.

Either I'm coming across garbled, or he doesn't get the reference because he gives me one more questioning look and then returns to his food.

The Mexican is still examining his half-eaten dinner when I leave the dayroom. I grab an empty Styrofoam coffee cup as I pass the serving cart. Nobody notices. Down by the Mexican's room, I slip into one of the bedrooms and piss in the cup, filling it almost to the top. The Mexican eventually limps down the hallway. Everyone else is still in the dayroom. His arms hang at his sides. His rough hands still have calluses and old scars, as if they used to carry bricks or some other heavy load.

When he's close, I splash the cup of piss across the tiled floor in front of him, move forward, and sweep him into my arms like a groom picking up his bride to carry her across the threshold. His weight drags at my arms, but I pull him to my chest and lift. The slippers on his feet flap on the ends of his legs as he struggles to find the floor. His thick, dark hair brushes against my nose, bringing the barbershop odor of witch hazel. His sideburn slicks against my face. We grunt in unison—the Mexican with alarm and me with the effort.

I bend sideways to the right, tipping his still-flapping feet toward the ceiling, and drive the back of his head down onto the tiled floor. His skull makes the same sound one of those full water jugs makes when the helpers change the water cooler in the dayroom. You'd think a head hitting the ground that way would sound like a dropped watermelon, but it isn't a soft sound.

The Mexican lets out a sharp, whooshing sound, sucks in another breath, and sighs. His eyelids twitch a little, but his legs no longer flail. He's on his back in the piss I tossed on the floor. In just a few seconds, blood pools behind his head. My knee is on the floor beside his shoulder, so I have to pivot to the side so the blood won't hit my pants.

His eyelids stop twitching, and he stares at the ceiling. I set my hand against his cheek and turn his face toward me. The back of his skull is flattened, so his head doesn't roll easily. But there's no more turmoil down there. All is quiet.

I walk down the hall and sit by the nursing station just as people start to leave the dayroom. Soon, there's a crowd around the Mexican. Later, some workers carry him away on a gurney. I crush the Styrofoam cup into a tight lump.

Chapter Ten

Mike Flores tossed a shelled peanut into the air and caught it in his upturned mouth. He grinned across the table at Kester.

Kester set his empty beer bottle on the table and whistled his appreciation. "There's something you don't see very often anymore," he said. "I wonder if these kids even try that these days." He surveyed the crowded bar. "I bet you're impressing the hell out of these little coeds, Mikey."   A fresh-faced blonde server brought two more full beer bottles to their table. A tattoo of vines and fairies covered the server's left arm. She wiped the litter of peanut skins onto the floor and glowered in mock disapproval. "God, you guys are so messy."

Mike pointed at Kester. "Can you believe it, Kimberly? Old Doc Grayson here thinks we're too old to hang out with you college kids!"

Kimberly placed their empty beer bottles on her tray. "Didn't you guys used to come here back when you were in pre-med?" she said.

"Well, yeah," Mike said. "The College Inn has been the best hangout in Fort Collins for generations."

"And you started coming here--what year?" She tossed her head, pulling her hair off a tanned shoulder.

"Legally?" Mike counted on his fingers. "Oh, that would be about 1983."

"So let's see," Kimberly said. She scrunched her face "That would be three years before I was born."

Mike Flores snorted in disgust. Kester laughed. Kimberly smiled and leaned over and kissed the top of Mike's head. "For what it's worth, you're still good-looking, Mikey," she said. She patted his shoulder. "Any girl here would be proud to call you 'Dad.'" She turned toward the bar as Mike frowned over at Kester.

"Jesus, Kes, do we stand out like turds in the punchbowl here? Why do we keep coming?"

"I don't know." Kester shrugged. "Habit, I guess." Students moved about the busy room. "I've always felt comfortable here, but sometimes I feel like I'm partying with grade schoolers these days."

"Yeah," Mike said. He sipped his beer. "I don't think of myself as old, but lately, coming here makes me realize time's passing."

"Well, I guess it's all relative," Kester said. Two football jocks playing pool nearby laughed, showing off for their dates. He turned back toward Mike. "I feel like a million years separate me from these kids. I feel old—old. He shook his head. "But this morning—on the ward—I felt like a youngster in a crowd of ancients."

"Yeah," Mike said. "A crowd that's getting smaller by the day, it seems. Lots of deaths on your ward lately." He tossed another peanut into the air. It bounced off his upturned chin and fell beneath the table. "You talk to Reggie about the guy who slipped in the pee?"

"I called him right after the emergency room at Poudre Valley called me," Kester said.

Mike leaned forward and rested his elbows on the table, turning his beer bottle with one hand. "And he didn't find it ironically humorous that one of our patients was done in by some incontinent neighbor?"

"Nope, not a chuckle from Reg," Kester said. He raised his bottle and sipped, then set it back on the table. "Reg called Gordy in housekeeping and told him he wanted an incident report on his desk by the end of the week. He said heads might roll."

"It's hard to put too much blame on the janitors," Mike said. "It's a wonder the floors aren't a Slip n' Slide, what with all the incontinent patients. I've skidded through a few pee pools on those wards myself."

"Yeah, it's too bad about Garza," Kester said. "I'd say 'bad luck,' but maybe it's not so bad to catch an earlier flight and skip that long wait in the terminal—if you know what I mean."

Mike held up a finger. "Wait a sec." He scooted out of the booth and stood. "All this talk about peeing is making my bladder hurt." He turned and hurried past the pool players and into the men's bathroom.

Kester rocked his half-empty beer bottle back and forth on the table. Conversations buzzed around him. Young faces glowed with health. Mike exited the bathroom and stopped to talk to the pool players. Whatever he said to them drew a laugh from the group. He slapped one of the football jocks on the back and walked over to the bar. Soon he returned with two fresh bottles and slid into the booth across from Kester.

"So how's it going with Clare?" Mike said.

"Oh, you know about that too?"

"Come on, Kes. Everyone knows. Including your severely demented patients."

Kester frowned. "We wanted to keep it under wraps for a while longer."

"Hey, I think it's great!" Mike said. "I think it's a good fit." He raised one eyebrow. "Getting pretty serious, is it?"

Kester grinned. "Pretty serious. She's the best thing that's happened to me in quite a while."

"So don't screw it up," Mike said. He raised his beer bottle and took a swig. "And speaking of screwing, I bet there's plenty of that going on with you two—am I right? I hope I'm right."

Kester laughed. He picked up a peanut and threw it at his friend. "None of your business." The crowd around the pool table cheered a shot made by one of the players. Kester flicked a peanut off the table. "I'm trying not to screw it up. Last night I sort of ticked her off, though."

"How? Did you take her to that crappy Italian restaurant you think is so good?"

"No, I took her there last week, and she likes it." Kester chuckled. "So I know she's the woman for me."

Mike pursed his lips and frowned. "So she has poor taste in men and in food. How did you tick her off?"

"We were talking about the whole end-of-life euthanasia thing."

"Like, at work? Or was it like bedroom talk?" Mike asked.

"Not at work. We were at my place."

"Oh, amigo, bad time to talk shop." Mike shook his head. "That's something Liz and I would talk about in bed, but we've been married for twelve years. When a relationship is at the stage yours is, you don't want to be talkin' shit like that." He reached across the table and tapped Kester on the forehead. "What you thinking?"

"Yeah, I know. But this whole thing's been working on me." Kester toyed with his beer bottle. "Tell me what you think, Mikcy. Should we be keeping those people alive—the ones who are gone?"

Mike turned sideways in the booth and rested his back against the partition. He propped his feet on the upholstered bench. "Oh yeah. Here we go. I feel some serious philosophical shit coming on." He rubbed his hands together.

Kester laughed. "Hey! I didn't mean to start a debate."

Mike waved his hands. "No, no," he said. "I love this stuff."

Kester set his elbows on the table and propped his chin on his fist. "So what do you think, Mikey? Don't you find the whole business—doctoring dementia patients—sort of soul-killing sometimes?"

"Sure," Mike said. "Just the day-to-day hassles in this line of work can get to you. And it always comes down to the big questions, doesn't it? Who would want to live like that? Do you care for them or kill them?"

Kester munched on a peanut and laughed. "Well, that's certainly putting it bluntly."

"No, think about it, Kes." Mike tapped the table. "None of the other stuff we do makes any difference, or even any sense, until you answer some pretty basic questions."

"So what do you think?" Kester said.

"I think you have two different sets of questions you're dealing with, first of all," Mike said. "One set as a member of society, and one as the guy in the trenches at the hospital."

"It sounds as if you've given this quite a bit of thought."

"I've studied the philosophical literature on euthanasia."

"Didn't you flunk that philosophy course back in pre-med?" Kester grinned.

"Yeah, but that was boring, abstract bullshit." Mike burped. "This stuff we're talking about now meets me every day in the hallway, every time I'm on the wards."

"Okay," Kester said. "So give me your take on this."

Mike took a swig of beer and cleared his throat. "Well," he said, "as a society, we are some very confused, ambivalent hombres about the issue of dementia and euthanasia. At least, most of us are. Most people find the whole thing creepy and abstract unless they've dealt directly with a relative. So they don't waste much time thinking about it."

"Okay, why is there so much in the news about it?"

"Those would be your outliers," Mike said.

"Outliers?"

"Yeah. The ends of the spectrum. On one side are the folks who would line 'em up along a trench and start bustin' caps or start selling 'em off to dog food companies. On the other end of the spectrum, those who think Monty Python's song 'Every Sperm is Sacred' should be the national anthem." Mike tossed another peanut into the air, turning his face skyward, mouth gaping.

"You've really given this some thought, haven't you?" Kester said. "And you're not one for wishy-washy language. I can see that."

"Well," Mike said, "I can give you the more refined philosophical arguments if you want."

"Just a sec." Kester held up a finger. "If this is going to get any more philosophical, I'm gonna need another beer." He slid out of the booth, walked to the bar, and returned with two more bottles and a dish of peanuts. "Figured you might want to practice your nut tossing some more." He slid the dish across to Mike and leaned back in his seat. "Okay, Doctor Flores, proceed."

"All right," Mike said. He grabbed a handful of peanuts and pushed the dish to the side. He carefully lined up five peanuts on the table in front of him.

"We'll eliminate the 'Kill 'em all and be done with it' bunch." He flicked the first peanut in the line off the table. "Can't reason with them anyway."

Kester nodded. "No soul in them."

"Right," Mike said. "And we'll eliminate the people at the other end of the spectrum—the ones who think we should hook 'em up to life support until the last brain cell flickers out."

"No brains in that bunch," Kester said.

"Right," Mike nodded and took a swig of beer. "Plenty of heart and soul, but you can't reason with them either." He flicked the peanut at the other end of the line off the table.

Kester nodded toward the remaining peanuts. "So, what do we have left?"

Mike cupped his hands around the three remaining peanuts. "These are the rest of us. We basically don't know what the hell to do about these end-of-life situations, especially when you're talking about active euthanasia."

"Why three peanuts? Why not one?" Kester said.

"Because when we flail around trying to figure out the right thing to do, we almost always frame the debate in one of three ways." Mike picked up one of the peanuts between his thumb and index finger. "Some people argue that it's all about autonomy. Who has the right to tell anyone whether or not they can end their life? Sure, we have living wills, and you might think that answers the whole question. But there's still plenty of suffering involved with that argument." He popped the peanut into his mouth and picked up another one.

"Second, we have people who get hung up on the question of mercy. Why do we let Grandma suffer if we put our old dog Fido down when he's in pain? Why can't we do the merciful thing and ease the old girl out? Endless debate on that question too." Mike placed the peanut in front of Kester. "Here," he said. "You eat those guys."

Kester tossed the peanut in his mouth. "You okay, Mikey? Kinda slurring your words.".

Mike raised his eyebrows and puffed out his cheeks. "That last beer is starting to hit me. I better finish my lecture before I forget the topic." He picked up the last peanut.

"This third group is people who argue about justice. How can we spend mucho dollars on Grandma when we could use that money to treat kids or poor people, or—take your pick? No shortage of arguments in that camp either." He chewed the last peanut and swallowed, then pointed at Kester.

"And here's the kicker, my poor, conflicted amigo. As the people in charge, we only get to ask one question. You and I and other docs who take care of the demented people at Foothills Hospital can have bullshit discussions until we're too drunk to drive ourselves home, and we'll still go on those wards every day and wonder what the fuck they mean by 'do no harm.'"

Mike reached into his pocket and solemnly handed his car keys to his friend.

Chapter Eleven

"Okay, let's get going." Nathan Mallory wiped toast crumbs from his sleeve and picked up his clipboard. Kester, Clare, Mandy, and the ward social worker, JoAnn Morton, looked on while Nathan read the first few pages.

Kester glanced across the conference table at Clare and winked. She winked back and then lowered her eyes to the papers on the table.

Nathan raised the clipboard and peered over his glasses at the list. "A lot of new names on the roster."

"We transferred Mr. Barton to a nursing home near Denver," Kester said. "Closer to family. Deaver and Jackson both went to Evergreen SNF. And then there are the recent deaths...."

Nathan glanced up and pushed his reading glasses higher on his nose. "Yes, I saw the autopsy report on Garza. Extensive occipital damage from the fall. 'Massive cerebral trauma,' I think they said."

JoAnn handed Nathan a slip of paper. "I talked to Rosa Garza yesterday. As you can imagine, she was upset but glad Manuel didn't suffer. I told her Manuel went quick and that we would make sure nothing like this happens in the future."

Nathan picked up the piece of paper and read it. "This is Rosa's number?"

JoAnn nodded.

Nathan stuck the paper in his pocket. "Okay, I'll give her a call later."

"Reggie got after housekeeping about the floors," Clare said. "They're working up some protocol for it, but Gordy thinks it won't really solve the problem. Just too many incontinent patients here."

"Helluva, way to go," Nathan made a face. "Lying in a puddle of piss with your head smashed open like a pumpkin."

They plodded through the rest of the morning report. Finally, JoAnn turned to Mallory. "After rounds, we need to meet with the Denton family. The younger daughter is in town now and has some concerns and questions for the team."

Nathan sat back and tilted his head. He removed his glasses and rubbed his eyes. "Are we dealing with the out-of-town-daughter dynamic here, JoAnn?"

"I don't know, Doctor Mallory. She was pleasant on the phone. We'll have to see how it goes when she gets here."

Mallory sat forward and adjusted the glasses on his nose. "Clare, let's make sure we have all our information correct,"

Clare lifted a chart from the rack and handed it to Nathan. He flipped through the pages before handing the chart across to Kester.

"Alzheimer's, very end-stage, DNR. Not really a psych issue anymore, Where are we with this, Kes?"

Kester picked up the chart but didn't open it. "Bed-ridden, non-communicative, not eating. Total care. I talked to Mary's older daughter, Paula, yesterday. She wanted hydration until the younger daughter flies in from Atlanta. Last night, we put an intravenous line in and moved Mary to room three across from the nursing station."

"She's stable?" Nathan flipped more chart pages, pausing occasionally to read.

Clare turned toward him. "She's comfortable and hasn't been much of a nursing problem. Very frail, but her vital signs are stable. She's refused food for six days now. No request for a feeding tube from the family."

Nathan rubbed his chin. "Afebrile?"

"So far," Kester said. "No sign of pneumonia. She may just slip away, but with the intravenous hydration, no telling how long we're looking at."

"All right," Nathan said. He handed the chart back to Clare. "This looks like it's going to be mostly medical on Denton, not psychiatric. You go ahead and take the lead, Kes." Nathan picked up his stack of index cards and stuck them in his coat pocket. "Okay. Guess that about covers it."

Everyone around the table pushed their chairs back and stood. Nathan turned to JoAnn. "We meeting them here or in Mary's room?"

"I thought we'd meet them in the visitors' lounge," JoAnn said. "It will be a little more like neutral ground."

"If they have any questions I can help with, just page me," Mandy said. "I'll be in the kitchen."

Clare headed for the nursing station. "I have another meeting to get to, but I'll be on my pager." She gave Kester a quick smile.

Darla Landry's round, plump face sat atop a short, stocky body. Her sister, Paula, towered above her—narrow and long-faced like their mother. Darla smiled, rose, and shook Nathan's hand as he and Kester entered the lounge with JoAnn. As head of the treatment team, Nathan began the discussion.

"So nice to finally meet you, Ms. Landry. I'm Nathan Mallory, your mother's psychiatrist. This is Doctor Grayson, who is taking care of her medical needs." Kester leaned forward to shake Darla's hand.

Nathan turned. "And I think you've already talked to JoAnn on the phone." Darla smiled and gave a little wave to JoAnn.

"And I think you know everyone, right, Paula?" JoAnn said. Paula smiled and nodded. "Let's sit down, and we'll try to answer any questions you might have," Nathan said, "although your mother's care will not involve me directly from this point on." He nodded toward Kester. "Doctor Grayson will be handling most of the issues for your mother."

The sisters resumed their seats. Kester, Nathan, and JoAnn sat on the couch facing them. Nathan looked at the sisters across the top of his reading glasses and motioned to Kester. "I thought Doctor Grayson might explain your mother's condition briefly, and then we can address any concerns or questions. Doctor Grayson?"

Kester opened Mary Denton's chart. Darla sat stiff and upright, her hands clasped. She smiled, but her eyes narrowed into a tight, accusing squint.

"Your mother is in the end stages of her illness," Kester said. "We're keeping her comfortable, and I don't think she's suffering. She's refusing food, but we've maintained an IV at your request, so she's receiving fluids." He closed the chart and shook his head. "Even the most optimistic prognosis doesn't see her living for more than a few more days."

Paula rested her forehead on her hand. Darla's face froze around her pursed lips.

Kester continued. "What we have to decide now is, should we continue the IV or let nature take its course? All our information and all the medical studies show that withholding fluids is not uncomfortable for patients in this final stage."

Darla rummaged through the large, black purse on her lap. She plucked out a square of paper and smoothed it open. Her smile disappeared as she turned away from Kester and addressed Nathan.

"Doctor Mallory, I have some questions and concerns."

Here it is, Kester tensed. Nathan smiled and leaned forward. "Certainly, Ms. Landry."

Darla held up the slip of paper and read, her voice quivering but indignant. "My mother has been here for nine months, and as far as I'm concerned, she has been in a living hell." She glanced at the three of them on the couch, pausing for a moment to see their reaction.

Kester's jaw tightened. *Her mother." Not 'our' mother.* No mention of Paula, who'd provided all of the care for their mother over the past few years. Nathan nodded and pursed his lips. Paula frowned.

"When we talked on the phone last winter," Darla continued, "you said the—Namenda?—would help her. But I don't think it helped at all." She glanced up at Nathan.

"Go on," Nathan said. He smiled. Darla coughed and continued.

"Now you say she has end-stage dementia, when before you said she had Alzheimer's disease. I don't think you,"---she raised her head and glanced at them again— "know what is going on with my mother. I know from looking on the Internet that there are all kinds of new tests and treatments, like vitamins, that can help her, and yet you have not tried any of them."

Nathan nodded again to indicate they were still listening. Paula reached out and touched her sister's shoulder. "Darla, we already talked about this..."

The younger sister folded the paper and placed it back in her purse. She grasped Paula's hand. "I know, but I just don't think everything has been tried for Mom." Her voice shook with indignation.

Nathan remained silent, in full psychiatric listening mode.

Darla's features softened. Her lip trembled as she struggled to regain control. "There must be something you can do!" She pulled a tissue from her purse and dabbed at her eyes.

Nathan removed his glasses and leaned forward. His voice went low and soft.

"Ms. Landry, let me see if I can address your concerns." He paused for a moment and cleared his throat. "You asked if your mother is suffering from dementia or Alzheimer's. Sometimes those terms are confusing. Alzheimer's is one kind of dementia—the most common kind. "

Darla wiped the tissue across her nose and sniffed.

Nathan continued. "Saying someone has dementia is like saying someone is in pain. It's a descriptive term, but it doesn't explain the cause. All dementia patients have lost brain function—the ability to reason and remember. Alzheimer's patients lose brain cells due to a particular disease process, but there are many things that can cause dementia." Nathan hesitated. "And I'm sure Doctor Grayson will agree with me when I tell you the disease does not get better with time. It is progressive and irreversible."

"The Namenda may have bought your mother a little extra time, Darla, but it was never intended to be a cure," Kester said.

Paula patted Darla's hand. "Really, Darla, the medicine did help for a while. I wish you would've visited Mother then."

Careful. Let's not get into a sister fight. Kester hastened on.

"We need to decide now how to keep her as comfortable as possible." Kester glanced at Paula, who winced.

"Well, I want her to at least have fluids," Darla said. There was still a note of defiance in her voice.

"We can do that if you insist. But as I told you, we don't believe your mother would suffer if fluids are withheld at this late stage." Kester said.

Darla bristled. "I'm sorry, doctor, but I do insist." She glared at Kester. "I think letting her die of thirst would be inhuman."

Kester nodded, his lips in a tight, thin line. He glanced at Nathan, who gave a tiny nod.

"Certainly, Darla, we can do that for you," Nathan said.

"Will she be on any medicine?" Paula asked.

"I've stopped all of her regular medications," Kester said. "I have an order for morphine to be given through her IV line if she shows any signs of discomfort, but so far, we haven't given her any."

Paula reached and grasped Darla's hand, and the sisters wept silently for a moment. Finally, Darla raised her head. "I'd like to see her."

"Let me take you to her room," JoAnn said.

Nathan checked his watch and stood. "I'm afraid I have another meeting." He rested his hand on Darla's shoulder. "Just page me or call my office if you have any further questions."

"Thank you," Darla said.

Nathan shook Paula's hand. "Doctor Grayson can be of more assistance than I can from this point on, but my door is always open." He nodded to Kester, then turned and left.

At the door to the lounge, JoAnn directed the sisters toward the nursing station and their mother's room. Kester followed.

Mary lay in the hospital bed, her head propped on a pillow. A clean white sheet covered her frail body. One arm lay atop the sheet, the hand palm up. A clear, plastic intravenous line ran from under the tape at her wrist, up along her shoulder, and to the bag of fluid hanging above the bed. The skin on her forehead was wrinkled but untroubled. Wispy white hair framed her face. Only her cheeks showed substance, swollen as freshly risen dough.

Darla bent and gripped her mother's hand, careful of the IV line. Darla's other hand rested on her mother's forehead, then moved slowly and lightly across the skin. Mary's eyelids fluttered but remained shut. Her mouth hung open, and her lips collapsed inward along toothless gums.

Paula stood back near the door, her face drawn and emotionless.

"Oh, Momma," Darla whispered. "I'm so sorry I didn't get back to see you sooner."

Kester checked the flow rate on the IV, then stood by in silence.

Darla studied her mother's face and talked softly to her for several minutes. Outside the door, the sounds of the ward rose and fell. Finally, Darla kissed her fingers and touched them to her mother's cheek. She turned to Kester.

"Please don't let her suffer," she said. A sheen of tears glistened on her cheeks. She walked to the door, hugged her sister, and left the room.

Kester rested his hand on Paula's arm. "We'll keep her as comfortable as possible," he said.

Paula slumped against the doorframe, her face slack with exhaustion. She turned to look at her mother and then back at Kester.

"Do what you can," she said, her eyes pleading. She turned away. JoAnn put her arm around Paula's shoulders in the hall and led her away.

Kester turned back to the bed. Mary grimaced. Her hand gripped the sheet.

Do what you can. And what was that? He could do nothing this late in the process except keep Mary quiet and hope for infection to steal into her lungs or bladder and end things quickly. Otherwise, it would be a slow death by starvation. If

Darla hadn't insisted on the IV, the end would come fast and without pain. Without water, her body would struggle to keep blood pumping to the brain, but in a short while, her tissues would dry and wither, and the pump would fail. The body could last for a long time—weeks sometimes—without food. But without water, death often came within hours.

He rested the back of his hand against Mary's forehead. Her skin was cool and dry. The fragile skin on her eyelids moved as if she might be dreaming. Did people even have dreams here at the end of things? Or were too few brain cells still making connections, fighting a losing battle to keep dreams alive in there?

Do what you can. Kester walked to the nursing station and leaned across the counter.

"Christina, get me ten milligrams of IV MS for Mary Denton, will you? She's been a little restless this morning."

"Just a second, Doctor Grayson," Christina said. "I just need to finish this chart note, and I'll get it." She kept her head down, intent on the papers on the desk.

Kester frowned. He reached across and clicked the door open, stepped through, and slammed it shut. "Never mind. I'll draw it up myself."

In the adjacent med room, he took the stock bottle of morphine sulfate out of the glass-doored cabinet. The med room was usually locked, but the nurses sometimes left it open during the day for convenience. He reached into a cardboard box and removed a three-milliliter plastic syringe. Holding the morphine bottle upside down in his left hand, he pushed the needle through the rubber access port in the bottle cap, drew out three milliliters of clear liquid, recapped the needle, set the morphine bottle back on the shelf, and turned to Christina.

"I've got twelve milligrams of morphine," he said, holding the syringe for Christina to see. "Can you write that down for me?" He turned the syringe so the numbers on the side were visible.

"Actually, Doc, you have more than twelve milligrams in there."

Kester shook his head and frowned. "No, four milligrams per mil—three mils—so twelve milligrams." He walked over and stood next to her.

"Except that's a bottle with twenty milligrams per mil. We don't have any four-milligram-per-mil MS right now. So you have sixty milligrams of MS in the syringe." She shook her head. "Doctors!"

"Well...." Kester pointed back into the med room. "What do we do? You want me to put it back?"

"No, that will technically contaminate the whole bottle," Christina said. She fluttered her hand. "Just go ahead and give Mary what you want to give her, and I'll fill out the paperwork to account for the wasted amount." She emphasized the word 'wasted.'

"Sorry," Kester said. He stuck the syringe in his coat pocket and stomped off.

He returned to Mary's room and found the IV access port—a small, tan nub halfway up the plastic tubing—uncapped the syringe and inserted the needle through the rubber cap. He pinched the tubing above the port to stop the saline flow from the IV bag. His thumb settled on the plunger of the syringe.

Paula's last command echoed in his head. *Do what you can.* He shook his head to stop the thoughts.

Let's see, Twenty milligrams per mil, and I want ten milligrams, so that would be half a mil. He pushed on the plunger, which moved from the 3 to the 2.5 on the syringe. The plunger slid smoothly, effortlessly. Moving it from 2.5 to 2, then to 1.5, and finally to zero would be easy.

Sixty milligrams of morphine delivered to Mary's waiting brain cells. It would settle on the nerves that kept her lungs inflating and deflating, bringing them to rest. It would bring her peace. One slight push on the plunger and Mary Denton would go to where she desperately needed to go.

He'd tell Christina he'd emptied the rest of the morphine into the sink. She'd believe him.

Amanda Pettigrew's stern face rose in his mind, pointing her finger. *Do what you should.* He pleaded with Amanda's accusing, commanding image. *But I cannot end her suffering without ending her life.*

Paula stood beside Amanda. *Do what you can.* He shivered, gripped by indecision and fear. The images of the two women waited, silent and judging.

His thumb trembled over the plunger. His mind raced, but a part of him stood aloof and detached as though waiting for some external force to decide. In the end, something deeper spoke. *I will not do this again.*

He pulled the needle out of the port and unpinched the IV tubing. The saline solution flowed, pushing ten milligrams of morphine into Mary's vein. The medicine would keep her sedated and comfortable but would not lead to a quick and painless death. Mary's chest rose and fell with her breathing.

He set the syringe on the shelf above Mary's bed. She would need another dose soon; best not to waste it. He patted her arm and left the ward.

Chapter Twelve

The scab man sits across the hall from me. He's asleep, with his empty mouth hanging open and his head to the side. He's one of the rocks in this place. The tray on his wheelchair holds him upright, or he'd fall right out of his seat. He can sleep anywhere. When he's awake, he runs his fingernail around a piece of newspaper the nurse puts on his tray—around and around like he's plotting a path out of this place.

There's a fresh scab on his bald head and a couple of older scabs, too. He's a picker, and if they don't give him something like the newspaper to fuss with, he picks at his scalp so much that it makes you think he has some purpose in mind. But I've looked down into his eyes, and there is no fire. It's as if he left on the spur of the moment, and now his body is trying to stay occupied until it can run off, too.

The helpers put mitts on his hands to keep him from picking, but he got really good at pulling them off, no matter how well they taped them on. Getting them off kept him occupied for a while, but then he'd go right back to putting new scabs on his scalp. I don't know who figured out the newspaper thing, but it keeps him away from his head sometimes.

I've been drowsing myself this morning. The sun slants through the big windows in the dayroom, lighting up the dust motes around the rocks lined up in front of the television. The rocks stand out extra pale in the bright light. Not much activity going on. Occasionally, a helper moves among the wheelchairs, stirring up the sparkly dust motes so the air swirls like water.

The nursing station is to my right. The chubby nurse is working today. She's at the desk, answering the phone and stapling papers together. She never moves much either—kind of like the rocks. Of course, I'm not moving much today myself. Something in my back gave out when I picked up the Mexican, and now I get a sharp pain if I move too fast. So I'm mostly sitting and dozing. Have I been doing more of that lately? Hard to say.

They moved the song lady into a room across from the nursing station, but I don't know how long she's been in there. When she first got here, she'd sing much of the time. Sometimes in a high, clear soprano, and sometimes just a quiet little hum, almost under her breath. So I labeled her the song lady.

She's a rock, like the scab man. At least she was last I checked, but I don't know how long ago that was. Am I right about this whole horse and rock thing? I hope so. At least every time I've looked into someone's eyes, I've been left with no doubt about which group they're in. Still, it would stand to reason that people don't go from horse to rock in the blink of an eye. It must be a process. Maybe they go through a phase where they're a horse part of the time and a rock part of the time. But so far, it's been one or the other.

Earlier, Doctor K and the doctor with the half glasses passed by with the clipboard lady, who talks to families most of the day. She's probably spoken to Maureen many times in the past. The clipboard lady's speech is always measured and soft. She talks to people in a hushed, almost funeral-home tone and then writes stuff down on her clipboard.

The three of them walked over to the visitors' lounge and were there for a while. Later, Doctor K and the clipboard lady go over to the room where they put the song lady. There were two other women with them. One is a younger version of the song lady—with a long, narrow face—and the other is like an older version of the chubby nurse.

From where I sit, it's a clear shot into the room. Doctor K fiddles with the water bag while one of the ladies cries and fusses and talks to the woman in the bed. Finally, she leaves the room with the other two ladies. She's got tears all over her cheeks, and the clipboard lady tries to comfort her. The other

lady, who looks like a younger song lady, isn't crying. She looks
tired and grim and watches the chubby one with slight disgust.

After they leave, Doctor K stares at the woman in the bed
for a long time. He rubs his chin and scrunches his forehead.
Probably thinking hard. He looks tired, too, and a little on the
undernourished side. His white coat hangs on him like it's on
a wire hanger. I don't know if he's a good doctor, but he looks
the part with his coat and stethoscope. I think he's a good man,
although I have no way of knowing that for certain either, but
he does have kind eyes and a nice smile sometimes.

He's still staring at the song lady. Then he reaches out and
puts his hand on her forehead. His head is cocked to the side,
sort of like the scab guy. His fingers trace around her hairline.
Maybe, like the scab guy, he's trying to figure a way out of this
place.

Finally, he returns to the nursing station and talks to the
chubby nurse. A cabinet door slams and Doctor K walks back
to see the song lady. He pulls the cap off a syringe, fumbles
with the tubing going into her hand, and pokes the needle into
the line. And then he's back to staring at the song lady. He's
taking an awfully long time to give her the medicine. His whole
body strains with the effort, but he can't seem to make the
medicine go in. His thumb holds steady on the syringe, but it
isn't moving.

It feels like he tries for hours, but then he drops his head in
defeat. His hand relaxes on the syringe. It still looks almost full

of medicine. His hand shakes as he pulls the needle out of the line and puts the cap back on.

Now Doctor K looks totally used up. Maybe trying to get the medicine to go in has sapped all his energy. He sets the syringe on the shelf above the bed, gives the song lady a little rub on the forehead again, and walks out of the room. The song lady slumbers on, but I'm worried now. Did Doctor K just decide to give up? What if she needed that medicine?

Doctor K passes by me, moving down the hall. He looks sad or maybe embarrassed by his failure. I doze but wake up to find the scab guy still snoozing across from me. The angle of the sunlight entering the dayroom is almost unchanged. The chubby nurse still works the stapler at the desk. I must've been sleeping for only a couple of minutes.

The chair scrapes as the chubby nurse stands and moves. Maybe she's going to try to give the song lady her medicine. But I hear her walk back to the break room. Soon, I hear the sound of the microwave door slamming and the electric hum as she warms something up.

The song lady rolls her head from side to side. I can just make out the sound of her moaning over the noise from the microwave. I walk across the hall, into her room, and over beside her bed. She's still moaning a little, and her eyes droop, half open. I've looked down into her eyes before, but I look again to reassure myself that she isn't a horse. Still cold and quiet down there. But I'm sure Doctor K wouldn't want her to be without her medicine, even if she is a rock.

The syringe of medicine is on the shelf above the bed. Maybe Dr. K wasn't strong enough to push the medicine in. I pick up the syringe, find the little rubber mushroom on the line, and push the needle into it. The plunger on the syringe moves almost by itself. There is no resistance, and the medicine goes right in. I put the cap back on the needle and set the empty syringe back on the shelf.

Then I put my hand on her forehead like Doctor K did. Her skin is cool and dry. The muscles in her forehead crinkle under my palm a few times, and then she quiets. I give her forehead a final rub and walk back to my chair by the nursing station. I feel good that I gave the song lady her medicine. She lets out a deep sigh and then is very quiet.

The scab man is awake now and back to tracing lines around on his piece of newspaper. I watch him for a while, and then I doze again.

Chapter Thirteen

Clare leaned her head on her hand and twirled the pen atop her notebook while her colleagues around the table listened to Jenny Lewis, the head of the Physical Therapy Department, drone on.

"But I'm saying the automatic lift system will more than pay for itself. Every time an aide goes out with back strain for a week or two, it costs us plenty." Jenny checked around the table for agreement.

Gerry Walters sat across the table from Clare. Gerry rolled her eyes. Clare grinned and nodded. Jenny Lewis' voice faded into a faint hum in Clare's ears. The committee was far from an agreement after months of debate.

Gerry scribbled on her tablet and pushed it across the table. *How's it going with Kes?*

Clare shrugged. Gerry pulled the tablet back and wrote again. She pushed it across and raised one eyebrow. *Nice catch, girl!*

Clare frowned, shook her head from side to side in mock anger, and smiled. Gerry returned to doodling on her tablet.

Kes is a very good catch, Clare mused. And not just because of his medical degree. She'd worked with many professionals over the years and had no illusions about doctors. There were good ones and bad ones, but there were just as many train-wreck personalities among the professional men she'd met in other walks of life. Some doctors came across as friendly and even personable but were so wrapped up in their work that they had no time for or interest in developing social skills. And some of the doctors she knew could only be described as natural assholes.

But Kes was different. He could've fallen into the 'nice guy/social nerd' camp, but he had a sense of humor and took his talent with a grain of salt. He had a somber—even dark and gloomy—side, but she was breaking down his natural reserve and discovering a complex, playful personality. Over the past three months, they'd spent almost all their free time together.

She hid a yawn behind her fist.

The Safety Committee suffered through more discussion until eleven-thirty. Clare gathered her papers. Gerry hurried around the end of the table and walked with Clare to the conference room door.

"I saw you yawning," Gerry said. "Not getting much sleep these days?"

"I could sleep for a week, and these meetings would still make me yawn," Clare said.

"I know," Gerry held the door open. "At this rate, we'll be lifting patients by hand for years to come. You want to get some lunch?"

"Sure."

They walked to the cafeteria, ordered salads and iced tea, and found a table by the window. Nurses, aides, and administrative staff milled around the crowded tables. The lawn outside spread down the hill, a dark emerald carpet. Staff sprawled on the grass, enjoying the summer warmth.

Gerry was a large, dark-haired, friendly woman with a wicked sense of humor.

She'd turned down several administrative promotions during her twenty years at Foothills, electing to continue in direct patient care. She concentrated on her salad for a few minutes, poking at it with listless jabs of her fork.

"You know," Gerry said, "I eat this crap almost every day, and I don't think I've lost a pound of fat in five years. God, I wish I'd had the cheese nachos!"

Clare toyed with her salad and laughed.

Gerry pointed her fork at Clare. "And you, on the other hand, probably still look good in a bathing suit. No wonder Doctor Grayson finds you irresistible."

Clare leaned across the table. "Well, to answer your earlier question—yes." Clare scanned the crowded cafeteria, then lifted her pinky finger with a theatrical flourish. "Kester and I are enjoying each other's company regularly."

"So is that your euphemistic way of saying you two are screwing like randy teenagers?"

Clare laughed. "Can't you see the bags under my eyes? I haven't had a full night's sleep in weeks!"

Gerry rested her elbows on the table and again pointed her fork at Clare. "Oh, it's all smoochin' and skootchin' now, but what about the long run? Is he a keeper?"

"I think so," Clare said.

"I mean, he seems like a great guy," Gerry said, "and he's way better than a lot of the docs I've worked with. But there's a big difference between how some of them do at work and how they do out in the real world."

"Kes does great out in the world," Clare said.

"Just be sure, sweetie," Gerry forked a chunk of lettuce into her mouth. "Back before I met my Howard—back when I was still lookin' good in a swimsuit too—I hooked up with a doc at University Hospital in Denver. Great looks, wonderful bedside manner—all the goodies. But he brought all that bullshit about doctors having god-like qualities home with him. Spoiled as could be and a real pain in the ass to live with."

"Gerry, I've seen plenty of guys like that, too," Clare said. "But Kes is the real deal. Funny, attentive, not too full of himself."

"No faults, huh?" Gerry said.

"Nothing major, so far." Clare hesitated. "Although we've kind of been having a debate—um, discussion—about the patients here at Foothills." She swirled her fork around the bottom of the salad bowl. "Kes is a little conflicted about taking care of terminal patients. He's even wondering if we should have some kind of euthanasia program." She waited for Gerry's reaction.

"Huh." Gerry concentrated on her salad.

"Nothing too sinister or creepy, but it rattled me a bit when he first mentioned it."

Gerry snorted. "Hell, that's not anything disqualifying. We've all thought it, even if we never said it out loud. It sounds like he's just being honest with you."

"I know," Clare said. "Still, he can't seem to get it sorted out. The poor guy is really conflicted."

"So, no other faults? No skeletons in the closet?"

"Nothing major. He was married once; to some respiratory therapist he met in school. It lasted five years, and he says it ended amicably, even though they don't keep in touch. She didn't want to have kids."

"And Kester does?" Gerry said.

"We haven't really talked much about that yet," Clare said.

They finished their lunch and carried their trays to the counter. Gerry clapped her friend on the back. "Well, if it doesn't work out, at least all the sex will be good for your complexion."

Clare laughed. "Thanks for putting it all in perspective for me."

After lunch, Clare walked back to C Ward. She spent the rest of the afternoon in the small nursing office, charting and finishing reports. At two-thirty, she met with the afternoon staff in the break room for the shift report.

Christina wheeled in the portable chart rack. The staff found seats around the table, on the couch, or stood along the back wall by the microwave.

"Sorry, I was off the ward all morning, Christy," Clare said. "The safety meeting dragged on forever."

"No problem," Christina said. "It was a quiet morning. Mary Denton died about eleven, but that was expected...."

"Wait—what?." Clare raised her head. "She died this morning? Why didn't you page me?"

Christina set her hands on her hips and shrugged. "Well," she said, "she was DNR, and we moved her to room three because we figured she would go soon. What's the problem?"

"The door was closed when I returned to the ward after lunch," Clare said. "I guess I assumed someone closed it for privacy."

Christy shook her head. "No, we closed it after the funeral home picked up the body."

"Did you at least notify Doctor Grayson or Doctor Mallory?"

"Mallory was on the ward at the time, so he pronounced her. He probably talked to Grayson."

Clare picked up Mary Denton's chart. "So she went quietly?"

"Not a peep," Christina said. "I went in about eleven, and she wasn't breathing. I checked for a pulse and then went and told Doctor Mallory in the conference room."

"I guess I'm just a little surprised she went so quickly since we had her on the IV," Clare said.

Christy held out the medication log. "She was getting a little agitated, I guess. Doctor Grayson gave her ten milligrams for MS earlier in the morning."

A red circle highlighted the notation for morphine sulfate on the log sheet. "Why is the MS order circled?"

"Because Grayson drew up the shot himself and screwed up the dosage. I had to go back and adjust it and list the extra fifty milligrams as wastage," Christy said. She gave a quick, skeptical snort. "Doctors! They'd be killin' patients left and right if we didn't keep track of them!"

A lump settled in Clare's gut. "So you destroyed the rest of the MS in the syringe?"

"No," Christy said. "I think he squirted it into the wastebasket or the sink." She shrugged. "They do that sometimes, even though we keep telling them that's against the regs. He put the empty syringe on the shelf in Mary's room." She laughed. "But at least he capped the needle. Most men are such slobs, and the doctors are no different."

Clare coughed, hiding her alarm. Sixty milligrams of morphine. A dead patient. Of course, they'd expected the patient to die soon, so maybe it was all coincidence. But the bedroom discussion with Kes was clear in her mind—the uncertainty that struggled against his compassion. Could he have done such a thing? It was hard to imagine. But, according to Christy, Mary was dead, and Kes was the last person to see her alive. And sixty milligrams of morphine sulfate was more than enough to kill someone.

Chapter Fourteen

Kester pulled into the parking lot just as the engine sputtered and died. He patted the steering wheel as if calming a horse. "At least it got us here. Maybe it'll get us back home, too."

She smiled but didn't respond. Kester slammed his shoulder against the door. It groaned open. "These Camrys can sure take a beating," he said. She opened her door and followed Kester into the restaurant.

The crowd at Bruce's Grill swarmed around the bar and out across the dance floor. Kester and Clare found a table near the back of the restaurant, away from most of the noise. Out on the dance floor, sunburned, t-shirted college students mingled with older couples and even a few ancient cowboys, all dancing to the music of a local western band.

Clare scanned the crowd while Kester read the menu. She reached across and clasped his hand, and Kester absently rubbed his thumb along her thumbnail. Finally, he looked up from his menu.

"I'm always amazed when I go someplace in this town, and I don't run into one person I know," he said. He studied her face for several seconds. "Why so quiet tonight, hon?"

She squeezed his hand. "Don't know. Tired, I guess. Long day at work."

Kester swatted her playfully on the arm. "Yes, and now you're away from there, and you're with this great guy in a fun restaurant, and you should loosen up."

Clare managed a weak smile but kept silent.

Kester frowned. "Something else wrong?"

Clare hesitated. "Mary Denton died this morning," she said.

"Yeah, I heard from Nathan. I talked to Paula afterward." Kester scanned the menu. "She sure went quicker than I thought she would."

He waited for her reply. When none was forthcoming, he lowered the menu and studied her from across the table. Clare avoided his eyes. "Kes, you have to be honest with me. I trust you, but I have to know. Did you have anything to do with Mary's death?" She raised her eyes to his.

He pulled his hand back. "I'm not sure what you mean."

She leaned forward and lowered her voice. "Christy said you gave Mary a shot of morphine this morning."

Kester hesitated. "Yeah, I gave her a shot when she became agitated."

"How much did you give her?"

"Ten milligrams."

"And that's all?"

"Yes, ten milligrams." His eyes narrowed. "Certainly not enough to kill her."

"Christy said there was sixty milligrams in the syringe. Are you sure you didn't give her too much—by mistake?"

"By mistake? No, I did not give her too much '*by mistake.*'" With the last two words, his voice hardened.

Clare reached across, grabbed his hand, and squeezed. "Kes, what did you do with the rest of the morphine? Did you throw it away?"

"No," he said. "I thought we might need to give her another dose, and I already felt bad about wasting the medicine. So I left the syringe on Mary's shelf. I meant to tell Christy, but I got busy and forgot." He leaned forward and rested his elbows on the table. "Why are you asking me this, Clare?"

The waitress brought their food. It sat untouched. Kester asked again. "What are you getting at?"

Clare let go of Kester's hand. She looked down at the table for a moment, then raised her head. "Kes, the syringe was empty when Mary died. Christy found it on the shelf, like you said. But all the morphine was gone. Now you're saying you didn't throw it away. So what happened to it?"

He turned, looked out across the restaurant, lifted his beer glass, and drank. Setting the glass on the table, he turned back and leaned toward Clare. "You think I gave her the whole thing?" he said, his voice filled with sarcasm. "Is that it, Clare?"

"Kes, I don't know what happened." Her hand moved back across the table, seeking his. Kester gripped the beer glass with his right hand and lifted it to his lips. His left hand fell into his lap. He drank and then set the glass on the table. "You think I killed a patient?" His eyes flashed with anger—and something else.

"I don't know what to think." She crossed her arms and watched the dancers twirl out on the floor.

Kester set the glass back on the table and spread his hands. "Look, I know it was dumb to leave the syringe in the room—I know that." He shook his head. "But I sure as hell didn't give Mary Denton sixty milligrams of morphine."

"But after what you said the other night—how you hate keeping some of your patients alive—can't you see why I'm upset?" Clare said. Her hand squeezed into a fist on the table, and her eyes narrowed.

"First, you talk about 'easing demented people out,' and the next thing I know, one of them is dead, and a syringe full of morphine goes missing."

Kester banged the flat of his hand down on the table. "Clare, I can't believe this shit. I don't know what happened to that morphine, and I know that was my responsibility." He nodded. "I did a stupid thing by leaving it on the shelf in the patient's room. I plead guilty to all of that. But I'm not a murderer."

Tears rolled down Clare's cheeks. She dabbed at them with the napkin.

Kester's voice softened. "Do you think I'm a murderer? Do you think I'm capable of that?"

Clare sniffed and dabbed her face again, then leaned forward and spoke in a low tone. "Kes, I think you're a good man. And I thought you were a good doctor. But you were in such anguish the other night. And now Mary is dead."

She sat back in her chair, away from him. "I don't know what I believe right now." One hand wiped across her eyes to clear them. "I have to think."

She rose from her chair, leaving her salad untouched. "I want to walk home. By myself. It's not that far. I'll see you at work tomorrow." She turned and walked through the dancers and out the door.

He paid for the uneaten meals and walked to the parking lot. The Camry started on the first try, but he was too distracted to notice. He drove west, back toward the hospital.

On C Ward, the evening shift rushed around, cleaning up from dinner and putting patients down for the night. Dinner smells lingered in the air. The empty wheelchairs lined the hallway while the housekeeping crew swept and buffed the dayroom floor. The night-darkened windows gave the ward a closed and insular feel.

Somewhere a female patient yelled, "Robert?" with a tremulous monotony. Calling for a long-dead husband? A son? Or was she 'sundowning'? Late in the day, patients still able to walk sometimes wandered the halls, rising from their complacency like a pot brought suddenly to a boil. Or, like the woman calling out for a loved one, falling into a confused melancholy. The plaintive call stopped.

Virgil Washington sat in his usual spot near the desk. His heavy-lidded eyes tracked the doctor down the hall. Kester squeezed Virgil's shoulder as he passed by. "Evening, buddy."

In the nursing station, the mid-shift nurse stocked her med cart. Nancy Thompkins was a skinny, middle-aged redhead who wore traditional nursing whites long after most RNs switched to regular street clothes or scrubs. She flinched, surprised to see Kester.

"Doctor Grayson, what are you doing here in the middle of the night? I thought Doctor Flores was on call."

"He is, Nancy," Kester said. "I was just checking on something." He smiled. "And it's hardly the middle of the night."

Nancy stood stiff and straight, almost at attention. "Is it anything I can help you with, Doctor?"

"I'm just wondering if you have the duty roster for day shift," he said.

Nancy turned and pointed to a paper tacked to the bulletin board. "There's the schedule for the week."

He scanned the roster. His request to see the list was probably raising some alarm bells with Nancy. Doctors seldom bothered to check on specific aide assignments.

Six staff members were working on C Ward when Mary died. The list didn't say which workers were assigned to which patients. That was usually decided at shift change. The

work assignments could be fluid, depending on the circumstances. Someone assigned to laundry or baths might help another aide with a difficult patient or cover during a break.

Nancy stood silently while Kester checked the list.

"Too bad about Mary Denton, huh?" Kester said.

"Yes, it was." Nancy returned to her cart and put two large pills into a metal press. She

brought a heavy metal handle down, crushed the pills, and mixed the powdered medicine with applesauce. Swallowing problems plagued many of the patients, forcing the staff to crush the bigger medications and mix them with pudding or applesauce.

Nancy looked up. "I grew up in the same neighborhood as the Denton girls. I remember their mother was a lovely woman. Very active in the church. Oh, and what a beautiful singing voice."

She crushed two more white tablets and poured them into a labeled paper cup. "That Paula was always a sweet girl, too. I talked to her this afternoon when she came by for her mother's things. She was so glad Mary didn't linger at the end."

Kester tried to think of how to word his question without arousing suspicion, but there was no way around it. "Do you know which day shift aide was caring for Mary when she died?" he asked.

Nancy hesitated. "I remember hearing that Lloyd Simpson was with her."

"I'm sorry," she said. "I'm not one to judge others, usually. This is a hard place to work, I know. Even good folks have a tough time caring for some of these poor souls." She brought the handle of the pill crusher down with extra force. "But some people just don't fit here from day one."

Kester nodded. "Yeah, I agree." He hesitated. "Maybe Lloyd's one of those."

Nancy's scrawny shoulders were hunched forward. "Yes," she said. "Some people can bring more trouble into a troubled world."

Chapter Fifteen

Lloyd checked his watch for the fourth time in ten minutes. *Nine-thirty already. Where are those shitbags?*

He'd tried the door to the house when he first arrived. You never knew about these druggy types. Rusty might've passed out in mid-afternoon and still be in a coma inside the ratty-looking house in a rundown part of Fort Collins.

He'd knocked on the front door and the grimy picture window but eventually gave up and returned to sit in his car.

A faded Buick with a tattered vinyl top turned into the driveway and stopped. The thumping bass and drone of rap music vibrated through Lloyd's car seat and into his groin. The Buick's driver shut off the engine and the headlights. The music stopped.

A tall, gaunt young man opened the driver's side door and stepped out. His shoulder-length hair hung in a ponytail. A wispy brown beard covered his chin. Wrinkled, baggy green cargo shorts hung low on his narrow hips. No shirt. He wore thin flip-flops on his long, grimy feet.

A short, square-built Hispanic with a large head—close-shaved as a tight-fitting skullcap—emerged from the passenger side. The tall man nodded toward Lloyd's car and said something to the passenger.

Lloyd knew Rusty, the driver, but he'd never met the other man. This part of the deal was always nerve-wracking, but he exited his car and walked to meet the two men by the front door. No handshakes.

Rusty reached out and squeezed Lloyd's arm. "Hey, man, thanks for waiting. I was out on some business and lost track of time. Let's go inside."

He unlocked the front door and disappeared into the dark living room. The second man gave Lloyd an "after you" gesture but didn't smile or speak. Lloyd hesitated, then stepped through the door as Rusty switched on a floor lamp. The living room brightened, revealing a jumble of clothes, trash, overflowing ashtrays, and general grime. The stink of a litter box mingled with a miasma of stale cigarettes, weed, and old hamburger grease. Muggy summer heat magnified the stench.

Lloyd slunk into the room and stood by the television. He slipped his hands into his pockets and rocked from foot to foot, then pointed to the man just entering from the porch. "Lloyd, this is Hector."

Lloyd pulled his right hand from his pocket and extended it to Hector. "Hey, man," he said.

Hector pushed his stubby brown fingers into Lloyd's palm and withdrew them without shaking his hand. "Yeah."

Lloyd kept his face impassive. He turned back to Rusty. "Where's Jackie? I thought it would be the usual deal."

"Jackie's gone," Rusty said. He didn't elaborate. "But my friend Hector here is in a buying mood." He nodded toward the man by the door.

This fuckin' vato ain't no friend of yours either, Rusty. Lloyd smiled.

Hector lifted his chin. "What you got?"

Lloyd reached into his pocket and pulled out a baggie filled with pills. "Sixty Vicodin fives, twenty Percodan fives, and thirty Ativan."

Hector put his hands on his hips and glared at Rusty. "You shittin' me, man? That ain't even enough for a fuckin' high school party."

Rusty froze, looked from Hector to Lloyd and back to Hector, smiled, and spread his arms. "Dude, I never said we were dealing with major quantities here."

Hector snorted in disgust. Lloyd stiffened again, then leaned back against the television and tried to look relaxed.

Lloyd's small bag of pills represented a lot of work. Staying close by when the med nurse made her rounds, offering to carry the little medicine cups to the patients when the nurse was in a rush or running late. Pocketing the pills and bringing

the wadded paper cup back to the wastebasket on the med cart
to show he'd delivered the medicine.

The old crazies sure as shit didn't act any different when
they missed their dose. They still went to sleep, screamed, or
babbled and pissed their pants the same as they always did, pills
or no pills. Hector's anger terrified Lloyd, but at the same time,
the man's dismissal of Lloyd's hard work was insulting.

Screw this little fireplug motherfucker. Lloyd stood with his
left hand in his pocket and the bag of pills dangling from his
right hand. He kept his eyes on Rusty, avoiding Hector's angry
glare.

Rusty grabbed the bag and held it out to Hector. "Sorry,
man. Maybe we can give you a good deal on what we got
here—for your trouble." He glanced back at Lloyd and then
back to Hector. "How about 350 for all of it? That's a lot less
than we usually get for this amount."

Hector grabbed the bag and tucked it into his pocket. "How
about 200 for all of it, and I'll forget how much of my fuckin'
time you wasted tonight." It wasn't a question.

Rusty nodded and thrust the bag at Hector. "That's cool."

Lloyd kept silent, his eyes riveted on Rusty and avoiding
Hector's eyes.

Hector took a wallet from his back pocket and pulled
out ten twenty-dollar bills. "Which one of you fuckin' drug
tycoons gets this?" Hector thrust the bills forward.

Lloyd reached out his hand.

Rusty moved around Hector and opened the front door. "I'll drive you back to your car, man," he said. "Lloyd, you want to hang out here until I get back?"

Lloyd shook his head. "No, I got to get home. But thanks." He followed Hector out the door past a grim-faced Rusty.

Rusty and Hector left in a cloud of exhaust and the thundering beat of rap music. Lloyd walked to his car, stuffing the bills into his pocket. His hands shook when he tried to put the key in the ignition.

That goddamn Rusty. All his work—all the risk he'd taken—for two hundred dollars. Rusty could stick his thumb up his ass and spin if he thought he was getting one cent of the money.

Lloyd started the car and drove down the dark street toward the center of town. On College Avenue, crowds of students milled along the sidewalks. Dozens and dozens of tanned coeds with tight summer shorts and tank tops. The sound of a rock band drifted over from Old Town, an area of upscale clubs and restaurants. Cars moved bumper-to-bumper, music blaring from every open window.

Lloyd joined the line of cars creeping along the avenue and scanned the groups of young women with a hungry intensity. He held no illusions about his chances of hooking up. A plain girl might take a chance, but things always ended badly. He came on too aggressively, pushing for quick physical contact that women found intimidating and shallow. They sensed his superficial interest and his contempt. Even the most desperate soon found reasons to avoid him.

He pictured Clare Williams, imagining what it would be like to have her in his bed. Daydreams about women occupied much of the time. In every scenario, the woman stood before him naked and compliant. And always silent. He couldn't imagine a conversation with any of them.

At Locust Street, he drove east six blocks to the tiny house he shared with his grandmother, Nora Simpson. His father disappeared shortly after Lloyd's birth, resurfacing only twice in the past twenty years, both times for only a couple of weeks. His mother dragged Lloyd through a series of homes owned by a string of boyfriends, who often let him know he was an unwelcomed addendum to his mother. He'd eventually cut loose from that life and wound up at Nora's house. She'd insisted that he finish high school and get a job. Otherwise, she'd left him alone. His grandmother made it clear that the free room in the basement didn't come with any amenities, affection included.

Lloyd parked in the driveway and climbed the wooden steps to the back door. Once inside, he didn't bother to look into the kitchen. His grandmother would be sitting at the table, a cup of warmed-over coffee in one hand and a Camel cigarette in the other.

The muffled sound of the television drifted through the doorway.

He stomped down the steep basement steps and flipped the light switch. The narrow room held a double bed, a tattered orange La-Z-Boy recliner, a small television on a heavy oak stand, and a desk from the same era. A computer sat atop the desk, illuminating the dark end of the room with a faint blue light. A cheap metal clothes rack stood against one wall, holding several empty hangers. Most of his clothes lay scattered around the room, draped on the unmade bed and heaped in piles on the maroon-tiled floor. Dark curtains covered two small basement windows.

Lloyd pulled the wad of bills out of his pocket and tossed them on the desk. Not much to show for all his work. His cheeks flushed when he remembered Hector's sneer. He dreamed of finding the C Ward med room open and unguarded and filling his pockets to bulging with Vicodin. Not for himself. But the money was good, or at least it was until Hector.

Stealing from the patients was a low-risk enterprise, so he'd mine that vein as long as possible. He smiled. At least the idiots on C Ward were good for something. Maybe they'd be glad to know they were still contributing to the economy if any of them had a brain left to appreciate it. He didn't hate them. They were part of his work environment—as inanimate as towels and wheelchairs, and pills. Some supplied other advantages, but he ensured nobody ever discovered him in that position. The older, frailer women were his preferred targets.

An image of the smooth-skinned college girls walking on College Avenue popped into his mind. He'd probably never have one in his room, so he'd take what he could get. Alone in a patient's room, with the door shut, he'd think of the coeds. Occasionally, he thought of Clare Williams—unclothed and splayed across his bed.

Chapter Sixteen

The day suited Kester's mood. Wind swept across the lake and swirled around the administration building. Low clouds the color of pewter pushed against the brown foothills to the west. Kester hunched into the wind and trudged along the sidewalk from the parking lot to the front entrance.

He walked alone. An awkward message from Clare on his phone said she planned to drive herself to work.

In the conference room, Reggie Wilson sat in his usual spot at the head of the table. The regular Morbidity and Mortality meeting wasn't scheduled to start for another fifteen minutes. Reggie and Kester were alone at the table. Reggie raised his heavy Notre Dame coffee mug to his lips, sipped, and then continued reading the agenda for the upcoming meeting.

"Morning, Reg," Kester said.

Reggie glanced up and nodded as Kester pulled a chair beside him. "How's it goin', Kes?"

Reggie took a stapled copy of the meeting agenda from the top of the pile on the table and scooted it across to Kester. "Great weather for discussing death and medical calamity, isn't it?"

Kester picked up the papers and scanned them. "Yeah, it's gloomy."

Mary Denton's name was on the list. All deaths came under the scrutiny of the M and M Committee, even those patients whose deaths were expected. The report indicated that Mary's body had already been cremated. Should he mention the morphine incident to Reggie? No, better to wait and see what was already known.

As far as the official record was concerned, the extra morphine was destroyed and recorded as a medication error. And as far as Kester knew, that was precisely what happened. Best not to muddy the water until he knew more.

There were only two likely scenarios: Either someone else discovered the syringe and emptied its contents into the wastebasket or sink, or someone emptied the morphine into another container and took it to sell or use themselves. Such things happened. But if someone stood in Mary's room and injected fifty milligrams of morphine into their own arm, they'd probably still be sitting there with tiny pupils and a blank stare.

The other possibility was that someone discovered the syringe and injected all fifty milligrams into Mary. Kester had to admit that Clare's suspicions made a sort of sense. It was no wonder his earlier talk of euthanasia set off alarm bells in her head. The morphine incident was already closed, according to the official record, but he still needed to find some way to convince Clare he hadn't killed Mary Denton.

Other committee members wandered into the conference room for the morning meeting. They worked through the agenda items quickly. Mary's death raised no red flags.

Shortly after eight-thirty, Kester unlocked the door to C Ward and walked to the nursing station. Clare sat at the desk, filling out an incident report. She glance up as Kester swung open the gate to the station and then quickly returned to her work. He reached for her shoulder but pulled his hand back when another staff member rounded the corner.

Kester stood straight and coughed nervously. "Why the incident report?"

Clare kept her eyes on her papers. "Mr. Blanden climbed over his bed rail this morning and fell on his right shoulder. I already put him on your clipboard." Her tone was flat and businesslike. "It's pretty bruised, but he was using the arm at breakfast, so I didn't know if you wanted to get an x-ray."

Kester stood in awkward silence next to Clare while she continued writing, then walked into the short hallway connecting the nursing station to the break room. A row of clipboards hung from hooks along one wall. He grabbed the one labeled "Dr. Grayson" and scanned the top sheet. It held the usual requests for medication changes or evaluation of minor complaints like coughs and constipation. The most recent entry said, *Blanden—bruised shoulder due to fall.*

He'd check Mr. Blanden before the nine o'clock ward staff report. The other entries could wait. He replaced the clipboard and walked to the dayroom.

Fred Blanden was the type of patient some staff called a "Mister Magoo." He was frail and thin, with a mottled, hairless scalp and a prunish face. He slouched low in his wheelchair among the front line of television watchers, his chin on his chest and his eyes closed. He wore a red, long-sleeved shirt with pearl snaps on the front and on the cuffs.

Kester found the med nurse dispensing pills to a patient farther along the line of chairs. "Tina, who has Fred Blanden this morning?" he asked.

Tina turned and pointed her spoon across the room to where a couple of aides stood next to the breakfast tables. "I think Lloyd does," she said.

Lloyd swung a damp towel in slow circles. The skinny, twenty-something girl beside him bent across a tabletop, wiping up crumbs, ignoring him.

"And the fuckin' idiot tried to tell me the car was".... Lloyd spotted Kester and stopped talking. The towel hung at his side. A white half-moon of gut protruded from the bottom of the red t-shirt across Lloyd's abdomen. His face went blank, except for his eyes, which shifted from side to side, unblinking and watchful.

"Lloyd," Kester said, "would you mind bringing Fred Blanden to the exam room so I can look at his shoulder?"

Lloyd turned and walked toward the line of wheelchairs without a word. The girl threw Kester a tight, relieved smile.

Lloyd stood with Fred Burger's wheelchair in front of the exam room. He waited for Kester to unlock the door and hold it open, and then pushed the wheelchair into the room and reached down and locked the brake levers on the wheels.

Fred Blanden's chin still rested on his chest, and his eyes were closed. Lloyd stood behind Fred, bent forward with his elbows resting on the back of the wheelchair. He stared at the far wall, his face as inanimate as the patient in front of him.

Kester closed the door and moved around in front of the wheelchair. "We'll need to get his shirt off," he said.

Lloyd scowled and straightened. "Okay." He reached his hands around the skinny chest and pulled the shirt snaps apart in one quick maneuver. Kester reached to help, but Lloyd grabbed both of the patient's shirtsleeves and tugged the thin arms upward.

Fred moaned. His head flopped backward as Lloyd pulled the shirt cuffs past the old man's pale, boney hands. Lloyd yanked again, harder, exposing the thin chest.

"For Christ's sake!" Kester said. He reached out and steadied the patient's flopping head. "Take it easy!"

Lloyd's face briefly contorted with anger before settling into a look of wary guilt. "Sorry." He tossed the shirt onto the exam table beside the wheelchair and crossed his arms on his chest with a bored deliberation.

Kester scowled. "He's not a goddamn stack of cordwood, Simpson." Kester knelt in front of the chair and examined Fred's shoulder. A large, purple bruise spread along the pale skin. He palpated the soft flesh, feeling the boney structures underneath. No deformity and no obvious tenderness. Fred didn't squirm or even change expression. It was hard to tell if the old man felt anything. Kester remembered dementia patients who hobbled around on a broken ankle or hip and showed no distress.

He raised the old man's arm and palpated across the shoulder joint and the collarbone. The bones moved smoothly under the thin muscles and skin. No sign of a fracture or dislocation and no evidence of discomfort. No need for an x-ray.

Kester reached for Fred's shirt and slipped the right sleeve over the old man's arm. "Let's get you back together, Fred. Okay?" he said. Fred sat with his head down, silent. Lloyd stood relaxed and indifferent. Kester wrapped the shirt around Fred's back and pulled the frail body forward. The movement brought a growl of irritation from the old man. Kester winced but continued. He glanced up and caught Lloyd smirking—either at the doctor's discomfort or the old man's reaction.

Kester finished and stood. "We'll just watch it for now," he said.

Lloyd bent and unlocked the chocks on the wheelchair. He turned the chair toward the door. "Okay."

Kester reached to open the exam room door but hesitated. "Say, Lloyd, I was wondering—were you there when Mary Denton died the other day?"

Lloyd pulled the wheelchair to a stop. His eyes flitted to the closed door.

Kester blocked his way.

"Yeah," Lloyd said. He rocked the wheelchair back and forth and stared at the door.

"I just wondered if you happened to see a syringe on the shelf over her bed." Kester laughed nervously. "I forgot and left it there, and I think one of the nurses—or somebody—came along and threw the medicine away."

Lloyd's face remained passive, except for his eyes, which studied Kester. "What was in it?" Lloyd asked.

Kester stammered. "What—in the syringe?"

"Yeah."

"Some morphine we were saving to give Mary later—if she needed more," Kester said.

Lloyd's eyes narrowed. "And you want to know if I got rid of it—or something?"

"No, no. I imagine one of the nurses came by and tossed it," Kester said. He waved his arm and shook his head in dismissal.

Lloyd pushed the wheelchair forward until the metal footrest banged against the wall. Kester turned the knob and pulled the door open. Lloyd pushed the wheelchair through into the hall until he and the doctor stood face to face. The noise of the ward cut the silence.

"You think I took it?"

"Hey, I'm just asking...."

"But you think I look like the kind of guy who'd take it, right?"

Kester didn't answer. The two men glared at each other for several seconds.

"No," Lloyd said, sneering. "No, you accusing asshole, I didn't see a fucking syringe."

Kester gritted his teeth and returned Lloyd's stare. "I'm not accusing you of anything, Simpson." He lowered his voice and leaned forward. "I just asked a question. I didn't accuse you of anything."

Kester started to turn away but turned back. "And if you ever call me a 'fucking asshole' again, I'll break your arm." He leaned in closer. "And if I ever catch you treating the patients like you treated Fred, I'll break more than your arm."

Lloyd started to speak but hesitated. His mouth snapped shut, and his face flushed deep red. He turned away and pushed the wheelchair down the hallway.

Chapter Seventeen

Katie Lattimer held the picture of a cat in front of Virgil Washington. Virgil sat stiffly in his chair, rubbing his hands back and forth across the tabletop.

"Cat," she said. "Can you say it, Virgil? Cat."

Virgil studied the card for several seconds, raised his head, and stared at Katie. He sat attentive but silent while she showed him picture after picture.

Katie placed the cat picture on the pile of cards to her left and picked one from the stack to her right. "Tree," she said. She showed him the card. "Can you say 'tree,' Virgil?"

He glanced at the card and then back at her. She fluttered the card in frustration before placing it on the left-hand pile. They'd met every Monday morning in the dayroom and every Thursday afternoon in the speech therapy room for over a year, but there'd been no breakthrough.

Virgil's hair was grayer, and his face sagged more than when he'd first arrived at Foothills. His shoulders and his neck still showed some definition. The gut below his shirt's University of Colorado logo ballooned out, adding to an overall sense of bulk. His hands were large and solid with flat, wide nails.

The door opened, and Maureen Washington entered. She wore her usual crisp white blouse and tan slacks. Katie waved her in. Maureen came and stood behind Virgil and reached out to pat his shoulder.

"Hi, honey," she said. She waved across at Katie. "They told me at the desk you were still here, so I thought I'd drop in and see how it's going."

Katie smiled and gestured to the seat next to Virgil. "Sure, Maureen. Good to see you."

Maureen sat with her purse in her lap. She opened it and pulled out a plastic bag. "I brought Virgil some cookies. Would it interfere with the session if I gave him one now?"

"Not at all." Katie reached and patted Virgil's hand. "He's being his usual silent self anyway."

Maureen handed him a cookie. Virgil's face hung loose and expressionless. He stood and shambled over to the window and nibbled the cookie. He pressed his nose against the glass and stared at the pine boughs rustling in the wind.

Katie arranged the picture cards into a neat stack.

Maureen nodded at the cards. "We're back to those again, I see."

"I know it's frustrating, but we've tried everything else at least once," Katie said. "Maybe it's a simple thing that will finally get a response."

Maureen set the plastic bag on the table. "Maybe. But it's been so long—eighteen months since the stroke. And not a single word."

Katie put the cards in her briefcase on the floor beside her chair. "We just never know what will happen after a stroke."

Maureen's mouth turned up in a tiny smile. "I have no illusions about Virgil's condition. I've had enough time to educate myself on strokes and aphasia. Plenty of long nights to study up." She picked up the plastic bag holding the remaining cookies and put it in her purse. "My life is so different now. Almost as different as his life," she said, nodding toward her husband.

"He must've been something back then," Katie said. "I've read his history, of course, in the chart, but that doesn't always tell the whole story."

"No, it certainly doesn't."

"What was he like?"

Virgil stuffed the rest of the cookie into his mouth and chewed slowly, his eyes riveted on something outside. "It's hard to remember sometimes," Maureen said. " You tend to erase all of the negative things after a while as if one big tragedy can cancel out all the other problems. Virgil was something to see, all right, like you said."

She opened her purse, brought out a wallet, and handed a picture to Katie. It showed a much younger and handsome Virgil standing behind a young Maureen. Virgil and Maureen were smiling. Two small children stood in front of them.

"That was taken right after we moved to Golden when Virgil went to work for Coors Brewing. He was so driven then, just like when he played football back in college."

"Did he enjoy his work?" Katie handed the picture back.

Maureen put the picture back in the wallet. "For the most part. But he worked so hard—such long hours. I think he was trying to make up for what happened with his dad, you know."

"I hadn't heard about that," Katie said. "What happened?"

"Right out of college, we moved back to Laramie. Virgil went to work in the family department store. Frank—his dad—built it up over about twenty years and was so proud of it. I think Frank was content to keep it small and local. Virgil came home with his new business degree and jumped in with both feet."

Virgil walked over and stood next to Maureen. She reached into her purse and pulled out another cookie. Virgil took it from her hand and went back to the window.

"Anyway, Virgil convinced his dad to expand the business. He took out a big loan from the bank and used it to expand the Laramie store and open a second store in Cheyenne."

Virgil stared out the window, his belly flat against the glass. "He was always one for action. Not much for dithering about things".

"So what happened with the business?" Katie asked. "I take it things didn't work out."

"No," Maureen said, "they didn't. Within a year, we were in trouble. Virgil worked insane hours, but we lost everything. Frank and Edna even lost their house. They never said it out loud, but I don't think they ever really forgave their son."

"How about you?" Katie said. "Did you forgive him?"

Maureen hesitated, her eyes narrowed. "You know, that's a good question, Katie. Did I ever forgive him?"

"I'm sorry," Katie said. She reached out and touched Maureen's hand. "I don't mean to sound like a psychiatrist."

"No," Maureen said, "that's a valid question. When you live with someone for so many years, you forget the questions, so you don't have to deal with the answers." Maureen made little rubbing motions on the tabletop, lost in thought. "I think I forgave him that," she said. "He was young and naïve, but his heart was good." She laughed and looked at the ceiling. "Yes, that I forgave. There were a few things—later—that I only forgave after his stroke."

Maureen sat silently for a moment. "He was good to us—the kids and me—in his own way. A good provider."

"But not good in other ways?" Katie said.

Virgil stood at the window, his eyes tracking the pine boughs swaying in the wind. "He was the proverbial hard-charging executive: working long hours, smoking, drinking too much—maybe even some infidelity." Maureen put her wallet back in her purse. "The youngest vice president in the history of the Coors Brewing Company." She hesitated again, then continued. "He knew about the high blood pressure. He'd been warned." She smiled at Katie. "Men. Such an exquisite ability to block things out."

"And the high blood pressure brought on the stroke?" Katie said.

Maureen nodded. "He was at a meeting in Denver. They called me and said they'd taken him to Denver General Hospital. When the kids and I arrived, he was out of danger and stable."

"It's so weird, you know?" Maureen said. " He looked about the same, but it was like looking at a photograph. No moving parts—no animation. And not one coherent word from that day to this."

Katie patted Maureen's hand again, nodded, and then checked her watch and stood. "Well, I have to get over to another ward. It was so nice to see you, Maureen," she said.

Maureen smiled. "I was thinking about his last words before leaving for Denver that morning. He said, 'Don't forget to pick up my shirts at the cleaners.' Nothing profound—just a simple everyday request." She stood and moved around the table to give Katie a hug. "Thanks for all you're doing, Katie."

"We'll keep working on it," Katie said. "You never know when you're going to have a breakthrough."

"Oh, Katie," Maureen said. She turned to go get Virgil. "I don't know if I would welcome a breakthrough or not." Her voice came out weary and plaintive. "Sometimes, I hope he's not even in there."

Chapter Eighteen

Reggie Wilson leaned back in his leather chair and lifted his feet and size-fifteen loafers onto the corner of his desk. He tossed a small rubber football from hand to hand as he thought about his meeting with Clare Williams a few minutes earlier.

He'd finished rounds on D Ward and was returning to his office in the admin building. Clare Williams opened the door to C Ward, then turned and locked it.

"Clare? Do you have a few minutes?"

She stopped. "Sure, Reg."

"I'm on my way back to my office right now. Come on." He draped his arm across her shoulders and guided her down the sidewalk. A grin broke out on his broad face. "Don't worry. This isn't about your ongoing, very illicit love affair with that Grayson fellow."

"Uh—you know about...."

Reggie jostled her shoulder. "I'm hoping you two either get engaged or break up before I gotta quit pretending I don't know about it. State regulations, you know."

They climbed the steps to the administration building.

"Actually, kiddo, it is about Kes—about the two of you—but not about your romantic situation. At least, I hope not," Reggie said as they entered his office.

Clare's shoulder tensed under his hand.

"Sit down," Reggie said, motioning to the upholstered chair in front of his desk. He moved around, picked up the small rubber football on the corner of the desk, and sat in his chair.

Clare sat, her body stiff and tight. "What's this about?"

"Our boy Kes has been acting strange lately, and so have you, according to people around here. It's my job to find out about these things." He tossed the football into the air and caught it. "Kind of like a snoopy reporter for National Inquirer."

He set the ball on the desk and studied her expression. "Something's up, and I'd sure like to know what it is that's got you two walking around like a couple of zombies."

"I don't know what you mean."

"Come on, Clare," Reggie said. "I'm not stupid. When you've done this job for as long as I have, you can sense when something's not right. Plus, people talk to me all day long around this place. Like I told Kes, there are no secrets in this institution. And something sure isn't right with you and him."

He reached over and spun the football on the desk. "Besides, Gerry already told me you two had a fight about something here at work—something on the ward."

He held up a hand. "And before you get all riled up about Gerry spilling the beans to me, let me say that she let it slip during rounds on B Ward and didn't go into any details. So don't go yelling at her. She's a good friend and wouldn't hurt you for the world."

Clare sat tight-lipped. Reggie studied her face for several seconds. Finally, Clare cleared her throat and spoke, her voice hesitant. "Reg, it's nothing—really."

"You need to let me be the judge of that, kiddo."

He twirled the football again. "I also had a little visit from Christina."

Clare's hands lay tightly gripped on her lap.

Reggie cleared his throat, then continued. "She was concerned about getting in trouble for a med error on your ward. Said she wasn't worried at first, but your response made her wonder. Said I should talk to you about it."

Clare took a deep breath and fidgeted in the chair, avoiding Reggie's eyes. Finally, she spoke, low and hesitant. "I don't know if this is a big deal or not. And I've had a hard time deciding if I should say anything. I was up all night thinking it over." She bit her lip and then let out a mirthless laugh. "I guess I should've kept my mouth shut around Gerry and Christina."

Clare stood and paced nervously in front of the desk. "This is hard for me"

She stopped pacing. "It has to do with Mary Denton," she said.

"The patient who died on C Ward the other day?"

"Yes," Clare said. "She was end-stage and DNR. We knew it was only a matter of time. And Kes and Nathan even met with Mary's daughters that morning to discuss all that."

Reggie tented his fingers under his chin. "Was the death unusual? I remember some of this from M and M, but I don't recall Kes saying anything strange happened. I guess I'm not sure what the problem is here."

"That's what I'm saying. I don't think there's a problem at all. It was just a misunderstanding."

Reggie studied her face. The pause grew uncomfortably long.

Clare finally continued. "The problem is, I don't know if her death was unusual or not. Kes gave Mary a shot of morphine that morning before she died, and he drew up a lethal dose by mistake."

Reggie sat up straighter in his chair. "He gave her a lethal dose of morphine?"

"No, no." Clare waved her hands. "He just drew up too much by mistake. He didn't give it to her. He only gave her ten milligrams."

"It sounds like a med error to me," Reggie said. He shrugged. "Heck, I've done that before. We all have, I suspect. Wasn't it recorded?"

Clare nodded. "Yeah. Christina did the paperwork."

Reggie looked puzzled. "What am I missing here?" He was met with silence. "Clare, what am I missing here?"

She hugged her chest. "Kes said he left the other fifty milligrams in Mary's room—on the shelf."

"Okay," Reggie said. He leaned back in his chair and propped his chin on his hand. "Now that sounds pretty stupid. But not a hanging offense, really. I'll talk to him later today."

Clare frowned.

Reggie sighed. "I hate this part of my job, you know. I always feel like an interrogator beating information out of somebody." He rubbed the back of his neck and waited. Finally, he spoke. "I didn't want to get to this point, but maybe you need to consider your obligation to the hospital and your profession. I hope that's enough motivation for you. I hope I don't have to drag Christina and Gerry back in here."

Clare hesitated, then took a deep breath. "The morphine in the syringe disappeared. Kes says he didn't empty it in the sink, and nobody else on the ward knows anything about it. Christina found the empty syringe on the shelf after Mary died. She thought Kes disposed of it, so she filled out the med error paperwork."

Reggie frowned. "Damn, Clare, this just gets worse and worse. Are you saying Kes may have kept the morphine for himself?"

"No way." Clare shook her head. "I know Kes well enough by now. He isn't using drugs. I've known doctors who did, and he isn't the type."

Reggie leaned forward and put his arms on the desk. "Well, I guess somebody on the staff could be lying." He stared at the football for several seconds. "Or Kes could've slipped up and given the patient a bigger dose of morphine than he meant to and then lied about it." He drummed his fingers on the desk for a moment and shook his head. "But Kes doesn't strike me as an incompetent physician or a liar."

Clare stood straighter. Anger flashed in her eyes. "Kes is no liar! He's a good man." She gripped the edge of the desk, regaining her composure. "Anyone can have some doubts in this place." She glared at Reggie. "Anyone."

"So." Reggie leaned back in his chair. "Tell me about this doubt Kes is experiencing."

"Oh, I don't know, Reg," Clare said. "He's been conflicted lately."

"How so?"

"He talked about active euthanasia the other night—about how maybe we should intervene somehow when a patient gets really bad." She shook her head. "It was just talk like we all do."

He nodded. "That's what Gerry said."

She continued quickly, eager to explain. "And it was probably just a coincidence that this thing with Mary happened so soon after that."

"Sure," Reggie said. "And sometimes patients die sooner than we expect." He picked up a paper from the desk, read it for a few seconds, then set it down. "Don't know where I put that report. Anyway, I seem to remember that Denton was cremated. Is that right?"

Clare nodded.

"So we can't check the body to see how much morphine was in her bloodstream."

Clare stiffened in the chair. Reggie sat forward. "To confirm that Kes didn't overdose her, of course," he added.

Reggie stood and walked around the desk. "Thanks, Clare, for bringing this to my attention,"

Clare walked with him to the door.

"I feel like I've betrayed him, Reg," she said. "I never should've mentioned any of this to anybody." Her voice trembled. "This has all got to be a big misunderstanding. Seeing him agonize about this kills me, but I don't know what to do for him."

"I know," Reggie said. He patted her shoulder and guided her to the door. "I'll have a talk with him—get this straightened up. Don't worry."

He closed the door and walked back to his chair, where he propped his shoes on the corner of the desk and began to worry.

Mikayla Thompson's diamond nose stud flashed in the sun, momentarily blinding Kester. He shaded his face with his free hand. "Mind if I sit with you?" he said.

Mikayla squinted up at him. "Sure, Doc, grab a seat."

Kester set his lunch bag on the concrete table and straddled the bench. Mikayla flashed a crooked smile. Her body slouched forward, thin to the point of emaciation. Her wispy, yellow hair outlined a narrow, sunburned face. Heavy eyeliner surrounded dark blue eyes. The yellow t-shirt covering her chest lay as smooth and flat as a child's.

Kester grinned. "Good lord, Mikayla, how can you stay so skinny? Every time I see you, food is going into your mouth."

Mikayla continued chewing. "Don't know, Doc. Calories don't stick to me. My mom weighs over two hundred pounds. Go figure." She shrugged her slender shoulders and took another huge bite of pizza.

Hospital workers filled the patio outside the cafeteria. A few cottony clouds drifted east from behind the mountains. Mikayla's and Kester's table sat near the south end of the patio, away from the rest of the lunch crowd.

After his encounter with Lloyd that morning, Kester stayed in the exam room for a few minutes, fighting the urge to rush out and slam the insolent little prick into the wall. He elected instead to do nothing while Lloyd pushed Fred Blanden back to the dayroom.

Maybe he should've kept quiet about the syringe. But after what Clare said, he needed to prove to her that he wasn't responsible for Mary's death.

And there'd been something odd about the way Lloyd denied knowing about the morphine. His fury masked an undercurrent of guilt about something. So far, Kester only knew that Lloyd's hatred for him was all too real and now very personal. The surly aide was capable of anything, Kester was certain. He needed to find out more about the man.

Kester and Lloyd avoided each other for the rest of the morning. At lunch, Kester studied the other ward workers before deciding Mikayla might have some answers.

He reached into his lunch bag and pulled out a sandwich. "If they quit selling Skippy Super Chunk, I may get as skinny as you," he said.

Mikayla laughed. Kester bit into the sandwich as she sipped her soda. "So, do you think you and Clare will move in together?"

Kester lowered his sandwich. "For the love of Pete! Is there some kind of spy network in this place?"

"There might as well be, Doc." She pointed the pizza at the other diners around the patio. "All these trained observers, ya know." She took another bite of pizza. "I like her."

"Who? Clare?"

"Yeah. She's always nice to me," Mikayla said. "And to the patients too."

"It's true," Kester said. "She has trouble being mean to anyone. Do you like the other people on C Ward?"

"You mean the workers?" Mikayla chewed and thought for a moment. "Mostly. By the way, Doc, thanks for saving me from Lloyd this morning in the dayroom when I was cleaning tables."

"Why?" Kester said. "Don't you two get along?"

She wrinkled her nose. "The guy is just too weird. I tried being nice to him when we first started working together, but he's creepy."

"What do you mean, 'creepy'?" Kester bit into his sandwich.

"The whole white coat thing, the attitude—all of it."

Kester laughed around the peanut butter. "Yeah, I think his white coat thing is kinda creepy too."

"And he can be a real shit when it comes to helping with stuff," Mikayla said. "Like with Wilma Carsten? That new patient we got in last week? All I asked was could he help get her out of the bathroom, and he just looked at me with that creepy, shitty grin and walked away."

Kester glanced out at the lake, feigning disinterest. "So he's not one of your favorites," he said.

"No way." She raised her eyebrows and pushed her palms against the table's edge. She chewed for a moment. Her mouth turned down in disgust. "Even when he's talking to you, it's like he's not really saying anything *to* you. But he stares like he wants to do something to you." Her thin arms shivered, although the day was warm.

Kester reached and patted her hand. "Well, tell Clare or me if he gives you too much trouble." He waited a few seconds and then asked, "So, isn't Lloyd close to anyone on the ward?"

"None of the women, that's for sure," Mikayla said. "The only guy I ever see him with is Dennis Enger, but he got moved to afternoon shift."

Kester finished his sandwich and gathered his trash, stuffing it into the brown lunch sack. "Well, back to work," he said, standing.

"Hey, Doc?" Mikayla squinted up at him again. "Why all the questions about Lloyd? Why just him?"

"Oh, I don't know," Kester said. "I guess because he's an interesting person."

"If by 'interesting' you mean a total creep, I agree." Her voice displayed no hint of humor. "Has he done anything?"

"Done anything?" Kester said. "No, not that I know of. Do you know of anything he's done?"

"Nothing I'd put down on paper and sign," Mikayla said. She glanced around the crowded patio. "But I think a guy like him could get away with some bad-ass things. He could just do them and never think twice about it."

She stood, wadded her lunch sack into a ball, and arched it perfectly into a nearby trashcan. "I sure hope you and Clare move in together," she said. "See you later, Doc." She turned and walked away.

Kester threw the rest of his sandwich into the trash can and stuck his hands in his pockets. He watched the workers laughing and talking around him and shook his head. "I'll be happy if Clare ever talks to me again.".

Chapter Nineteen

A mind at perfect peace with God; Oh what a word is this!
A sinner reconciled through blood; This, this indeed, is peace.

The preacher mumbles along with the hymn, hunched forward in his wheelchair with his ever-present bible on the tray before him. I don't think he knows the words of the song. It looks like his mouth is moving in a random chewing motion. But he's definitely watching the minister who's up in front of the room and nodding a little bit to the music.

The minister is wearing a shiny purple robe. Some young guy this time. He's holding a hymnal up, but he must know the words by heart because he's looking out over the small crowd of patients and helpers and waving his hand in time to the music— bobbing his head a little—just like the preacher.

If he's trying to get more enthusiasm out of this crowd, he's wasting his time. Even the plump woman playing the piano in the corner is having an off day.

Most of the patients in the crowd sit silently or look around while some helpers and a few visitors sing. The preacher is at least paying attention to the minister. But then, the preacher didn't lose his spiritual zeal when he lost his mind. He's pretty far gone now, but when he first got to the ward, he could recite scripture like crazy.

He'd stagger around with that bible stuck on the end of his arm like a permanent body part, yammering on about the righteous and the damned.

I bet he could give a damn good sermon in his day. In fact, I wonder if he's sitting there wishing he could go up and knock that young minister aside and get this crowd on its feet. Probably not. Like I said, he's pretty far gone.

The song ends, but some old guy to my right goes on making noise. It's just a faint rumbling sound, so I don't know if he's trying to sing another verse or what.

The young minister has his arms outstretched, spread out like a big, shiny, purple bat, while he says a prayer. His eyes are closed. I peek across, and the preacher sits back in his chair, clutching his bible to his belly. He's all skin and bones except for a plump, round lump in his middle. Some old guys go like that, thinning down from the perimeter until they look like stick figures, with all their reserves concentrated in a last stand around their belly buttons.

The prayer must've been the benediction because the crowd begins to stand and mill around. Helpers push wheelchairs back to the ward. The hallway outside the activity room is drenched in golden sunlight, making a nice, cheery finish to the Sunday service. The patients and helpers in front of me move through the bright light like souls arriving in heaven. I follow along to the ward and to lunch.

Two helpers show up in the afternoon to take some of us fishing. We walk down the path to the lake and stand on the dock, where they bait a couple of hooks and cast out into the water. One of them hands me a pole and gives the other pole to the farmer, and we stand there watching the bobbers. I think I've fished with the farmer before. He's in his usual faded overalls. He tugs on the fishing pole but doesn't reel it in. The other two patients nod and drowse in their wheelchairs and show no interest in fishing. One of them glances at the water but not at the bobbers. There's a breeze off the lake, ruffling his hair into a bunch of little whitecaps. I've checked both of them out, and they are definitely rocks.

The helper guys are over by the shore, smoking and talking. Once in a while, they look over to check on us and watch the red and white bobbers.

I am trying to remember when I started going to Sunday services. I don't think I was a religious person back before the stroke. But for some reason, a fair amount of religious stuff is still stuck in my head. Not like whole passages from the Bible or anything—just general stuff.

Maybe they made me go to Sunday school when I was a kid. I remember my dad and mom, dressed up and standing next to me in a pew, holding books and singing. I can even smell the furniture polish, and the scent of old books, and the starch in my stiff, white shirt.

So there's some religion in my past, although, like I said, I don't think I was religious. The idea of church and some kind of belief comforts me, though perhaps more comforting as a pleasant childhood memory than anything spiritual.

One of the helper guys ambles over. He takes the fishing pole out of my hands and reels in the line. The hook is empty. He roots around in a Styrofoam cup full of dirt, pulls out a fat night crawler, sticks it on the hook, loops it around, and pokes the other end over the barb. Both ends of the worm snap around and strain upward toward the sky, like the minister giving his benediction. The helper guy whips the pole through the air, sending the worm and the bobber sailing out into the lake, then sets the drag and hands the pole to me.

Sometime later, he reels it in. The worm lies thinned out along the hook, motionless and drooping. We catch no fish.

Back on the ward, I sit by the nursing station. There's someone else in the bed where the song lady used to be—another rock. The song lady passed away shortly after I gave her the medicine, so I guess it didn't do her any good. It would be nice if Doctor K knew that I at least tried to help. If I'm reading his face right, he's been so troubled lately. Maybe if he'd been at the Sunday service this morning, he would've been uplifted. But I don't know if he's religious, either.

It was so pleasant afterward, walking down the hallway with the sunlight shining everyone up and the dust motes hovering around us like souls who'd gone to heaven welcoming us home.

Dickweed races down the hall wearing his white coat. He's pushing the preacher along in a wheelchair. The preacher sits open-mouthed, like a man who's lost control of his car on a mountain road. His eyes stand out big and scared, and he's clutching the side of his activity tray with one hand while his other hand holds his bible like a lantern showing the way.

Dickweed is scowling, as usual. He's ramped up his campaign against the patients lately, getting in a few more smacks and jabs and tossing bodies around like sacks of flour.

The other day, he fondled an old woman's breast while he rubbed his groin along her arm. He checked around first to see if anyone was watching, but I blend into the background, so I don't think he took me into account. Even while he was squeezing and rubbing, he looked like someone beating a dog.

They round the corner like a careening getaway car and skid to a stop in front of the washroom. Dickweed sticks his butt against the door to open it and backs in, pulling the wheelchair after him. The door shuts, and the sound of running water drifts out.

Maybe the preacher's faith followed him to this place, but it's hard to know, considering how he acted when he arrived. I don't think you get a ticket to this ward without a history of raising a little hell, so it's doubtful his decline has been all roses.

He must've been too big a handful for someone—acting up and yelling or something.

He went around sort of wild-eyed at first, with his big mane of white hair and fevered speech, like he was crazy or maybe a prophet filled with the Holy Spirit. Has it stuck to him through it all— his faith? Maybe a good, strong helping of the Holy Spirit is just the thing to make the slide from horse to rock less terrifying. He clutches that book like he's trying to keep a grip on something important.

The ward is always quiet on Sunday nights. A lot of the patients get tucked in a little earlier than usual, and the helpers gravitate to the break room or the television or slip outside for a smoke.

The mountain man walks out of the dayroom and opens the washroom door. The preacher's head sticks up over the top of the big metal bathtub. The mountain man motions to dickweed, and says something. Dickweed comes out of the washroom wearing his usual pissed-off expression and follows the other guy down the hall after a quick glance back at the preacher.

The washroom door glides shut. I walk over and push it open. The warm steam and the smell of shampoo hit my nose. The preacher sits propped up in the metal tub, staring straight ahead with his hair slicked back like a white helmet and his knees sticking out of the soapy water. His bible rests on the seat of his wheelchair.

I tiptoe across the wet tile, but water seeps into my socks anyway. The preacher turns to look at me when he hears my footsteps. I squat next to the tub, my hands resting on the rounded rim. He reaches out with his hand and covers mine as warm as sunlight through a window. His eyes are calm now, impassive, neither welcoming nor judging. I look down inside, for once truly afraid of what I will find. So afraid I almost stand up and turn away. But his hand rests on my hand with gentle pressure, almost like a caress.

I look into his eyes again and get an overwhelming sense of disappointment and sadness. The fires burn bright, swirling and writhing with unbearable heat, forcing me to close my eyes for a few seconds and drop my head, dreading what must be done.

My hand pushes on his head, and he slides underwater with a frictionless, fluid motion. Twice he tries to rise, his heels pushing against the end of the tub, forcing his head partway out of the water. The third time I push him down, he stays under. A fist-sized bubble of air rises from his mouth and roils the water's surface, and then he drifts, loose in my grip. His hands float to the surface, the fingers relaxed and waving like palm fronds in a breeze.

I keep a grip on his hair for another minute before lifting his head out of the water. His left eye is closed, but his other eye cracks open enough so that I can look down inside. The terrible fires have been washed away. His head slumps forward on his chest when I let go of his hair. It makes me think he's back, leading his flock in prayer.

The bible lies in his wheelchair seat, and I consider taking it with me. But, like I said, I'm not religious, and I don't suppose it would help me now.

Chapter Twenty

Pastor McNair's feet extended beyond the edge of the sheet, splayed out at a forty-five-degree angle, white and lifeless. The body lay covered, awaiting a ride to the coroner's office.

The ward was dark, except for the light from the nursing station. Kester sat at the desk, finishing his chart notes. Staff moved in and out of the circle of light with almost no sound. When they spoke, it was in hushed tones. The gurney holding the body sat against the wall by the washroom, imposing an unusually somber mood on the workers.

Kester was watching television in the call room when the operator phoned to tell him of the emergency. He'd arrived on the ward to find the naked and still-wet Pastor McNair stretched out on the washroom floor. The ward nurse pumped rhythmically on the pastor's breastbone. Another staff member, John Logan, pressed a ventilation mask to the narrow, wet face with his left hand and squeezed an Ambu bag with his right after every fifteen pumps.

Kester knelt beside them on the wet tile. "What we got, Nancy?"

Nancy glanced up but continued pumping. "He was in the tub. Down maybe five minutes now," Her speech came in short, staccato bursts. "Don't know what happened. Maybe an MI."

Kester's fingers moved along the pastor's neck. A faint pulse ticked under his fingertips with each chest compression.

"All right, hold up a sec," he said.

Nancy rocked back on her heels, her breath coming in short gasps. She brushed a loose strand of hair from her eyes with the back of her hand. John Logan pulled the mask away from Pastor McNair's face. Kester lifted the pastor's right eyelid and played his penlight across the pupil. The large, black circle didn't shrink in the light.

"Fixed and dilated," Kester said. "Let me spell you, Nancy."

He placed his right hand on top of his left hand and pressed his palm against the middle of the chest. The skin was still warm because of the bath water or because life continued to flicker in the body. John placed the mask back over the pastor's face.

"Get the AED," Kester said. "Let's be sure before we decide if we need to call it."

Nancy struggled to her feet and left the washroom, returned with a portable automatic electronic defibrillator, and knelt beside the body. John used a towel to dry a spot on the Pastor's upper chest and another over his left rib cage. Nancy peeled the backing from two defibrillator pads and slapped the pads against the now-dry flesh.

Kester nodded at the patches. "Go ahead and hook 'em up."

Nancy snapped wire leads onto the pads and pushed the button on the AED panel. The small display on the unit brightened. A thin line ran straight and level across the screen.

"It looks awfully quiet," Kester said. If any energy moved through the pastor's heart muscle, the machine would automatically evaluate it and announce that a shock should be given. The machine's computer-generated voice remained mute.

The skin under Kester's palm grew cooler as heat left the body. Nancy looked at the AED screen and then at Kester. John continued to count out every fifteen compressions, ending each count with another squeeze of the Ambu bag.

Kester relaxed his arms and sat upright. "Let's call it," he said. John gave one last squeeze on the bag before lifting the mask away. Kester glanced at his watch. "Time of death, 9:15 P.M." Kester's knees ached from contact with the hard tile floor. He pushed back until his weight rested on his feet and raised his knees away from the wet surface.

Nancy removed the wires from the AED pads. She picked up the towel and draped it across the naked hips and lower belly. John and Nancy stood, brushing the wet patches on their knees. John frowned and mouthed a word. "Shit."

"What happened?" Kester said.

Lloyd Simpson and another aide, a large, bearded young man, stood in the doorway, watching the code. Lloyd gripped the doorframe and stared at the pastor's body, avoiding Kester's eyes. His face showed no emotion. Only his eyes showed any activity, shifting from the body to the empty tub. He turned and walked down the hall.

Nancy bent and picked up the AED. Kester squatted next to the body, checking the cooling, pale skin for signs of trauma.

"Lloyd was giving Pastor McNair a bath. He says he just quit breathing," Nancy said.

"Where were you when it happened?"

"I ran to the supply room to get some Chux pads." She wrapped the AED wires around her hand. "I was only gone for a few minutes. When I got back, Lloyd and Dennis were lifting him out of the tub."

"Was he a full code when you found him?"

"No breathing, no pulse. Still warm, but he was just out of the hot water. And they told me he'd only been unresponsive for a minute or two." Dennis stood in the doorway, his hands in his pockets. "Is that about right, Dennis?"

"Yes, ma'am," the man said. His thick-framed glasses and a full, black beard masked his expression.

"Lloyd was givin' him a bath, and I was comin' down the hall when he yelled." He looked from Nancy to Kester and then at the body. "We dragged him out of the tub and put him on the floor. I was going to go for help, but Nurse Thompkins,"---he nodded at Nancy—" showed up just then."

Nancy walked out to the hall and returned, pushing a gurney. The three lifted the Pastor and placed him on the wheeled cart. Nancy unfurled a clean sheet. It settled around the hills and valleys of the body until just the feet poked out, sallow and naked at the end of the gurney. She parked the gurney against the wall in the hallway and hurried off to call the coroner's office.

Kester signed his name at the bottom of the chart entry and closed the metal cover. Samuel McNair's congregation would awaken tomorrow morning to hear about the death of the former pastor of the United Methodist Church. Kester had seen him preach once at a funeral service for one of Kester's high school classmates killed in a car accident.

McNair talked about the sorrow surrounding death at a young age, his voice mellow and reassuring as he spoke of God's grace and the promise of everlasting life. When Kester admitted him to the ward, the pastor stuttered and rambled, the victim of a barrage of tiny brain strokes. Dementia gradually closed him down until he wandered the ward with his bible and with a wild, unfocused look in his eyes.

Nancy walked from the darkened hall into the nursing station. "I told Dennis he could go out and smoke." She looked back over her shoulder. "He's really shook. Lloyd went with him."

"Isn't Simpson usually on the day shift?" Kester said. He walked over to the chart rack, slipping the metal chart cover into its assigned slot.

"Usually," Nancy said. "But if we need a fill-in, he volunteers sometimes. He and Dennis Enger are friends, it seems." She frowned.

"Not a fan of either one?" Kester asked.

"No," she said. "And something doesn't ring true about their story tonight."

"You mean the nervousness?"

"Well, a code is always stressful," she said. "But there was something else."

"Yeah, I felt it too," Kester said. He crossed his arms. "Think they're lying?"

Nancy thought for a moment, then walked into the break room and returned with two mugs of coffee. She handed one to Kester and leaned against the countertop. "I'd be reluctant to make any accusations," she said. "I don't like either of them, I'll admit. But I don't want that to falsely accuse anyone, either."

Kester sipped the bitter, warmed-over coffee. "Same here. I had a run-in—kind of—with Lloyd the other day. But I don't want to read too much into this."

They stood in silence for a few moments. The coffee calmed him.

"Oh, by the way," Nancy said, "the coroner said no autopsy's required because it was an in-hospital death in an essentially terminal patient. So I'll call the funeral home if you want." She picked up the phone.

"Sure," Kester said. He took another sip from his cup and walked to the break room, pouring the remaining coffee into the sink and setting the cup on the counter.

Lloyd and Dennis appeared in the doorway.

"Uh—Doc?" Dennis said. He stuck his hands in his pockets and lowered his head. A faint clicking sound came from his coat pocket— the snap of a Zippo lighter closing. Dennis clicked the lighter with a staccato rhythm.

Kester kept his eyes centered on Lloyd, who returned Kester's stare with unblinking contempt and defiance. Any guilt or fear the younger man might've displayed earlier was now safely hidden behind a mask of hatred.

Kester turned back toward Dennis. "Pretty rough night, huh?" He kept his tone neutral. The bearded aide shrugged, still avoiding Kester's eyes.

"Yeah, a rough shift." Dennis hesitated. "Too bad about the old guy," he said. "You think it was a heart attack or somethin'?"

"Don't know," Kester said, his voice neutral. "Probably." He waited for a few seconds and then shrugged. "I guess the coroner will figure it out."

The clicking sound in Dennis's pocket quickened. "Oh," he said, "so the coroner will take a look at the body?" he said.

"Yeah," Kester said. "They always check out cases like this. He should be able to tell us if it was a heart attack—or drowning or something."

The clicking sound became even faster. Lloyd reached over and jostled Dennis's arm. "Quit it."

Dennis raised his eyebrows. "Huh?"

"Quit clickin' the fucking Zippo," Lloyd said. He stared at Kester. "It's annoying." The clicking stopped. Dennis took a deep breath and coughed nervously. "Doc...."

Lloyd nudged his friend again. "Shut up, Enger." It came out as a sharp command.

Dennis turned toward his friend, his face twisted with worry. "Shit, Lloyd, they're going to find out when they do the autopsy thing anyway."

"Shut the fuck up, man," Lloyd said. He glared at his friend.

Kester placed his hand on Dennis's shoulder. "Hey, Simpson," he said. His tone sharpened. "Why don't you shut the fuck up and let Dennis speak for himself?"

Lloyd's cheeks flushed. His eyes blazed with hatred. He shoved Dennis in the back, jostling him into Kester.

"Thanks, Dennis, you dumb, spineless shithead," he said. He turned and stalked out the door.

Chapter Twenty-One

Gene Rogers leaned forward and rested his elbows on the conference table in Reggie's office. Gene pointed the pen in his right hand at Kester. The pen thrust forward with small, jabbing motions.

"Doctor Grayson was clearly out of bounds on this issue," he said. Gene leaned back in his chair and rotated it sideways, lifting one leg and resting his polished, black cowboy boot on the knee of his pressed jeans. The pen turned and pointed at Reggie Wilson, who sat at the head of the table.

"The collective bargaining rules are clear on this, Reg," he said. The union shop steward almost matched the Medical Director in height but carried a sizeable paunch across his middle. His job title at Foothills was listed as 'custodian,' but his position in the employees' union gave his words a powerful air of authority.

Reggie frowned, as much from Gene's words as from the gravity of the meeting. He hated it when Gene Rogers called him 'Reg.' Reggie managed the hospital with friendly informality. He seldom insisted that any staff address him as 'Doctor Wilson,' but it always irked him when Gene used this power play in their meetings and negotiations.

"Okay, Gene," Reggie said. "I'm aware of the union rules—Mr. Simpson's rights," he added, nodding toward Lloyd.

The aide sat next to Gene. Today he'd left his white coat at home and wore a pressed shirt and a pair of black slacks. His eyes avoided Kester, who sat across the table. Lloyd clasped his hands on the tabletop, his face impassive.

"I'm also aware of Doctor Grayson's responsibility in this matter," the medical director continued. He tapped his finger on the sheet of paper in front of him. "But the fact is, we have a statement from Dennis Enger saying the patient was left unattended." He shook his head from side to side. "You know, Gene, we can bullshit all day long—arguing about how long those two boys were off doin' something else—but we're still going to get back to the fact that we got a dead patient and a negligent staff member."

Kester swiveled his chair from side to side. The fingers of his right hand drummed softly on his copy of Dennis's statement.

After Lloyd stormed out of the break room on C Ward, Dennis told Kester everything. He explained how he'd asked Lloyd to help him get a patient out of the bathroom and back into bed. Dennis insisted they'd been away from the washroom for only a few minutes before Lloyd returned to attend to Pastor McNair. The rest of the aides were on the opposite end of the ward at the time. It was doubtful any of them knew how long Dennis and Lloyd were away from the washroom.

Dennis responded first after Lloyd's panicked call for help. He arrived to find his friend pulling the old man out of the tub. Dennis grabbed the legs while Lloyd hoisted the torso up and over the tub rim onto the floor. They squatted next to the body for about a minute, checking for any signs of breathing or movement. By the time the nurse arrived and began CPR, they'd already whispered frantically back and forth, establishing their story.

In the break room, Dennis gave Kester his new account of the incident in short, nervous sentences, accompanied by the rapid clicking of the cigarette lighter in his coat pocket. Kester spent several minutes talking to Dennis, confirming the details of the incident, and then asked him if he was willing to write it all down. The frightened aide agreed once Kester assured him he wasn't in trouble. Since Lloyd was responsible for the pastor at the time of the incident, Dennis couldn't be held liable.

"Maybe so," Dennis signed his name to the bottom of his written statement. "But I've lost my only friend." Dennis looked toward the darkened doorway. "And I sure don't like the idea of Simpson as an enemy."

Gene picked up his copy of Dennis's statement. "Reg," the union man said, "if you try to use this thing as a true account of what happened the other night, we'll have one of our lawyers in here so fast it'll make your head swim." Gene slapped the paper back down onto the tabletop, then turned toward Kester, studying him with a tight frown.

"Doctor Grayson, why didn't you go through the proper procedure with Dennis? Pete Dugan is the union rep on evening shift. He could've come over and advised him of his rights under union rules."

Kester hunched forward, puckered his lips, and glowered at the union steward. "Well, let's see, Gene. My patient was dead in the bathtub, I wasn't sure what killed him, and this guy—" he pointed his thumb at Lloyd—" and his buddy were the last people to see him alive. Besides which, they were acting guilty as hell."

Gene held up a hand and shook his head. "Mr. Simpson already admitted he and Mr. Enger were nervous due to the circumstances of the patient's death and the subsequent attempts to revive him."

Kester pictured Lloyd's impenetrable silence in the break room.

"And as for calling Pete Dugan over to feed me a bunch of union bullshit, well—no. That wasn't real high on my list of priorities. I was more interested in finding out how Sam McNair wound up dead when Simpson here was only supposed to wash his hair." He thrust his finger at Lloyd.

The union rep tented his fingers, pondered this for several seconds, and then turned to Reggie. "Despite Doctor

Grayson's sardonic explanation, I'm telling you that this will bring out the big legal guns if you try to use any of Dennis Enger's statements against Mr. Simpson."

"Oh, for chrissake, Gene, don't bring in a bunch of lawyers," Reggie said.

Gene turned back to Kester. "Lloyd has given his statement concerning Sam McNair's death. Lloyd had a union representative present when he dictated and signed his statement. At this time, that makes it the official record of what happened on C Ward." He flicked the paper on the table before him, sending it skidding halfway across the smooth surface. "Mr. Enger's statement would be inadmissible in any legal proceeding."

"I'm afraid Gene is right about this, Kes." He turned to the union rep.

"Okay, Gene, for now, Mr. Simpson is off home leave and back on duty." He glared at Lloyd. "Unless—or until—any further information comes to light. That's it for now." Reggie shoved the stack of papers on the desk and stood.

The wheels under Gene's chair squeaked against the floor as he pushed away from the table. Lloyd still sat motionless, his eyes riveted on Kester.

"C'mon, Lloyd," Gene said.

Lloyd stood and started toward the door, then hesitated and turned back to face Kester. "Wait," he said. "How about an apology?"

"An apology?" Gene said, puzzled. Reggie stood motionless at the head of the table.

Lloyd's eyes held steady on Kester. "Yeah. I think the Doc owes me that."

Kester let out a bitter laugh.

Reggie cleared his throat and pointed at Lloyd. "Don't push your luck, son," he said, his eyes flashing an angry warning.

"Lloyd, let's go," Gene said. He put his hand on Lloyd's back. "It's over and done."

Lloyd stood motionless, staring across the table at Kester, who gritted his teeth.

"I just want him to say he's sorry for dragging me into this," Lloyd said. The corners of his mouth curled up in a malevolent leer.

Kester laughed again. He looked at the ceiling momentarily, then dropped his gaze back toward Lloyd and thrust his index finger out. "Okay, you devious shit. Here's your apology." He stood up and leaned across the table. "I'm sorry I didn't kick your pathetic ass when you threatened me in the exam room the other day."

Lloyd stuck an unlit cigarette in his mouth and leered at Kester. Then he turned away, with Gene practically pushing him out of the room.

Reggie waited for them to leave and then walked over and closed the door. Kester paced the floor. He ran his hand through his hair in irritation.

Reggie stood. "What the hell was all that?"

Kester continued pacing, lost in his anger. "I can't believe that little prick wants an apology," he said. "Lying through his teeth and expecting me to tell him I'm sorry?"

Reggie moved around the table and rested his hand on Kester's shoulder. "Sit down, Kes. I've got more to say." Kester stopped pacing and sat. Reggie pulled another chair close to the still-muttering Kester and sat facing him. Kester twisted back and forth in his chair, staring at the far wall.

"I don't much care for this either, son," Reggie said. He leaned forward with his elbows on his knees. "No doubt about it. This was pure crap on a cracker. But I've been dealing with Gene Rogers and the union for a long time. Old Gene may only be a custodian, but he knows the union like the Pope knows religion. If he says this will blow up in our faces, you better duck and cover."

Kester paced next to the table. "Jesus, Reg, I can't believe this place."

Reggie reached over and patted Kester's knee. "Sometimes I can't believe it either, my friend." He stood, walked to his desk, opened a drawer, and pulled out a bottle and two glasses. Back at the table, he set the glasses down, unscrewed the cap on the bottle, and poured each glass half full of clear liquid.

"What's that?" Kester said.

Reggie slid one of the glasses over in front of Kester. "Tequila. After what we just experienced, it's probably a good time for a little numbing medicine."

"Isn't this against hospital policy?" Kester asked. He raised the glass and sipped.

Reggie downed his in a single gulp. "Sure as hell." He winced and swallowed. "And maybe if we get an affidavit and sign it in blood with a union rep and a team of lawyers present, they'll bust us for drinking on state property." He set the empty glass on the table. "Until then, fuck 'em."

Kester smiled and finished his drink. "So what happens now?"

Reggie leaned against the edge of the table. "Well, when Dennis Enger calms down, and when he finds out the coroner didn't examine the body, and when he discovers the statement he gave you is just so much toilet paper, I imagine he'll decide he was terribly mistaken and will change his story to match Lloyd's."

He paused for a moment. "And if that scary, ice-cold young man we just saw in here gets an opportunity to be alone with poor Mr. Enger for a few minutes, I can almost guarantee that the 'official' version will receive a unanimous vote."

Kester tipped his glass up and gulped the rest of the tequila.

"We'll keep our eyes peeled for any new information," Reggie said. He carried the glasses and the bottle back to his desk.

Kester stood and walked over to the window, his hands in his pockets. A thunderstorm roiled over the mountains. Wind disturbed the surface of the lake at the bottom of the hill. Lightning flickered between the soot-gray lower side of the storm and the foothills behind the steel-colored water. At this distance, there was no clap of thunder.

Kester turned toward Reggie. "I think I need some time off," he said.

Reggie blinked in surprise. "Because of this?"

"This and—other things," Kester said.

"Is this about the morphine and Mary Denton?"

It was Kester's turn to look surprised. "You know about that?"

"Yeah," Reggie said. "Did you give her too much?"

"Did I kill her? No."

Reggie nodded. "I never thought you did. I know you're telling me the truth."

Kester turned back to watch the storm. "I gave her enough to stop her pain. But sometimes I wonder why I couldn't give her enough to end her suffering for good." The sound of thunder finally rolled in across the lake from the approaching storm. "Does that make sense?"

"You think you're the only doctor who ever thought about pushing the ethical limits?" Reggie snorted. "I don't think you're that naïve, son. Most of us think about it. We just don't go ahead with it." He shrugged. "Probably for many different reasons, but we somehow find a way to keep to that Hippocratic Oath."

Kester dropped his head and rubbed the back of his neck. He didn't respond.

Reggie spoke quietly. "Kes, take a couple of weeks off. Try to forget about what happened today." He walked over and rested his hand on Kester's back. "But I want you to think a lot about that second thing—how much morphine you need to give a terminal patient. When you answer that, you'll know whether you should return to Foothills."

Chapter Twenty-Two

I'm going to stay in bed for a little longer this morning. Lifting the Mexican did something to my back. Most of the time, it's not bad enough to keep me in bed, but it's worse than usual today. One of the helpers tried to get me up earlier, but eventually, he left me alone.

We've got another screamer down the hall. I plan to check her out sometime soon, to look down into her eyes and see if she's screaming from the fire. Some of them scream out of frustration, not pain. It's easy to become frustrated here—I know.

The back spasms aren't as bad if I stay rolled over on my side. Plus, it lets me keep at least one of my ears against the pillow, blocking some noise. This is a busy place most mornings. There are better places to try to get some extra sleep.

Even with all the clanging, screaming, general buzz of the ward, and back pain, I've dozed a little this morning. My memory is better lately. There are still giant gaps, but parts of my past are starting to fall into place. Even so, my dreams and memories tend to mix when I'm semi-awake, like now. One minute I'm in a bathroom, staring into a mirror. Maureen stands in the doorway with her arms folded across her chest. We're arguing about something—I don't know what. Maureen is a little younger. In the mirror, I am too. Shaving cream covers my jaw. There's even a little splash of water on the mirror and the scent of the soap. And I hear the anger and frustration in Maureen's voice. What are we arguing about? My work? The kids? Infidelity?

I'm in a car the next minute, trying to get up an impossibly steep, rocky hillside. The car strains, the engine whining with effort. The vibrations of the wheels travel through my legs and back, and the stench of burning rubber stings my nose. The car moves backward and down the slope while I angrily bang the steering wheel.

Maybe they're both dreams. Or both memories. Or one of each.

The pain in my back is easing a bit. I swing my legs over the side of the bed and sit up. The noise out on the ward comes through louder. The television buzzes in the dayroom, and there's the sound of water running somewhere.

My stomach growls, reminding me I've missed breakfast. I can make out the clatter of food trays as someone loads them onto the cart in the dayroom. Well, lunch will come soon enough.

The preacher's death remains vivid in my mind, too, another indication that my memory is returning. With it has come a new unease about what I've been doing to help the horses. The preacher, the gray guy, and all the others were consumed by the fire down inside their eyes. There is no doubt. I know what I saw. But now there are all kinds of emotions along with the memories. One of them may be guilt.

My slippers are on the floor by the bed. When I slip my feet into them, the old scar that wraps around the side of my right foot catches against the sole. It's been there since the summer between fifth and sixth grade when my buddy Jerry pushed me off the raft we built. My foot came down on a sharp rock in the North Platte River, laying the flesh open and exposing the white, round fat cells under the skin of my instep. I mistook the fat for worms, or fish eggs, or some other horrible thing. Along with that memory is the memory of fear and disgust when I plunked my foot back down in the fast-flowing water to wash the wound.

That's the thing about memories—not one comes without an emotion stuck on it. And maybe it's like something I read once about table salt. How it's made up of sodium and chlorine. Either of those alone will poison you dead. But if you put them together and sprinkle them on your food, all you get is a salty taste.

When I first came to this place, the fear and perplexity almost drove me crazy. Raw emotion, not much memory. Pure poison. Maybe when I look down inside the horses, I see all that emotion blazing hotter and hotter, but there's no memory—no context—to cool things down.

When I stand up, my back gives another little twinge. The pain makes me lean a bit sideways in the bathroom while I pee.

I worked one summer in high school for the Miner Feed Company up in North Park. Long, hot days bucking hay bales onto flatbed trucks. A sweet-rot odor rose when we kicked the heavy bales over to let the wet undersides dry in the morning sun. Ten-hour days of bending and lifting until our hands cramped from grasping the hay hooks. The pain-itch on the skin of our flat bellies where the sharp straw poked through our t-shirts. We'd lie down at night with our backs shrieking. But in the morning, we'd be good as new. After lifting the Mexican, my back will not be as good as new anytime soon.

In the hall, the cute nurse stops me by the med cart. She hands me a cup of pills and a cup of water, and I down both. She's almost always chirpy with energy and joy, but not today. Obviously, she and Doctor K have a thing for each other, but something must've happened. They're back to a stuttering, awkward formality when they encounter each other. She gives me a sad smile and a pat when I hand her the cup.

It's easy to find the new screamer. It's not a constant wail she's giving off, but it's regular enough that I can turn left at the corner and follow the high-pitched sound down to the end of the hall.

Late-morning sunshine bathes the room. The sheets on the hospital bed blaze white. The new screamer is propped up at an angle with a pillow behind her head. The skin on her face is almost as pale as the pillow. Deep-set, dark-rimmed eyes, the lids closed but fluttering. Nubbins of hair cover her scalp like a black, stubbly five-o'clock shadow. Over her left ear, there's a long rainbow-shaped scar and a depression in her skull, as if someone used an ice cream scoop on her head. Up close, the odor of urine and body lotion, and the detergent smell of the clean sheets.

She's young. Maybe mid-twenties. The skin across her face lies as smooth as the sheets on her bed. But then her brow furrows and her mouth twists open in a scowl. She lets out a wail of anger, or fear, or frustration. Or maybe pain. Whatever is inside her works up from her lungs like the blast of an air horn. She arches her neck a little while the wail builds, and then she relaxes back on the pillow.

I pry up her smudge-colored eyelids and reveal beautiful, dark-blue eyes. They're the same blue as my daughter's. The young screamer's pupils fix on a point toward the foot of the bed, but her eyes are out of focus. I don't want to look down in there for the fire. My gut clenches with the hope that everything is cool and dark all the way to the bottom.

Even her face is shaped a lot like Mia's. The young screamer arches up again and lets out a blast of noise.

A memory hits me of a five-year-old Mia arching that same way. She'd crept into our bedroom and wedged her warm, tiny body between Maureen and me.

"Daddy," she'd whispered, "I feel so bad." And her slender back arched upward and then curled into a C-shape next to me. She'd let out a soft moan, jarring me awake. Her skin practically glowed with heat. In the dark, I'd reached out and pushed on her board-like belly, drawing another shriek of pain.

Mia cried and moaned during the frantic trip to the emergency room, quieting only when they slipped the little oxygen mask over her drawn face and wheeled her off to the operating room. She'd recovered from her burst appendix, but the memory of her suffering still brought an ache to my gut.

Either I look into the young screamer's eyes or give up and leave the room. I bend forward until my nose almost touches her soft, warm cheek and look down. No flames but a whole universe of glowing coals. Waves of heat shoot out of her pupils and into my own close-held eyes. So hot it makes me stutter-step away from the bed.

My back explodes in pain, and I limp to the door, ignoring the searing in my back. I sit by the window in the hall until I can breathe again. My eyes still water from my pain and the agony radiating from those eyes. Maybe the coals burn so hot because of her age. Whatever the reason, I'm suddenly left with a horrible dilemma. With the other horses, there'd been no doubt about their suffering. I'd never lost my direction with them. But now I hesitate. Is it her resemblance to my daughter? Maybe the young screamer's agony burns like Mia's inflamed appendix. Maybe, as bad as it is, it could ease off at some point, and she'll no longer arch her neck and wail. Her incredible blue eyes might take in the world again, and her lips might turn up in a smile instead of a twisted sneer of suffering.

The rest of the day passes with little recollection. At some point, I must've gone to lunch or dinner. Hunger has vanished, at least. I'm back by the nursing station. The pain in my back has settled into a dull ache. Shadows fill the quiet hallways. Even the young screamer makes no sound. Has her pain eased, as mine has?

I stand and walk into the semi-darkness of her hallway. Light spills through her door. Soft weeping drifts out along with the light. It's sad, but at least a human sound. Maybe she's awakened and is only now discovering her shorn scalp and the concave defect in her head.

There are four people standing around the bed. The crisp, white sheet covers the young screamer from her feet to the top of her poor, damaged head. An older woman is by the bed. This woman weeps while a young man wraps his arm around her shaking shoulders. A nurse mutters something to them in soft tones.

I duck back out of the light before they spot me. Back in my room, I sit on my bed for a few minutes and then ease onto my back. Tears fill my eyes. The young screamer's voice whispers in my ear.

"I feel so bad."

I roll to my left side, away from the voice, ashamed that I didn't help end her suffering.

Chapter
Twenty-Three

The Poudre River shimmered in the mid-day sunshine. The long stretch of rippled water ended in an upstream granite and white water jumble. Clare settled the sunglasses on her nose and breathed in the smell of the mountains. Kester drove with his right hand resting lightly on the steering wheel, his left arm draped along the open car window. A swirl of warm summer air ruffled his hair.

"I'm glad we decided to do this," Clare said. "We both needed a break."

"I'm glad too." He smiled. "And I'm glad we're in your car and not that piece of crap I own."

The road turned in sharp curves, paralleling the fast-moving river. Steep canyon walls rose on both sides with a slash of cloudless blue sky above.

Kester breathed in the fresh mountain air. "Ahh, I've always liked this drive to Steamboat Springs. It's a tough road in the winter, but Dad loved skiing Mount Werner, so we made the trip a lot."

A large, slow-moving RV in front of them forced Kester to hit the brakes. They crept around a couple of curves at thirty miles an hour, slow enough to hear the rush of the water. Eventually, the two-lane highway straightened, allowing Kester to pass. He quickly accelerated.

"You're pretty good at this mountain driving."

Kester laughed. "Years of practice."

It was good to laugh again after the past couple of weeks. They'd worked together on the ward with strained professionalism, with no personal conversations. She avoided seeing him outside of work, too, not even calling. When he suddenly took a leave of absence, she was confused and worried but also relieved. He'd called yesterday, inviting her along for the weekend.

Kester yelled above the wind noise. "My dad's brother, Uncle Nick, still lives up there. Aunt Cora died a couple of years ago. Mom's been after Nick to move down to Fort Collins, but he doesn't want to leave. Real bad lung problems, and the altitude doesn't help. I told Mom I'd check on him and try to convince him to follow her advice." He laughed. "Fat chance. But it'll be a nice weekend."

They passed through Walden, climbed to Rabbit Ears Pass, and then dropped down the steep, winding road into Steamboat Springs.

Clare walked around the parking lot of the Steamboat Grand Hotel while Kester checked in at the front desk. The lower ski runs on Mount Werner rose up in front of her like wide, green rivers. Summer bikers and lone hikers dotted the brown trails that cut back and forth across the face of the mountain. The air smelled of warm pine needles.

Kester walked toward her across the asphalt parking lot. *He fits right in here.* As tan and trim as the group of bike riders passing alongside him. She couldn't see his eyes behind his sunglasses, but at least his face was relaxed and untroubled. She was glad he'd asked her along.

They drove through town and headed north along the Elk River. Kester turned in at a gravel drive and followed it back through a grove of aspen trees. The trees thinned, revealing a large log home tucked in among a jumble of granite boulders next to a stream.

A fat, yellow Labrador retriever rose from in front of the cabin door and waddled down the steps to greet them.

An older version of Kester sat in a chair on the porch. He wore thick-framed reading glasses, and his white hair began a little higher on his forehead than Kester's, but his body was straight and trim when he stood. He waddled a bit when he walked, just like the dog. Uncle Nick and the dog both grinned. The dog wagged his tail while the man waved his arm in greeting.

Kester opened his car door and stood up to look across the hood. "Well," he said, "So you're both still alive up here! Mom will be glad to hear it." He walked around the car and hugged his uncle.

The dog shuffled over and rooted along his pant leg. Kester squatted to pet him. "Huck, you must now be the oldest dog in the known universe."

Clare opened her car door and stepped out onto the gravel drive. Huck walked over and nuzzled the front of her shorts.

Nick laughed. "He always likes the women." He shuffled over and shook Clare's hand. "He always did have good taste," he said.

Clare wasn't sure if he was referring to the dog or Kester. She smiled. "A pleasure to meet you, Mr. Grayson." She scanned the neat, solid cabin and its spectacular surroundings. "Such a beautiful spot."

"Yeah," Nick said. He turned toward the river. "I first saw it in 1958, and I still think it's the center of the universe."

After a lunch of fried trout and fresh-picked salad, the three spent the rest of the afternoon hiking along the river. At dusk, they returned to the cabin, where Huck ambled out to greet them.

"He used to run around this property like a jackrabbit," Nick said. He scratched the old dog's head and motioned Clare to one of the rockers on the cabin porch.

"Have a seat, and we'll cool off before dinner," Nick said. "Kes, run in and grab us some cold beers."

Nick's breathing came in short, labored squeaks. He lowered into the rocker with a sigh of relief.

Kester returned and handed a bottle to his uncle and one Clare. They sipped the cold beer in silence.

Nick lowered his bottle and sucked in a lungful of air. "Whew," he said. "Maybe I should've stayed here with Huck!"

Kester set his bottle on the railing and leaned against a log column. "You know, Nick, it's not going to get any easier for you up here." He crossed his arms. "Mom thinks you should think about moving down close to her."

Nick winked at Clare and smiled. "I wondered when he'd get that out," he said.

Clare blushed.

Nick slapped Kester on the back. "Nephew," he said, "you tell Maggie to find another project."

Kester picked up his beer. "Mom takes my orders about as well as Aunt Cora took yours."

His uncle laughed. "Oh, that's right. You tell her thanks kindly, but I'll stay here." He turned back to Clare. "Living with a woman of Irish extraction is like walking around with a firecracker up your ass. It's only a little annoying unless you light the fuse."

Clare laughed. "You know, Nick, I'm one of those Irish women myself."

Nick raised his eyebrows in mock alarm. "Oh, Kes, you have my sympathy, lad."

They finished their beers as the last sunlight sparkled across the waves on the water.

Nick rocked back and forth in his chair. His breathing now came slow and easy. "No," he said quietly, "I think this is where I'm supposed to be when it all goes dark." He stared past the light pouring from the front door, out into the shadows falling along the Ponderosa pines across the driveway. His eyes twitched with memory. "I could walk this property and see every rock and tree, even on the blackest night. There's a great deal of comfort in that," he said.

He smiled at Kester. "So tell your mother I truly appreciate her concern, but I'll stay in the center of the universe."

Later, they grilled steaks and ate them with baked potatoes and glasses of red wine. Clare listened to the two men's affectionate banter. At the end of the evening, Nick hugged Clare at the door. "You remind me of Cora," he said. "A young, fiery Irish woman. Take care of Kes. He's a good kid."

Back at the hotel, Clare reached for Kester as soon as he'd closed and locked the door to their room. She buried her face in his chest, drawing in the smell of sweat, wood smoke, and wine. He smiled and pulled her close. They peeled off their thin t-shirts and tossed them into the dark room. Clare grabbed his hand and led him silently to the bed.

In the morning, they hiked along the trails above the town. The sun beat down hot and bright in the thin air. Just before noon, they stopped by a small stream at a shady spot, ate apples from their backpacks, and drank tepid bottled water.

Another steep climb brought them near the summit. They rested in the shade. Kester tugged his sweat-soaked shirt over his head and laid it on a rock to dry. He took a deep breath, and his chest expanded until the skin stretched tight and slick over his ribs. Clare pictured Uncle Nick struggling to recover from their previous leisurely hike.

"Quite a climb," Kester gasped.

"But it's worth it," Clare said. She sat at his feet and looked out over the valley. The Yampa River ran as a silvery squiggle through the town below. The Elk River meandered off to the north. The sky glowed blue-white in the summer heat.

They rested in silence for a couple of minutes. "You reminded me a little of your uncle just now, with that heavy breathing," Clare said.

He lifted his water bottle and poured a thin stream onto his head. "Yeah, except I climbed an entire mountain to get that winded. Nick just had to stroll along the river on level ground."

"Are you sorry Nick said 'no' to leaving here?" Clare asked.

"Not really. I think I'd make the same decision."

She leaned back against his bare legs. "You mean, just let nature take its course?"

"Yes."

"Even though he'd have more time—and better quality time—if he moved out of these mountains?"

"Yeah."

She drank from her water bottle. "Then I guess I don't understand why you have so much trouble letting our patients at the hospital do the same."

He rubbed her damp hair. "What do you mean?"

"Just let nature take its course. You say that's okay for Uncle Nick but not for someone like Mary Denton."

"It's not the same at all, Clare." There was exasperation in his voice.

She grabbed his hand. "God, Kes. I never know what to make of you. One minute you seem fine, and the next, you're acting so strange I can't believe it." She raised her arms in frustration. "Do I trust what you say? Do I not? Are you being sincere? Are you feeding me a line of bullshit?" She struck a palm against her forehead. "It's driving me crazy!"

"You're bringing that up now?"

"I'm sorry. But it's still hanging out there. Nothing's been resolved."

His hand rested on her hair, unmoving. "I'm sorry too. Sorry, I don't have your trust. Sorry I can't get it figured out for you." He pulled his hand away from her head. "And by the way," he continued, "it sounds like you're still not sure about the whole morphine thing either."

His anger washed over her, but she sat silent and trembling.

He stood and walked around to stand in front of her. "So what is it, Clare?" Still think I bumped off poor old Mary?"

Her lip trembled. He sat cross-legged in front of her. Sweat trickled along his jaw and collected on his chin. She raised her eyes.

"You want to know why I decided to leave the hospital for a while?" he said. "Because even though I couldn't push that whole syringe full of morphine into Mary's IV line, I tried to. I tried really hard. And I couldn't."

He reached out and rested his dust-caked hand on her knee. "And then I spent every day feeling ashamed that I didn't go through with it." He threw his arms out wide and rolled his eyes.

"Do no harm? What a joke that Hippocratic Oath turns out to be in our little corner of medicine!"

Clare recoiled with shock and sadness at his outburst.

Kester leaned forward. "Uncle Nick is making a rational decision. He's looked at his life and said, 'This is the logical next chapter—the last chapter I will ever be able to write myself.'" He sighed and closed his eyes for several seconds. "He's dying, you know. He's probably only got a few months left."

Kester looked past Clare, out over the valley. His mouth hung open. Finally, he turned back at her. "Nick may be sad about coming to the end of his story," he said, "But at least it's still his story to finish. I think our patients are caught in an ending they didn't choose. And they're past sad." He paused, his eyes studying the ground, and then shook his head. "I think they're clear past that, into a place we can't imagine."

His brow wrinkled. Sweat trickled down through the dust above his eyes. "And may God forgive me, Clare. I can't help but wonder if our job should be to ease them out of their story if it becomes too painful."

Clare wiped her eyes and drank from her water bottle. Her voice was soft, quivering. "I'm only saying—you seem so defensive about all this. Okay, so you didn't give Mary the overdose. Okay." She wiped at the corner of her eye again. "But this whole thing—should we kill them, should we not— it's eating you up, love." She rubbed his knee. "You have to find some way to deal with this."

He pushed her hand away. "That's easy for you to say." He stood, jammed his water bottle into the pack, and slung it over his shoulder. "You're not the one they come to. You're not the one they ask." He started down the trail. "I'm tired of this crap. I don't want to talk about it anymore."

Tears cut little rivers through the dust on Clare's cheeks. She stood and moved silently down the trail.

Later, the drive back to Fort Collins seemed longer than the trip up.

Chapter Twenty-Four

Lloyd glanced up. *Jesus. The old bitch is going to drop it in the eggs again.* The ash on the end of his grandmother's cigarette sagged above the frying pan.

"And it's not like I'm getting all that much in Social Security, ya know," Nora said. The cigarette between her lips bobbed up and down as she spoke. She turned to the side as the inch-long ash fell to the linoleum floor.

Lloyd ate his bowl of cereal in silence.

"I know you buy your own food, but heat and electricity ain't free." The cigarette swung back over the pan. She plucked it from her mouth and tapped the glowing butt against the edge of a coffee can on the back of the stove.

He snickered. *Shit, there's more ash on the floor than in that fuckin' can.*

His grandmother's husky voice droned on. "I know you make okay money at that hospital, ya know. You could be contributin' more to run this household."

Lloyd ignored her and concentrated on the newspaper next to his cereal bowl. He ran his finger down the ads under 'Guns and Ammo' in the classifieds.

For sale. Ruger Security Six .357 magnum. Six-inch barrel.

Excellent condition. $400. He tore the ad from the paper and stuck it in his pocket.

Nora scraped the eggs onto a plate and walked to the table. Lloyd stood

and carried his cereal bowl to the sink.

She gave a dismissive wave of her hand. "Nice talkin' to ya," she said. He walked to the door without a word. "And thanks for rippin' up my goddamn paper," she yelled after him.

In the car, he dialed the number from the gun ad. The man who answered gave him an address in the east part of town.

"You're not, like, a gun dealer or anything, are you?" Lloyd asked.

The seller assured him it was a private sale. No waiting period. No paperwork.

Lloyd drove to the address. The seller turned out to be an elderly man. "I used to keep it by the bed in case somebody broke in," he said. He placed the leather-holstered pistol on the kitchen table. "The wife died, and I'm off to live with my daughter." He frowned. "She hates guns, so I'm getting rid of it."

Lloyd slipped the revolver out of the raw leather holster. Its heft drew his wrist down. He turned the metallic-blue barrel toward him and peered into the muzzle. The black hole at the end of the barrel moved back and forth in front of his eyes, as big as a bucket.

"Nice gun," Lloyd said. The weight of the pistol in his hand and the smooth, cold feel of the metal made him tremble.

"The ammo goes with it," the old man said. "I never even shot it."

Lloyd handed over a thin stack of bills. "Four hundred dollars, right?"

"Yep," the man said. He took the money. "She's yours."

At the hospital, Lloyd left the gun and the box of ammunition in the glove compartment. It was against the law to have a firearm anywhere on hospital property. Lloyd didn't give it a thought. There was almost no chance his car would ever be searched. He locked the car, walked a short distance to C Ward, hung his jacket in the closet in the break room, and slipped on his white coat.

The hospital placed Lloyd on administrative leave after the old man's death in the tub. He'd spent a week at home, his mood swinging from white-hot anger at Dennis to worry that he'd be held responsible for the patient's death and would lose his job. Or even go to jail.

The meeting with the medical director and the union steward went better than he'd hoped. Watching that prick, Grayson, fume was a bonus. It was a gutsy move, asking for an apology. But even now, he grinned when he remembered the look on Kester's face.

Aides and nurses wandered into the break room for shift change. A couple of people greeted him, but most ignored him. They'd all heard about the incident with the old man and the inquiry. Lloyd didn't give it much thought. His co-workers had never been very friendly, even before the incident.

Lloyd's co-workers moved about the ward. He pursed his lips into a thin smile. *Fuck you guys,*

After rounds, he walked to the dayroom and helped with breakfast trays. Lloyd spooned oatmeal and eggs into Kenny Bilmire's gaping, rubbery mouth. The mixture oozed back out onto Kenny's chin and bib. He pinched the back of Kenny's neck in frustration.

"Cut that shit out!" he whispered into the old man's ear. Kenny winced. Lloyd spooned more oatmeal into the open mouth and clamped the jaw shut with his left hand. Kenny let out a muffled cough. His face turned from pale to purple. Lloyd released his grip, and Kenny coughed deeply, spraying flecks of oatmeal onto the breakfast tray. Lloyd glanced around. All of the other aides tended to their own patients. Kenny coughed again.

"I told you to cut that shit out, man," Lloyd whispered. Kenny smacked his lips. His eyes blinked and roamed, blank and uncomprehending. The rest of the oatmeal went into the garbage.

Lloyd continued his shift—moving patients, changing diapers, shaving the men, and toileting the few who could still make it to the bathroom. He moved through the morning chores with mechanical indifference. It left him plenty of time to consider Dennis's betrayal.

Lloyd had no other friends. And in truth, the two men were improbable companions. Both were loners, but Dennis possessed a gentle nature. He kept to himself out of extreme shyness and a sense that his plodding intelligence made him a target for ridicule.

At first, he'd recoiled from Lloyd's cold, resentful attitude. Working together every day on the ward gradually led to a guarded, superficial friendship. Even this was more than Lloyd experienced with anyone else. To have Dennis betray their relationship made Lloyd seeth with anger. Such a betrayal demanded punishment.

He finished his shift and walked to the break room. Dennis sat on the couch while two other aides drank coffee at the table. Dennis glanced up at Lloyd and looked away.

Lloyd smiled and nodded. "Hey, Dennis, how's it goin'?" he said.

Dennis nodded. "Um—fine."

Lloyd waited until the other workers left the break room. When they finally finished their coffee and walked into the hallway, Dennis followed them out the door, avoiding Lloyd's stare.

After Dennis left, Lloyd took his coat from the rack and put it on. He walked down the hall and found Dennis alone in one of the patient rooms. Dennis looked up with alarm when his former friend appeared in the doorway, then went back to spreading a sheet over the bed. Lloyd hustled over, grabbed one side of the sheet, and helped tuck it in and smooth the top.

"You know, I've had time to think about what happened, and I guess you were right, man," Lloyd said. He punched Dennis playfully on the arm, picked up a pillowcase from the dresser, and threw it to him.

"I guess I just panicked, Dennis. You did the right thing. And anyway, I'm off the hook now, so no harm done."

Dennis hesitated, then grinned across the bed. "Thanks, bro. I thought you hated my guts."

"No way, man," Lloyd said. "Friends stick together."

They finished making the bed and walked toward the door. Lloyd slapped the big man on the back. "Hey, what you doing after work?"

Dennis scratched his head. "Goin' home, I guess. Why?"

"Well, tomorrow's Saturday. I'm off. How about I pick you up after your shift and get a drink?"

Dennis smiled. "Sure, man. No sense wasting a summer night. Maybe we can go to Old Town and find some nasty women."

"Okay. I'll pick you up at your place at eleven-thirty." Lloyd jostled Dennis's shoulder. "It's good to have my friend back."

The late evening sun still hung over the mountains west of town. A dark cloud rose along the line of peaks to the northwest. Lloyd finished pumping gas into his car and bit into the sandwich he'd bought along with a six-pack of Coors beer. The beer rested in a Styrofoam cooler in the trunk of the car.

In the parking lot outside the convenience store, he reached across, opened the glove compartment, and took out the pistol. It nestled in his hand, heavy and promising. The gun held six hollow-point cartridges.

Slipping the shells into the cylinder sent a shiver up his spine. He held the gun low in his lap and glanced around. Just a couple of empty cars parked in front of the convenience store.

Over the next couple of hours, Lloyd drove around town. At eleven fifteen, he pulled into the parking lot of an older apartment complex. Within a few minutes, Dennis rode along the sidewalk on his bike. He spotted Lloyd's car and waved. Lloyd waited while Dennis parked his bike in a stairwell and chained it to a post. He walked over to the car.

"Hey, Lloyd," he said. His grin was back.

Lloyd nodded and opened his car door. "Just a sec," he said. "Gotta get the beer." He walked around and opened the trunk, grabbed the cooler, and slammed the trunk lid. He set the small cooler on the console between the front seats and started the car.

Dennis slid into the passenger seat and opened the cooler. "Man, I need one of these." His shirt clung to his chest and stomach, dark with sweat. "That ride from the hospital was brutal." He popped the top of the can and swigged.

Lloyd pulled out of the parking lot and turned east on Mulberry Street. "I've got something to show you," he said. He reached under the seat and pulled out the pistol, holding it below the level of the dashboard as he passed it across to his friend.

Dennis took it in his free hand. The glow of the dashboard lights reflected off the barrel. "Shit!" Dennis said. "Where'd you get this?"

"Bought it this morning," Lloyd said. "I can't wait to see how this fucker shoots."

"Yeah," Dennis said. He turned the gun and peered down the barrel. "It's like a fuckin' cannon."

Lloyd slapped the barrel down. "Hey, idiot, it's loaded. Want to blow your fuckin' face off?"

Dennis grinned. "Sorry, dude." He handed the gun back across the console.

Lloyd stuck it under the seat. "Why don't we give it a try now?"

"You mean tonight?" Dennis said. He laughed. "Shit, we might as well. Probably no nasty women for us downtown anyway."

Lloyd drove east. Mulberry Street became Highway 6, running straight from the city to the farms and ranches of Larimer County. They crossed over Interstate 25 and into the dark countryside.

Warm, heavy summer air swirled inside the car, bringing the rich odors of feedlots and cornfields. Lightning flashed to the northwest, illuminating enormous cumulus clouds.

"Hey. Let's find an old farmhouse, or a silage pit, or something, and give this thing a workout," Lloyd said.

Dennis glanced over his shoulder as another flash lit up the sky. "We better hurry. I don't want to get soaked."

"I know a great spot," Lloyd said. He turned onto a gravel county road and drove along an irrigation ditch. Tall grass rustled in the breeze pushed ahead of the storm. Lloyd pulled onto a rough side road. The headlights lit up a dilapidated farmhouse. Weeds grew tall in the yard and along the crumbling front walk. Broken glass from the darkened windows littered a few bare patches of ground along the front of the house.

Lloyd stopped the car and shut off the engine. He left the headlights on. Dennis tossed his empty beer can out the window and took a full can from the cooler.

"Looks like the folks aren't home tonight," Dennis said. He laughed and took a swig of beer.

Leaves rustled on a stand of overgrown trees next to the house. The low grumble of distant thunder rolled across the dark, empty fields.

"C'mon," Lloyd said. "We don't have much time."

They got out of the car and moved into the light. Lloyd held the pistol at his side. Dennis set his beer on the car hood and looked around for a target. He spotted the empty beer can he'd tossed earlier.

"Hey, Lloyd," he said. "How about this?" He picked up the empty can.

"Sure," Lloyd said. "Set it up on the porch."

Dennis walked toward the house. Lloyd raised the gun, aimed it at the window next to Dennis, and pulled the trigger. The gun bucked in his hand, and a hole blossomed in the weathered clapboard siding. Lloyd shivered with an overwhelming feeling of force and power. Even the sound made him grunt with pleasure.

Dennis crouched near the porch, his hand up as if shielding his right ear from the noise. He peered back into the headlights, his eyes wide with fear and surprise.

"What the fuck? Man, that isn't funny!" he said.

Lloyd reached down and grabbed a handful of gravel, and threw it at the crouching man, who winced and turned his head away.

"You rat motherfucker!" Lloyd screamed. His ears rang with the report of the gun.

Dennis gaped into the light. "What the hell are you talking about, bro?"

Lloyd's face knotted with rage. "Telling on me like that!"

Confusion spread across Dennis's face. "I thought you said we were cool about that." He stood and took a tentative step toward the car. Lloyd leveled the gun, working to hold it steady. Dennis stopped and raised his hands up along his shoulders. "Man, I said I was sorry. Let it go, Lloyd."

Lightning flashed, close enough now to add the stink of ozone to the air. Thunder quickly followed.

"Fuck you, man." Lloyd jiggled the gun from side to side. "Sorry don't make it right. You really fucked things up for me, you know."

Dennis dropped his hands to his sides. He peered into the light, anger in his eyes. "You mean like you stealin' pills? Or you bangin' the old ladies?"

Lloyd's hand shook with the weight, sending the barrel around in small, jittery circles. "What the fuck do you know about that?" he said.

"Why do you think I asked for a move to afternoon shift, man?" Dennis said. "I didn't want any part of that shit. But you were a friend...." His shoulders slumped. He held his hands in supplication. "Just take me back to town, man. Let's forget this."

The barrel of the gun steadied. This time, Lloyd braced for the kick. Even so, the slam of the shot and the flash at the muzzle left him momentarily stunned.

Dennis twisted to the left. Lloyd caught a glimpse of something spinning off into the dark, away from the left side of the big man's head. He lowered the gun. His ears rang—a high-pitched, electric sound.

Dennis sprawled in the weeds by the side of the porch. His legs swished from side to side in quick, jerky movements. Lloyd edged toward the house. The body lay in the shadows among the tall weeds. Even so, it was evident that a large piece of the man's left ear, and a cup-sized chunk of the skull, were gone.

Blood dark as tar and bits of tissue speckled the weeds and the siding on the house.

Dennis grunted. His open eyes shone white, large as silver dollars. The grunting turned into a gurgling sound and then cut off.

Lloyd stood over the body for a couple of minutes until the silent rise and fall of the chest slowed and stopped. The eyes remained open but motionless.

He ran to the car and turned off the headlights. The lights of Fort Collins illuminated the roiling clouds overhead. The sound of leaves and stems clattering in the rising breeze replaced the ringing in his ears.

It struck him that someone may have heard the report of the gun. How close was the nearest farmhouse? Would it sound like the approaching storm to anyone within hearing? Lloyd grabbed the flashlight from the glove compartment. Panic crashed over him, and he leaned against the side of the car for several seconds, sucking in air, then ran back to stand by the body.

Dennis's face glowed chalk-white in the flashlight's beam, framed by his black beard and blood-soaked scalp. Clots of white brain tissue tinged with blood peaked through the hole in his skull.

Lloyd trained the beam on the farmhouse. The weeds along the foundation cast long shadows against the gray concrete. He spied a basement window along the foundation. One kick disintegrated the dirty glass pane. Stooping, he played the light into the dark opening. Dry, dusty shelves, and below them, a grime-covered basement floor.

He returned to the body and grasped a pant leg with each hand. The thick weeds bent beneath the body, making moving the heavy weight easier.

Lightning sparked, momentarily blinding him. Thunder followed within a couple of seconds. The wind reeked of rain. A couple of drops landed on his bare arm, startling him. Panic rose in his throat again until he swallowed it down.

The window proved just big enough to receive the body. It slithered through and fell into the darkness. From below, a thud as the body hit the concrete floor and then a faint grunt of expended air.

His heart beat in his chest with a terrible force, thrumming with the exertion and the clawing fear. He stuck the light back through the window. Dennis sprawled on the floor. Billows of gray dust still floated around the body in the faint light.

A voice gibbered in his head, commanding him to run to the car and drive away now. A calmer voice spoke, telling him to make sure the job was done. The rain came with a building roar. The pool of blood where Dennis fell in the weeds seeped into the ground along with the rain.

Lloyd bent under the downpour, dashed to the front door, and pushed it open. The desiccated odor of dust and plasterboard replaced the smell of the storm. Yellowed newspapers lay scattered across the dirty, cracked linoleum.

Someone had broken holes in the plaster walls. The exposed wooden lathe stood out as stark as ribs.

He found the basement door and went down the narrow, wooden stairs. The basement was small, dug under only a portion of the house. Three walls and the floor were concrete. The fourth wall consisted of dry, packed dirt.

Dennis lay where he'd fallen. A puddle of blood—smaller than the one in the weeds—spread around his head. Lloyd played the light over the face. The eyes were closed now. The chest was still. He nudged the body with his shoe. No response. He grabbed the pants again and dragged the limp body to the dirt wall.

Twisting around, he spied an old galvanized bucket. He picked it up and scraped its rim along the dirt wall, then turned and tossed the dry, gray grit across the floor and onto the bloodstain. Then he used the bucket to scrape dirt onto the body. Fear kept him at it. Soon, Dennis's outline disappeared under a mound of clods and loose dirt.

Lloyd fell against the wall, panting, sweating, and choking. The air hung heavy in the small space. The storm thrashed the weeds outside the basement window, but no wind penetrated the small opening.

Outside, Lloyd squatted in the cold rain until his clothes hung wet on his body, leaving him cold and shivering. He staggered back to the car just as the thunderstorm moved to the east. The rain eased until only occasional large drops fell onto the windshield.

The gun rested on the seat where he'd left it. He sat in sodden clothes and drank the beer Dennis had placed on the car hood, then reached over and stuck the gun and the flashlight back in the glove compartment.

When he started the engine and turned on the headlights, the farmhouse stood out white and desolate. The weeds showed no trace of blood. The basement window swallowed the light. Tears mixed with the rainwater on Lloyd's cheeks. He sniffed and wiped his nose.

Chapter Twenty-Five

Kester's foot slipped on the narrow wooden stair. His knee struck the edge with a dull thunk. "Ow! Quit pushing, Paddy," he yelled up the stairs.

His brother's head appeared from behind the box they carried between them. "Oh, sorry, dude,"

Kester set his end of the box on the wooden step and rubbed his knee to ease the pain. "Aren't you a little old to be calling people 'dude'? You sound like one of your students."

Paddy laughed. "I don't know what my students say these days, but I think they've probably evolved past 'dude.'"

Kester picked up his end of the heavy box of books, and they maneuvered it the rest of the way down the stairs and set it on the basement floor. They stood with their hands on their hips and panted.

"Where you want it?" Kester surveyed the cluttered basement. "And for that matter, why do you want it?"

His brother pointed to the shelves in the corner. "Over there. And I want it because these are rare historical treasures." He punched Kester's shoulder. "Nah, just kidding. It's my old Playboy collection. Ma never comes down here. They'll be safe." He patted the box.

Paddy Grayson was two years older than Kester. The brothers were opposites in many ways, especially in temperament. Paddy stood a shade over five feet six inches with a square-built head topped with jet-black hair. His thick, sturdy legs and barrel chest made people think he might be a laborer, maybe a longshoreman.

Professor Padraig Grayson taught European History at nearby Colorado State University. Somehow, he'd corralled his rowdy Irish personality and channeled his energies into academia. His students worshipped him. Kester did too.

They pushed the heavy box into the corner and climbed the stairs. Maggie Grayson sat at the kitchen table, slicing strawberries into a large glass bowl.

"Did you get your magazines all tucked in down there?" she said. Paddy grinned at Kes. Their mother raised her cup of coffee and smiled.

"How does she do that?" Paddy said.

Kester grabbed a strawberry. "Beats me."

"Forty years as a high school teacher, my boy," she said. She sipped her coffee. "I can smell guilt."

Kester and Paddy sat down at the kitchen table.

"Well," Paddy said, "just about moved back in." He patted the table. "It's weird being back living in the old house." He popped a strawberry into his mouth. "Sure you want me back underfoot, Ma?"

Maggie reached over and patted his hand. "I've already told you, Paddy. You're doing me a favor. It's been so quiet in this house since your dad died."

"Yeah," Paddy said. "It's still weird not having him around."

The clock on the kitchen wall ticked in the sudden quiet.

Kester coughed to break the silence, then smiled and raised his hand. "Hey, Ma, can I move back in, too?"

Maggie set the knife beside the bowl and stood, a look of amusement on her face. "Should I make room for Clare Williams also?"

Kester knocked his forehead against the tabletop in mock frustration. "Lord, does everyone in northern Colorado know about Clare and me?"

"Yeah, just about everybody," Paddy said, ruffling his brother's hair. "Ya know, I like that girl. Better than Lori," he said, referring to Kester's first wife.

"Oh, Lori was a nice girl," their mother said. She set her coffee cup on the counter by the sink and sat and picked up the paring knife. "Just a different kind of soul—a different personality." She picked up another strawberry.. "It just wasn't to be."

Paddy winked at his brother. "I thought she was a nut job," he said.

Maggie pointed the knife at Paddy and shook her head. "Be careful what you say about people, Paddy. You never know what devils are chasing them."

Paddy nodded. "Right you are, Mother dear." He turned back to Kester. "But I do like Clare. Think this one will stick around?"

Kester popped another strawberry into his mouth and chewed thoughtfully for several seconds. "I was beginning to think so. He swallowed and picked at the dishtowel alongside the bowl. "Until Steamboat."

"I bet Uncle Nick scared her away," Paddy said.

Maggie finished slicing the strawberries and wiped her hands on her apron. "Quit it, Paddy. I think Kes is serious." She turned to her younger son, a look of worry on her face. "Nicholas didn't scare her away—did he, Kes?"

"They got along fine." Kester picked at the corner of the towel. "We had sort of a disagreement."

Paddy stood and walked to the refrigerator. "Doctor Grayson the Younger was found to be disagreeable? Hard to believe." He rummaged in the refrigerator door and pulled out a can of soda.

Maggie picked up the dishtowel and threw it at Paddy. "If Doctor Grayson the Elder is going to be sarcastic, he should probably leave now." She pointed toward the door. "Go clean your room."

Paddy pointed the can at his brother. "Did you ever think we'd hear Ma say that again?"

Kester flashed a brief, tight smile.

After Paddy left, Maggie leaned forward. "Do you want to talk about it, Kes?"

He traced a finger along the wood grain in the table, avoiding his mother's eyes. After a few seconds, he said, "You know, back when Dad got his diagnosis, and he knew he was going to die from the cancer, we spent a lot of nights just talking. Religion mostly."

Maggie squeezed his hand. "I remember that. It bothered him—a little—you being an agnostic."

Kester shrugged. We went back and forth about it." He shook his head. "I was so stupid. I told him he was scared to die."

He raised his head and looked at his mother. "We went round and round about that, I finally realized I was wrong. He wasn't afraid to die. He was afraid to lose his life—his memory—of himself. And you. And Paddy and me."

His mother studied his face for several seconds.

Finally, she stood. "Just a second. Let me show you something." She went to her bedroom and returned with a shoebox full of papers, sorted through it, and found what she was looking for.

"Don't judge it on quality." She handed the yellowed paper across to her son. "The man was a science major, not a poet."

Kester unfolded the paper and recognized his father's neat printing. He read the poem aloud:

"The Thief of Moments
We are swept along the river,
Throwing our nets to capture each moment.
We fill our lives like fishermen, hauling
Each shining memory aboard,
Until we ride low in the water with remembering.
If we fish well, we gather enough to
Sustain us on this journey.

But the thief of moments prowls the shore,
Waiting to slither out and drift alongside.
It reaches in with stealth and cunning.
Its sharp, quick fingers claw each memory
Across the gunwale and away.
We float on, just as before,
But so high—so high.

"Like I said, your father didn't have a poetic bone in his body." She read the poem again, silently mouthing the words, then folded the paper and placed it back in the shoebox.

"I felt resentful too, just like you kids did at first. How could he end it like that?" Her voice was plaintive—wistful. "After I found this, I understood why someone might decide to hurry along to whatever comes next. I think he captured something—something important in this poem."

Maggie placed the lid on the box. "So, I guess he cut his losses before whatever was left of him trickled away to nothing." She stood and walked to the kitchen counter. Her face brightened. "How about a sandwich? It's almost noon."

"Um—sure," Kester said. The kitchen was silent except for her soft humming. She didn't see the anguish on his face.

She set the plate on the table, and Kester leaned back in his chair and folded his arms across his chest. "Tell me something." He pursed his lips and stared at the table for a moment. "If Dad had been too sick to end it himself—and you'd known how he felt—would you have helped him?"

She sat and slid a plate across to him. "You mean would I have stuck the gun in his mouth and pulled the trigger?"

He stiffened. "No, I didn't mean...."

She smiled. "Sorry, didn't mean to be melodramatic." She pondered the question for several seconds. " No, probably not," she said.

"Why not?"

She set her sandwich back on her plate and sat with her head down for a moment. "Because there's never a defining moment in situations like that. Or at least I suppose we never see them as such."

Kester frowned. "I'm not sure I know what you mean."

His mother wrinkled her forehead, considering her reply. "Because it's a process—when the death comes along slowly—isn't it? It's not a single event. The dying and the way we react to the dying stretch out. We start out hoping for a miracle." Mary studied her hands. "Later, after the worry has worn us down, we just hope for an ending—one way or the other."

She bit into her sandwich, chewed and swallowed, and then continued. "It's a rare person who can decide to take action. Most of us simply endure."

Kester smiled and picked up his sandwich. "Is this something you learned during all those years as a schoolteacher?"

Maggie stood and carried her plate to the sink. "Of course not, Kes. I learned it from your Grandma Agnes. Talk to an old Irish mother if you need an expert on death and suffering."

After lunch, Kester made another sandwich and carried it upstairs to his brother. Paddy sat on the bed in their old room. Books and boxes lined the walls.

"There was a lot more room in here when we had the bunk beds," Paddy said. "Don't know where I'm going to put all this crap."

Kester set the sandwich on the bedside table. "Wishing you hadn't given up your apartment?"

"Nah," Paddy said. "Ma needs the help, and I'm saving a ton on rent." He looked around the room. "It'll work out."

Kester sat on the edge of the bed while his brother ate. "So, what's the big problem with Clare?"

Kester hesitated. "It's—sort of what you might call a philosophical difference of opinion," he said.

Paddy swallowed and waved the sandwich at his brother. "Oh, for Christ's sake, Kes! You two should be slobbering all over each other. Instead, you're busy pissing her off with some damn 'philosophical difference'?" He snorted in disgust.

Kester punched his brother's shoulder. "Hey! This is serious, you asshole."

Paddy chewed thoughtfully. "Okay, so tell me what the problem is."

Kester stood and paced the small room. "Clare thinks maybe I killed one of my patients at the hospital."

Paddy stopped mid-chew and stared straight ahead. "Wow." He looked up at Kester.

"Wait," Kester said. "Let me backtrack."

He told Paddy about his conversation with Clare and about Mary Denton's death.

"And Clare accused you of killing this woman with an overdose of morphine?"

"She didn't exactly accuse me, really—" Kester said. "But you can see why she might be confused."

"So? Did you kill her?" The question was matter-of-fact, as if he'd asked if his brother had gone to the store for milk.

Kester sputtered. "The patient? Hell no, I didn't kill her."

Paddy chewed on his sandwich. "I didn't think so." He licked mayonnaise from his finger. "It's not in your nature." He finished the sandwich and set the plate on the nightstand. "Of course, there is the issue of whether you *should've* killed her. I suppose that's what has you all screwed up."

"Jesus. That's cold."

"Cold or not, tell me that's not what's eating you."

Kester sat on the bed. "Okay, yes. And I can't figure it out—at least so far. I don't think Clare thinks I'm some kind of murderer, but....."

Paddy stood and walked to a bookshelf in the corner. "Heck, little brother, I'd be surprised if there weren't a whole bunch of fucked up people at that hospital."

"What do you mean?"

Paddy ran his finger along a row of books and pulled one from the shelf. "You ever read *The Inferno* by Dante?"

"Way back in college, I suppose," Kester said. "Why?"

Paddy thumbed through the book. "I think it was right at the beginning someplace," He turned a few more pages. "Yeah. Here it is." He held the book open in his left hand, poking the page with his right index finger. "Let me explain this to you since I imagine you slept through it in college." He shook his head. "Pre-meds."

He looked down at the open book. "So, Dante is being escorted through Hell by this Roman poet. Dante's all bummed out about his life and his sins. This is a little part about what the poet says they'll see along the way." He took a deep breath and read aloud.

Therefore I think and judge it for thy best
Thou follow me, and I will be thy guide,

And lead thee hence through the eternal place, Where thou shalt hear the desperate lamentations, Shalt see the ancient spirits disconsolate,

Who cry out each one for the second death;

Kester listened in silence, then smiled and shook his head. "Are you this weird in your lectures?"

Paddy waved his hand back and forth in frustration. "No, man. I have a valid point to make here." He looked back down at the page. "See, these souls had died and gone to Hell. They're suffering, so they're crying out to die again, to end the anguish and get to Heaven."

He looked at Kester. "Does any of this sound like what you deal with at that hospital?"

"Are you saying Foothills Hospital is some kind of Hell?" Kester asked.

"Well, no. Of course not," Paddy said. "Not *the* Hell. But maybe a kind of hell for some of your patients."

Kester considered his brother's words for several seconds. He nodded. "Okay."

Paddy went on. "I remember when you first started working out there. I came to see you, and we went onto the ward. You know what I thought when I remembered this passage from The Inferno?"

"What?"

"I thought, What if all these people got their wits back for five minutes? We could line 'em up and ask for a show of hands.

We could say, 'How many of you like where you've wound up? How many like it here?'" Paddy shook his head, his face solemn. "There wouldn't be any raised hands. I'm betting half would run screaming from the building. The other half would probably try to kick you in the balls."

"So you're saying they've already died a first death—sort of— which is their dementia."

"Yeah."

"And if they could, they'd—as you say—'cry out for the second death.'"

"Yeah," Paddy said. "Dante pitied the poor bastards he ran into in Hell but couldn't do anything about their situation." He put the book back on the shelf. "And that's the point, you see. Just because you're a doctor, I don't think that gives you the right—or the responsibility—to send those folks off to the second death. At least, not actively send them off. That's above even your pay grade."

"But they're suffering. What if I can stop that and I don't?"

Paddy sighed. "They're suffering, sure. And it's a terrible thing. But who put you in charge of the world? Did you get a little badge with that diploma, one that says, 'It's all up to me'?"

Kester sat silently on the bed.

Paddy set the book back on the shelf. "Society can't just say 'fuck it' and make you decide. We all have to make the decision together."

Paddy shuffled over and rubbed Kester's head. "You're a good man, little brother. I just think the conflict and the agonizing go with the job. I know you better than you know yourself sometimes, so I'm not worried about you killing your patients. Don't you worry either."

Chapter Twenty-Six

Lloyd's clothes dried on the drive back to town. He left the window down, even though the cool air following the storm raised a chill along his arms. Adrenaline set his body trembling and twisted his stomach into a knot.

Images of the farmhouse played sharp-edged in his head, welling up out of the dark, illuminated by lightning. The gun jarred his hand again, and Dennis spun and fell over and over.

Fear of discovery sickened him. Maybe even now, someone stood in the basement of the old farmhouse, kicking at the pile of dirt, uncovering a hand or a tag end of shirt. A vision of Dennis rising from the mound of earth and staggering out of the basement flashed bright as lightning in Lloyd's mind. He gritted his teeth in fear and horror. A choking lump in his throat threatened to strangle him or leave him forever speechless.

Lloyd crossed over the interstate and marveled at how ordinary the city appeared. His hands cramped on the steering wheel. His breath came in rapid little gasps.

The dark windows meant his grandmother had gone to bed. The clock in the basement bedroom read one fifteen. In the bathroom, he knelt by the toilet and vomited warm beer and the sandwich he'd eaten earlier in the evening. His stomach unclenched for a few moments. The gun! It was in the glove compartment, and the car sat unlocked in the driveway.

The stairs creaked with his weight. The cool air outside stung his skin, and the wet grass soaked his feet so that he tiptoed daintily across the lawn. When he opened the car door, the dome light swept across the yard like a beacon. Dread and cold set him shivering again.

The scent of gunpowder still clung to the cold, blue metal. He hid the gun under his shirt despite the dark and deserted street.

Back in his room, he buried the gun under a pile of clothes in his bottom dresser drawer. Scenes from the farm and horrible visions rattled like hail in his brain, but sleep came quickly and free of dreams.

The clock showed ten thirty when he awoke. An involuntary shudder swept over him. The pictures still played in his head. He spent the rest of the morning in his room, burdened by the horror of the act and a paralyzing vision of police knocking on the door.

Hunger drove him upstairs to the kitchen. Sunshine slanted through the windows, forcing down the dark pictures of the night before. He found orange juice in the refrigerator and drank it from the bottle.

The screen door slammed. His grandmother stood in the doorway. He studied her lined face, half expecting to see a look of discovery and horror. The ever-present cigarette hung from her lip.

His terrible secret sharpened all of his senses. The orange juice glowed like something molten through the glass of the bottle. The odor of cigarette smoke, the lilacs outside, the juice on his lips, and even the detergent in his grandmother's denim shirt hung in the air. The sprinkler in the backyard ticked loudly in its circle like a watch held close to his ear.

His grandmother set her purse on the counter. "What the hell happened to you?"

Something reached inside and squeezed his heart. "What?" An image of Dennis' mangled scalp flashed through his mind.

His grandmother walked over and tapped her cigarette against the coffee can on the stove. "Your hands are filthy." She frowned.

He looked. Dirt caked his fingernails. Streaks of mud ran up both arms. His palms were brown with grime. He put the orange juice bottle back in the refrigerator. "I got stuck last night. Had to dig the back wheel of the car out of a rut."

She sat at the table and surveyed him with disgust. "I bet your goddamn sheets are a nice sight." She picked up the newspaper and snapped it open. "Well, I'm not washin' 'em. You're on your own with that. If you want to live like a goddamn pig down there, go ahead."

He ignored her. Back in his room, he opened the bottom drawer and pushed the clothes aside. The gun glowed blue-black in the dim light. He shut the drawer and went into the bathroom to shower.

In the afternoon, he drove to Jax Sporting Goods and bought a waistband holster for the gun.

On his way out of the store, he passed by a display of Buck knives. On an impulse, he picked one up. Not as imposing as his gun, but it settled in his hand with its own kind of power. He bought the knife too.

He spent the evening in front of the television in his basement room and slept well again that night with no dreams.

On Sunday, he drove over, parked two blocks from Dennis's apartment complex, and walked toward it, expecting to see something. Maybe police cars with flashing lights or yellow crime scene tape holding back crowds of onlookers. But nothing moved in the neighborhood. A few cars sat in the parking lot. Dennis's bike still leaned against the pole under the stairs. He walked on by and circled around to his car.

Back home, Lloyd took the gun out of the drawer and slipped it into the waistband holster. It formed a visible bulge at his side, even concealed under a coat. He stuck it in the small of his back, but the bulge was still too obvious.

On Monday morning, he slipped the Buck knife into his coat pocket and the gun and holster into a brown paper bag. The bag he tucked behind the spare tire in the trunk of his car.

The horror that overwhelmed him during the weekend was gone. The power and comforting weight of the knife and the gun tamped down the twist in his gut. The images of Friday night still played in his head, but now like something he'd witnessed but not been a part of. Now he approached the workweek with anticipation rather than dread.

Lloyd kept the knife in his coat pocket at the hospital and left the gun in the car. He considered wearing the holster under his white coat, but it was too visible.

The ward looked unchanged. Clare Williams walked out of the nursing office. He smiled. "Good morning, Clare."

She turned to look at him. "Good morning." She didn't smile. Her eyes followed him until he passed by. Her discomfort almost set him to giggling.

He hung up his jacket in the break room, put on his lab coat, then palmed the knife and slipped it into his coat pocket. During the meeting, he slid his hand into his pocket, cupping the knife, stroking the edge of the folded blade with his thumb. Those workers who happened to look his way were met with a bold, glassy stare.

The day passed. At shift change, the nurse asked if anyone had seen Dennis Enger. Lloyd fought the urge to stand up and explain that Dennis lay cold and bloody under a pile of dirt in an abandoned farmhouse east of town and would not be joining them for the meeting. Instead, he shrugged his shoulders along with the rest of the people in the room.

That night, he returned to the sporting goods store and bought an ankle sheath for his knife.

Before work on Tuesday, he strapped the knife to his right leg above his sock and made sure it wasn't visible when he sat down.

The following day, the ward routine continued unchanged. The television in the dayroom still poured its light and sound against the line of wheelchair patients. The nursing staff and aides still moved about tending to their business.

In the morning meeting, Clare asked if anyone had heard from Dennis. She glanced over at Lloyd before scanning the rest of the room. Again, nobody answered. A small thrill fluttered in Lloyd's chest.

The killing and its aftermath led him to a new place. At odd moments, his gut still clenched, and images flashed in his head, but now it was more like wonder than terror.

He found an opportunity to approach the busy med nurse during the morning and offered to take pain meds to one of his charges. He pocketed the pills in the patient's room and tossed the medicine cup into the trash.

By the end of the week, the ward bubbled with rumors of Dennis Enger's disappearance. Lloyd ached to gather them all in the break room and tell them his secret. He'd show them the gun and knife and display their power. He'd explain how Dennis's betrayal demanded retribution. They would look at him with awe, overcome by the audacity and the rightness of his actions.

He'd remove the knife from its sheath and use the razor-sharp blade to cut a line across Clare William's sleek, tight uniform, exposing her pink flesh.

Instead, he smiled and remained silent.

Chapter Twenty-Seven

Kester bent a paperclip into a Z-shape and twirled it between his fingers.

Mike Flores leaned over and whispered in his ear. "Now, don't you wish you'd taken another week off?"

Kester turned and smiled and nodded.

Reggie Wilson sat at the head of the conference table, his heavy-lidded eyes locked on Georgia Nelson, the nursing director. Reggie leaned forward, his face relaxed but attentive. Only his slumped shoulders betrayed his boredom.

Georgia droned on. Mid-morning sunlight filled the room, heating the air and adding to the lethargy around the table.

"We're still short three nursing positions," Georgia said. "Night shift is tired of all the overtime, and none of the day shift nurses are crazy about working doubles."

Reggie frowned and toyed with the papers in front of him. "Well, Georgia, I don't know what to tell you. We've put ads out for nurses, but no bites so far. Just make do for the time being."

Now Georgia frowned.

Reggie looked around the table. "Let's see. We've discussed the budget cuts, the new reporting requirements from the boys in the Denver office, the fact that no nurses want to work for us, and the roof leak on B Ward. Any more good news for me today?"

Dan Franklin, the head of Human Resources, put his fist to his mouth, cleared his throat, and looked across the table. "Yeah, Reg, one more item."

Reggie sighed and put his hands on the table. "Okay. Shoot."

Dan continued. "The Fort Collins Police Department called me this morning. Dennis Enger, one of our afternoon aides, has been missing for almost a week."

Reggie thrust his chin at Georgia. "Did you know about this?" he asked.

"He didn't show up for work Monday. The nurse on C Ward let me know the next morning. We called and left him a message on Tuesday. On Wednesday, we called his mother in Boulder and found out she hadn't heard from him either. She must've contacted the police."

Reggie turned to Kester. "Wasn't Enger involved in that McNair situation?"

"Yeah," Kester said. He set the bent paperclip on his pile of papers. "I don't know him very well, but I think he's a good kid. Just got caught up in a lie, for his friend's sake. I don't know much about him."

Reggie looked at Dan. "Do you think he said 'the hell with it' after the McNair thing and took off?"

Dan shrugged. "Well, it wouldn't be the first time someone walked away without letting us know they were quitting. But I think the police are treating this more like a missing person deal."

Kester picked up the paperclip and twirled it between his fingers again, but the words 'missing person' brought his fingers to a halt. The hair on the back of his neck stood up. An image of Lloyd Simpson formed in his head.

"Okay, keep us informed on that," Reggie said. "Meeting adjourned."

Mike Flores walked next to Kester as they left the building. The morning sun warmed their skin. They squinted in the sudden light.

"Well, that was about as boring as watching paint dry," Mike said. "Right up until that missing person deal."

Kester stuck his hands in his pockets. "I hope the kid's okay," he said. "He's dumb as a rock but a sweet guy."

"Welcome back," Mike said. He slapped Kester on the shoulder. They stopped in the shade of a pine tree, enjoying the soft breeze from the lake.

"You all set to get back to work?" Mike said. "Did you get all your problems settled?"

"Yeah, I think so."

"And things are okay with Clare?"

Kester shrugged. "I don't know yet. She's avoiding me. I left her several voicemails, but she never called back."

"Maybe she still thinks you're a psychopathic killer," Mike said. He looked out at the lake. "That can't be good for a relationship."

Kester laughed. "I'm going to leave before you cheer me up so much I have to cut my wrists."

On the ward, the hum of morning activity greeted Kester. Virgil sat by the nursing station. He looked up when Kester's footsteps approached.

"Hey, Virgil, how we doing today?" Kester leaned down and squeezed the thick, sweat-shirted arm.

Virgil reached up and clutched his hand. *Still a lot of strength there,* Kester twisted out of Virgil's grip and stood upright. "Got to get to work, buddy. Have a good morning."

Virgil's eyes tracked him around the counter and into the nursing station. Virgil looked out at the ward with new attention. Kester made a mental note to check with the therapy staff. Maybe Virgil was making some progress.

He found Clare in the med room. Her light perfume mingled with the smell of pills and applesauce. The summer sun had lightened her hair and darkened the skin along her arms. She stood with her back to him, stocking the med cart.

He reached out and placed his hands on her shoulders, and she turned, startled.

He whispered close to her ear. "You got anything for heart pain on that cart?"

She smiled. "Why? What's wrong with your heart?"

"Oh, it's just lonely.

She rolled her eyes and laughed. "That's the worst make-up line I've ever heard."

He put his arms around her and pulled her close. "Well, let me kiss the top of your

head and tell you how much I've missed you." He buried his nose in her hair.

She hugged him. "I've missed you too, Kes."

"I'm sorry about how I've acted lately," he said. "I'm sorry I've made you wonder about me."

"It's okay," Clare said. She hugged him again and turned back to the med cart. "I talked to your mom, and she told me about your dad and how hard his death was on you and Paddy. I can understand why you might have felt a little confused."

"You talked to Mom?"

"She called me earlier this week." Clare turned and put a bottle on the cart. "And I talked to your brother, too. He said he straightened you out, and I wouldn't have any more trouble with you."

Kester laughed. "Yeah. For a history professor, he's a pretty good therapist."

She threw an empty applesauce container into the trash and closed the drawers on the med cart. "So what did Paddy say?"

"He said I shouldn't kill my patients."

"That seems simple enough." She licked a gob of applesauce from a spoon. "How is Paddy at relationship counseling?"

"Considering his past record with women, we probably shouldn't hire him for that." Kester looked at the floor and hesitated. "Actually, he told me it's fine to worry about my patients, and it's okay to question how far I can go on the suffering thing."

Clare walked back to the front counter. Kester followed her. "And that resolved your conflict?" she said.

"No." An aide passed close by. Kester lowered his voice. "I think I'll always feel like I'm somehow failing these guys. But it's not something I'm supposed to solve."

"Isn't that sort of washing your hands of the whole issue?" she said.

"Sure," he said. "The point is, who put me in charge of a solution?"

"Then, who gets to decide?"

Kester shrugged his shoulders. "Everyone—society—I don't know." He looked across the counter. Virgil sat in his chair with his head turned toward them. His eyes tracked Kester's movements. His mouth hung slack and motionless.

Kester turned back to Clare. "Until society, the Church, the American Medical Association, or somebody with more authority than I have around this place finally decides what the heck our policy should be, I'm going to refuse to play God."

Clare studied his face for a few seconds. "And you're okay with that?"

"No, not entirely. But at least it lets me get on with my job."

Clare leaned over and kissed his cheek. "Welcome back to the mainstream, baby."

Kester looked past Clare's head. Virgil sat slumped in his chair. His eyes were closed, and

his breathing was slow and regular.

Chapter Twenty-Eight

I know dickweed stole the young screamer's picture album.
It was one of those cheap, plastic things they sell at Wal-Mart
for a couple of dollars. Her family probably brought it and
filled it up with pictures of dogs, brothers, and birthday
parties. I suppose families do that, hoping to jar loose a
memory or two.

Why would dickweed want that? Just a goddamn klepto,
probably. Nobody's missed it so far.

The young screamer's mother came by for her stuff today.
She was crying, and I suppose she forgot about the pictures.
So much stuff gets lost in here—or stolen. Dickweed's stupid
little pilfering habit is bad enough, but it's not the worst thing
about that guy.

The young screamer shook me up. Watching people die is
one thing when you figure they've had a pretty good run. But
she got cheated out of a lot of years. I had to ask myself if I got
rattled about helping her because of her age.

Ultimately, I remembered how much she suffered. It took a while to get over the shame of not doing what I knew was right for her. It's just a lucky fluke that she went ahead and died anyway.

I've made a promise to myself. From now on, when I see the fire, and I'm sure of it, I won't hesitate.

The farmer has some new pictures in his room. His son brought them by a couple of days ago—a big, stocky man like his dad. Most days, the farmer wears a faded pair of bib overalls, washed out and so soft they drape over his belly like a second skin. He has on a green ball cap with 'DeKalb' across the front, and when he tilts it back on his forehead, a tan line shows, like a permanent tattoo, just above his scraggly eyebrows. Meaty arms stick out of his white t-shirt, going to fat, but he still looks like he could spend a whole day bucking hay bales.

The pictures in his room—two of them, taped to the wall by his bed—will stay there until one of the other patients wanders in and pulls them down. They may walk off with them or leave them lying on the floor. You never know what they'll do.

I went in and looked at the pictures right after he got them. One shows him standing with his arm around a tiny woman with one of those poofy, 1960s-style hairdos and pointy glasses. Probably his wife. The farmer is wearing a blue Hawaiian shirt with a string of flowers around his neck. He's standing there smiling but still looks like a fish out of water. No cap but that same tan line on his forehead.

The second picture shows him a few pounds lighter, standing beside a big, green tractor. He's turned toward the camera with one foot raised, caught stepping up into the cab. There's a smile on his face in this one, too, but he's not faking it. Same kind of overalls he's wearing today, over a smaller belly.

He's in the dayroom, over by the window. His big, denim-covered butt is pushed back in a chair, and he's bent forward at the waist with his elbows on his knees. He has that ball cap in his hands, and those sausage fingers are working it over good like they don't know how to be still. He's staring out at the trees and the clouds. He looks puzzled, like he's not sure why he's in here, instead of breathing in rich barnyard smells and finishing the plowing. If he keeps working them over like the one he's wadding up, his son will need to bring him a new supply of ball caps.

Maybe the farmer can no longer imagine himself back out on that tractor, watching behind him to make sure his plow cuts a nice, straight furrow. I think that's one of the things a lot of folks lose in this place. I know I said before that if you lose your mind, it's no problem. I stand by that. But losing only part of it is way worse than losing most of it.

Those pilots who got shot down way during that war—some jungle thing—said they got along better in captivity if they could escape in their minds. They'd think of things back home, and that helped. I don't think you have to be locked up in the jungle for that to kick in, though. I think we all do that every day. I think the farmer is probably trying to do that right now, but his brain can't quite get him back to his farm and driving that tractor.

I get up, walk into the dayroom, and go over to where he's sitting and twisting that cap. He looks up, and I get that same zing when I recognize how stuck he is down in there. Definitely a horse.

Maybe a big old draft horse like his grandpa used to keep for plowing those same fields.

I move over to the craft area in the corner and look at the underside of the table. One of the helpers always sticks wads of gum under there. Sure enough, I find some, pull it off, and stick it in my mouth. A faint taste of mint leeches out onto my tongue as the gum softens. I tuck the gum down by my teeth and return to my seat.

Later, I go in for dinner but don't feel like eating. The gum is still tucked down there in my cheek, and I give it a little chew from time to time.

They get us all tucked into bed at bedtime, and the helpers head for the dayroom and the television. I stay quiet for a while, thinking about how to save the farmer. Finally, I reach under my bed and feel around the metal frame. I find the part I'm looking for and bend it back and forth until it breaks loose. It tapers down to a sharp point, like a big old framing nail.

I get out of bed and check to make sure the helpers are still watching TV, and then I move down the hall to the farmer's room. The little light on the nightstand is on. The farmer's belly rises and falls under the blanket. A pair of heavy shoes are lined up under his bed. I give the wad of gum a good chewing and can tell it is Doublemint.

If I mess this up and the farmer gets those strong fingers clamped on me, I'll be in real trouble, so I move quietly. I pick up one of his shoes and hold it in my right hand. The piece of bed frame is in my left hand. I reach across the farmer's face and put the pointy end of the metal piece into his hairy ear hole. He's making little snoring noises. His warm breath blows against my left arm, just above his mouth. The gum is up near the front of my mouth, where I can get it quickly.

There will be only one chance at this, so I pause for a second before I raise his shoe and bring the heel down against the end of the metal. The spike disappears into his ear like a magic trick, and there's a little "thunk" as it breaks through into his brain.

I drop the shoe onto the farmer's chest and reach up to pull the gum from my mouth. He's flopping around like a fish on a riverbank now, and I have some trouble getting the gum into his ear hole to plug it up. A drop of blood darkens the pillow under his ear before I get it sealed.

I'm sprawled across his thick chest, pinning him to the bed, but he's no longer struggling. He lets out one last little gurgle and goes silent. His eyes are closed, but I know the pain isn't down in there anymore. The gum is holding, and no more blood leaks from his ear.

I place his shoe under the bed and line it up with the other one. I'm glad I did a tidy job and plugged his ear up so the pillow stays nice. A little bit of blood got out, though. The farmer was probably a stickler for neat and tidy on his farm. I hope he's back watching those long, straight furrows stretch out behind him.

Chapter Twenty-Nine

Carlotta Martinez peeked around the partition. "What's up?"

Ed Ralston, lead sergeant for the Larimer County Sheriff's Office Investigation Division, motioned her into his cubicle.

"Sit down, Carly," He pointed to the chair in front of his desk. "You aren't going to believe this one," he said. "I just got a call from Dave Lee over at the coroner's office."

Carly set her coffee cup on the desk and sat up straight. Her feet barely reached the ground. "Okay."

"Dave has a body from Foothills Hospital," Ed said. "Some guy named Frank Gustafson."

"A patient or staff?"

"Patient. One of their dementia folks. Guy was a farmer out in Weld County." Dave picked up a piece of paper and looked at it.

Carly waited for Ed to continue.

"So Dave gets a call from the hospital that this farmer's been found dead in bed with blood on his pillow. The nurse who found him looks in his ear, and it's packed with gum."

"Gum?"

"Yeah, like chewing gum. And apparently, this guy is one of their healthier patients and wasn't sick or expected to die soon."

"He stuck gum in his ear?"

So the nurse calls the doc. He looks in the guy's ear and decides to call for an autopsy."

"Do they know why the gum was there?"

"Probably so his brains wouldn't leak out. Dave x-rays the dead guy's head, and there's a big metal spike rammed into his brain through his ear hole."

Carly picked up her coffee cup and sipped. "And I get to figure all of this out?"

Ed smiled. "Yeah, I thought you'd like to take a stab at it."

"Gum—Jesus." She took a notepad and pen out of her jacket pocket. "Do you have a contact name at the hospital for me?"

"Not yet. Get in touch with the director. He'll help you find the people you need to talk to."

Carly put the notepad back in her pocket and stood. "This will be kind of weird for me--seeing Foothills again."

"Why's that?" Ed said.

"Back in high school, they bussed us out there for a tour. It was a state mental hospital back then." She hunched her shoulders. "Spooky place."

"I think you'll find it's changed a lot," Ed said. "My uncle was out there for a while before he died. I visited him a few times." He stood. "Anyway, go see Dave over at the Medical Examiner's office, then you can get out to the hospital and get started."

Frank Gustafson lay on a stainless steel table. Dave Lee ran a bone saw around Frank's skull and pried the top half away from the brain. He grinned at Carly.

"Quit it, Dave." She smiled at the short, pudgy medical examiner. "I'm not going to barf like last time."

Dave set the cup-shaped piece of the skull on the table. "I thought you might like to be here when I took this thing out," he said. He inserted a forceps into Frank's left ear. There was the snick of metal against metal. Dave tugged, grunting with the effort. A five-inch sliver followed the forceps out of the ear cavity.

"Huh," Dave said, rotating the forceps. He placed the metal on a tray next to a ruler. "I'll get some measurements and pictures for you after I finish here."

"What is it?" Carly craned her neck to see across the table.

"Don't know." Dave studied the metal sliver. "Not a manufactured spike or nail. It looks like it was broken off of something bigger." He turned back to the body.

Carly walked around the table and looked down at the metal sliver and then at the placid face below the exposed brain.

"You know this guy?" Dave said.

"No, but there are a bunch of Gustafsons over around Greeley, where I grew up. Mostly farmers. She looked at the large hands and thick forearms. "Physically, he looks like he could still do a full day's work."

"Yeah, still in good physical shape. But he must've been pretty far gone mentally if he was out at Foothills." Dave picked up a scalpel and steadied the brain with his left hand. He slid the sharp blade through the tissue, cutting it into thin slices like fresh-baked bread.

Carly left the coroner's office and drove north on the interstate and west toward the mountains. The hospital came into view, nestled against the first rise of parallel ridgelines. It looked much less ominous than she remembered. With its neat lawns and tranquil setting above the lake, the grounds were almost park-like.

The administration building fronted the campus. Inside, tile floors and deep, rich woodwork reminded her of that long-ago high school field trip. The hallway was cool and dim after the summer heat outside.

Carly found the information desk. The middle-aged secretary smiled and greeted her. "You must be from the Sheriff's Office. They called earlier and told us you'd be here today." The secretary stood and walked around the desk. "Doctor Wilson is expecting you."

They crossed the hall, and the secretary knocked on a thick, wooden office door and opened it. "Doctor Wilson, the lady from the Sheriff's Office is here."

The formidable man behind the desk rose and walked toward them. "Thanks, Janet." The secretary stood aside to let Carly pass and then left and closed the door behind her.

Carly glanced around the room. A lot of football memorabilia, mainly from Notre Dame.

"Reggie Wilson," the man said. He stuck out a hand that engulfed hers. His handshake was warm and delicate.

"Carly Martinez," she said.

He motioned her to a pair of chairs in the corner. "Let's sit here," he said. "It's a nice view of the water."

Carly looked out the window. The lake sparkled in the summer sunlight.

"I'll tell you the truth," Ms. Martinez, I've dealt with a lot of unusual issues around this place, but never a murder investigation." He sat in one of the chairs and crossed his legs. "I'm not sure how this all works, but I'll help in any way I can."

Carly remained standing. "I appreciate that, Doctor Wilson. And if you don't mind, I'd like to see the ward and Mr. Gustafson's room as soon as possible."

The medical director stood up. "Oh, sure. I'll take you over right now." He hurried to the door. "We closed off the room as soon as they left with the body."

They walked down the hall to the entrance door. Carly was tiny next to Reggie. "You were a football player, huh?"

"Yeah," he said. "That was a while ago."

"Notre Dame?"

"Yup. Go Irish."

"My brother played for Nebraska.," she said, smiling.

Reggie grinned. His shoulders relaxed as they walked out the door. "A Cornhusker, huh? Well...." He laughed. "We can't all be Fighting Irishmen."

They strolled along the treelined sidewalk.

"How did you go from football player to doctor?" Carly said.

"Family tradition," Reggie said. "We play football until our brains are knocked out, and then we go to medical school."

Carly laughed. They turned right and entered one of the buildings.

Reggie took a ring of keys from his belt. "This is C Ward." He unlocked a double door and swung it open.

Carly braced for a blast of horrible—perhaps unidentifiable—odors and sounds. To her surprise, the air carried only a trace odor of excrement and urine and a faint smell of medicine and disinfectant, and all of it overlaid with the scent of fresh-baked bread. The soft drone of a television came from down the brightly lit hallway.

"I'll introduce you to the ward physician and nurse," Reggie said. He locked the double door behind them and slipped the key ring back onto his belt. They walked toward a horseshoe-shaped counter with a wooden half-door at each end.

An upholstered chair stood against the wall by one of the half-doors. The man in the chair sat slumped forward.

Carly froze for several seconds. *Young, probably mid-fifties. Big. Very big.*

Reggie grinned at Carly's reaction. "That's Virgil,"

He looks kind of young for this place,"

"Most of our folks are older. But we have some even younger than him. Virgil had a stroke and became a problem at home and in the nursing facility, so we got him." He looked back at Virgil. "He's usually fine these days, but he can't talk or care for himself, so he's kind of stuck here."

Carly looked over her shoulder. Virgil sat watching them. "Sad."

A petite, blonde nurse rounded the corner and stopped.

"Hey, Clare," Reggie said. "This is the investigator from the Sheriff's Office."

The nurse shook Carly's hand. "Hi. Clare Williams, supervising nurse for the ward."

"Carly Martinez."

The nurse crossed her arms. "This is such a bizarre thing, Reggie. Did you talk to the family yet?"

"Yeah, I talked to Frank's son earlier. He's waiting to hear from the coroner. I told him we don't know too much at this point either. I'll give him a call again later."

"Doctor Wilson," Carly said. "Is there someplace I can meet privately with you and the ward physician?"

"Sure," Reggie said. "Clare, get Kes and meet us in the ward conference room."

Reggie escorted Carly to the conference room, where they both found seats at the table. While they waited, Carly jotted down a few notes.

Carly looked up from her notepad as Clare and the physician entered the room. Carly introduced herself. He walked to the table, shook her hand, and sat next to Reggie.

"First of all," Carly said, "let me tell you that this is a homicide investigation."

Kester crossed his arms and sat back in his chair. Clare stole a glance at him.

Carly reached into her coat pocket and pulled out a small tape recorder. "I'll be taking some notes and recording all of this," she said. She raised her eyes and looked around the table. "Is that okay?"

"Sure," Reggie said. The other two nodded.

Carly turned to Kester. "Doctor Grayson, the nurse on duty, found the body, right?"

Kester sat up straighter in his chair and clasped his hands atop the table. "Well, one of the aides found him and called Clare. Clare found the gum in Mr. Gustafson's ear and called me. I removed the gum. The ear canal appeared traumatized."

"Could you estimate how long he'd been dead?" Carly said.

"The body was cold, and there was some rigor mortis, so it must have been several hours," Kester said.

Carly scribbled on her notepad. "I talked to the coroner earlier, and it appears that Mr. Gustafson died because someone pushed a five-inch piece of metal into his brain through his left ear." The faint scratch of her pen on the notepad was the only sound in the room.

Finally, Reggie spoke. "So sometime last night, somebody went into Frank's room and rammed a piece of metal into his ear?"

Carly nodded. "Yes, and then plugged his ear with gum."

Reggie ran his hand through his hair. "Well, this is gonna make the papers."

Carly spent the next hour collecting information. Clare provided her with a list of all staff on the ward the previous night and a list of visiting family members.

Later, they walked to Frank Gustafson's hospital room, where Carly examined the bed and the pillow. A single stain of dried blood was the only abnormal finding.

"I'll have somebody over this afternoon to check for prints and other evidence," Carly said. She noted the pictures on the wall and the shoes lined up neatly under the bed.

Reggie excused himself. "I need to call my boss at CDHS and let him know about this." He hurried from the room.

Kester turned to Carly. "I need to get back to my rounds if that's okay." He hesitated. "Did Doctor Wilson mention our staff member who's been missing for a week?"

"No, I wasn't aware of that. Has it been reported?"

"Yeah, the police are looking into it."

Carly scribbled in her notepad. "I'll check on that. What's the name?"

"Dennis Enger."

"Okay, thanks." She turned to Clare. "I'll want you to lock this room until our forensics

people have a chance to look it over. I'll be back later to begin talking to the night staff."

Clare locked the door behind them and escorted Carly to the nursing station. The big patient who'd been sleeping in the chair was gone.

Carly turned to Clare. "How many patients do you have here?"

"On the ward? Usually around thirty. There are five wards, so the entire hospital has about a hundred fifty."

Carly told her about visiting the hospital years earlier. "It's quite a bit different than I remember it," she said.

"Yes, I'm sure it is," Clare said. "We don't have any general psychiatric patients here like they used to. The state transferred all of those to other facilities. We only deal with difficult geriatric patients. Mostly dementia, and a few brain injury people."

Carly surveyed the nursing station, the hallways, and the dayroom. "It's strange, the stereotypes we form about these things." She closed her notepad and stuck it in her pocket. "I'll be back later. Thanks for your help, Ms. Williams."

"I'll have to unlock the ward door for you," Clare said. She hesitated. "So what happens now? Who gets investigated?"

"To start?" Carly said. "Basically, everyone."

Chapter Thirty

The bread is still warm in my hand. The lady with the bread machine spreads butter across the top of my slice and hands it over.

"Let it cool a bit before you eat it, Virgil."

The yeasty smell is a nice change of pace. She comes every week and makes bread in her machine. It makes this corner of the dayroom a little cozier.

They say smells can bring on powerful memories; lately, I agree. My memory, in general, has been getting better. The days can still jump around with no rhyme or reason for me, but some things are coming into sharper focus—some of the time.

I bite into the cooling bread and get a strong image of my grandmother's kitchen. I can see the speckled, dark linoleum floor and the white metal cabinets. She always made six loaves at a time, and the first couple were fair game for whoever was around when they came out of the oven.

I finish the bread in three bites and sit by the nursing station. The rush of activity from earlier this morning has died down. I didn't see the farmer's face when they wheeled him out, but I think he was glad to get out of here. He used to get the warm bread, but he never looked any less homesick.

The sound of a key in the ward door sort of wakes me from a nap, but I don't want to open my eyes. It's easy to tell that the voice belongs to the football doctor. He works with Doctor K, but I don't see him on the ward very often. He looks like the guys I used to have across from me on the line back when I played football.

Whoever is with him sounds young and moves with short, clicking steps. The football doctor says my name, but I don't open my eyes until they pass by. Then I open my eyes and see the little dark-haired lady with the football doctor. She turns back and looks at me.

I'm glad I helped the farmer, even though it took some hard thinking to come up with a way of doing it. I'm good-sized, but he would've been a handful, even for me. The spike worked just fine. And I didn't leave much of a mess.

I skip lunch because of the bread. I walk down the hall in the afternoon and look in at the wreck. The wreck has a room off by himself because he gets to yelling sometimes. But not like a screamer. I think he just gets pissed off about a lot of things. I can't blame him for being angry. He's quite a bit younger than anyone else on the ward, except maybe the young screamer, who's gone now.

His leg pokes out from under the sheet, and the infection looks worse. I check on him daily because his leg's redness moves up and down like a thermometer. Some days, it's only red to the middle of his calf. On other days, it's like the heat's been turned up, and his leg gets red and swollen all the way up to his butt. He yells more on those days, and sometimes they take him off somewhere for a couple of days and then bring him back.

I call it yelling, but it's more of an angry wheeze. I've never heard any sound out of the wreck's mouth. There's a tube coming out of the front of his neck, right below his Adam's apple. The air comes whooshing out of it along with a fountain of phlegm, and his face looks angry as hell. So that's how I know he's yelling.

The only time he's genuinely calm is when he's jerking off. I'd call him the masturbator, but I feel sorry for the poor guy. He's never out of that bed, and I've never seen him do anything but suck air through his neck and move the sheets up and down where his groin is. That and the leg are probably why he's off down here alone. It has to be lonely for him.

I think he's here because of a car wreck or something. So I call him the wreck.

Something's been bothering me, so I'm going to check it out today. After the young screamer died, I thought I was okay with the job I've taken on. Her fire was different from the earlier ones. That really rattled me more than I admitted to myself. The farmer's fire was just like the gray guy's and all the others, so helping him was the right thing to do.

The problem is, if the young screamer's fire was different, maybe there are all kinds of fire, and that's what bothered me. The wreck isn't exactly like all the others, so I've come to look down into his eyes.

He's leaning up on his right side with that leg sticking out. They always prop him up some, too. The leg is apple red up to his knee today. The room contains nothing but a bed. No television, no pictures, no clothes hung up. Just the bed and him.

Up close, he has this little pattern to his eye movements, as if he's watching a horse gallop back and forth across the room. The air from his neck hole smells like morning breath. His hands lie under the covers, but the sheet isn't bouncing around down near his privates. His mouth is a bigger version of the hole in his neck and just as unmoving.

It's hard to see down into his eyes because they jerk around. Finally, I pick up the rhythm as they scan from side to side, and I get glimpses.

It's hard to even describe it. The nearest I can come is to say it's like the spark of metal against stone. Sharp, white-hot flakes shoot off in all directions and disappear into the dark around the edges of his pupils. Except it happens over and over down inside there.

The sound of a shovel scraping through a pile of gravel on concrete used to give me the willies. If there was a soundtrack with the sparks down in those eyes, it would be that sound.

I back off and turn to go. This time, there's no panic like with the young screamer. This time I was prepared. But there's a lot to think about now.

I sit in the dayroom for a change and watch the helpers tend to the wheelchair people. It suddenly hits me that both groups are okay—the helpers because their bodies and brains are alive and nimble, and the rocks in the wheelchairs because their fires are out down inside.

Maybe the helpers have fires going down inside, but all their moving around in the world cools the flames. Then—if they're particularly unlucky, like some of the people they take care of—they wind up like the horses, without a cool breeze to keep the fire damped. And maybe if they're unlucky too soon, and something happens to them like what happened to the young screamer or the wreck, it turns that fire into something even worse.

It's astonishing how complex the whole thing is becoming.

They wheel in the food cart. The dayroom fills with the odors of ham and potatoes. One of the helpers comes over and pats me on the knee. "Come on, Virgil," he says. "Sit at the table, and I'll get you started first."

I walk over and sit at the table. A couple of other people wander in to get an early seat. The helper brings my plate. While he's setting it down, I try to look into his eyes to test my theory, but he's moving too fast. It's too fast to let any fires flicker up anyway.

After dinner, I walk back down to the wreck's room. They give him regular food but mush it up in a blender or something first and spoon it in like baby food. A smear of the mushed potato and ham is stuck on his chin.

I gave it a lot of thought during dinner, and I'm splitting hairs on this issue. I'm too stuck on the kind of fire I'm seeing when I should concentrate on the pain that goes with it. Flame, glowing coal, spark, or whatever—all misery.

The wreck has his eyes closed. The tube sticking out from the hole in his neck is about as big around as my pinky finger, so my thumb covers it pretty well. I grip the sides of the slick tube with my middle and index fingers like I'm holding a cigarette. The wreck sucks in, and my thumb makes a little squeaky noise along the edge of the tube. I press in harder and get a better grip with my fingers. It's hard because the junk on the tube makes my fingers slide.

His mouth works open and shut, but no air whistles out. That's a bit of a surprise. I was ready to clamp my other hand over his mouth if necessary. I'm also prepared for him to start thrashing around some, but he rests in the bed as relaxed as can be.

The room turns murky with the sunset. It's so quiet I hear the trees rustling outside the shadow-filled window.

After a few minutes, I let go. There's a little red circle around the fat of my thumb from the tube. It's just visible in the gloom. I wipe my hand along the sheet to dry it and turn away. There's no need to look down inside the wreck. I know he's gone.

The odor of ham and potatoes still fills the air all the way back to the dayroom. The smell follows me to my room. During the night, I dream of Easter dinner. We're all sitting at the table—Maureen, me, and the kids. The wreck joins us. His black dress pants cover his poor, messed-up leg, but somehow, I know the flesh is no longer red and swollen. The tube is gone from his neck. He bows his head and says grace, then takes a bite of a warm, buttered roll and smiles.

Chapter Thirty-One

The pillow blocked his view of the alarm clock on the nightstand. He raised his head to see the glowing numbers. Six fifteen.

Clare turned beside him. Her hand came to rest on his right hip. Kester rolled over and admired her smooth, untroubled face buried in the pillow beneath a nest of yellow hair. She rubbed her hand along his thigh, although she wasn't entirely awake. Things were starting to settle between them.

He slipped from under her hand and sat on the edge of the bed. Clare would sleep for at least another hour, he knew. In the kitchen, he made coffee and read the newspaper. In the two days since the murder of Frank Gustafson, no mention of it appeared in the local or any of the Denver newspapers. Kester talked to the victim's son, but otherwise, he'd avoided discussing it.

His phone rang.

"Are you up and awake?" Mike didn't sound happy.

"Barely." Kester yawned. "What's up, Mikey?"

"I thought you'd like to know. Danny Toth died last night. I was on call, so I pronounced him about eleven o'clock."

Kester stood and paced the kitchen. "I almost hate to ask. How did he die?"

"Nothing suspicious so far. Everyone is goosey as hell around here because of the murder, so the body went right to the coroner."

"What do you think about the cause of death?"

"Like I said, nothing unusual. No trauma. The guy was a time bomb anyway, with the bad leg and the blood clots. I'm guessing another pulmonary embolus, except this one was big enough to kill him."

"Well, thanks for letting me know," Kester said.

"No problem. I didn't mean to ruin your day off, but I thought you'd want a heads-up."

"Yeah. How are things on the ward?"

"A little tense. It's like in those mystery movies where everyone is suspicious. Amy Ruiz found Danny, so now she's just about shitting her pants, worrying she'll be blamed for his death. Fun times, amigo. See you later."

Kester set his phone on the table and picked up his coffee cup. He filled another cup, carried it into the bedroom, and put it on the nightstand. Clare rolled toward him and opened her eyes. He bent and kissed her on the forehead.

"Good morning, love," he said.

She stretched her arms wide and smiled. "Oh, you dear man. Did you make me breakfast?"

Kester laughed and handed her the coffee. "Yes, and it's all in this little cup."

She sipped the coffee and set the cup back on the nightstand. "Ahh, the perfect breakfast."

He sat on the edge of the bed and told her about his conversation with Mike Flores.

Clare pushed up, leaned back against the headboard, and crossed her arms. "What do you think?"

Kester stood. "Right now, I think it's probably a coincidence. We lose five or six patients a month out there, after all. It's just the nature of the place. And Danny was never in good shape to begin with."

"Such a sad case," Clare said. "So young. Just like Colleen the other day."

"The head injury kid we had for a couple of days?"

"Yeah." Clare shook her head. "So terrible."

She swung her legs over the side of the bed and hugged him. His old blue shirt hung to her knees. "You're right, sweetie," she said. "There's no sense jumping to conclusions. Let's try to enjoy our day."

Later, they rode their bikes to Old Town. The mid-summer sun burned bright. A cool breeze from the mountains cut the heat. They found an outdoor restaurant and ate a late breakfast.

Afterward, they biked to City Park and sat at an empty picnic table. College students and families lolled on the grass or played Frisbee.

Kester drank from his water bottle as Clare sprawled atop the table. "Most women don't look good in Spandex bike pants. But your ass looks terrific."

Clare laughed and splashed him with water from her bottle.

A car pulled up on the road near their table and parked. Lloyd Simpson stepped out and sauntered toward them. He wore jeans and a t-shirt covered with a light nylon jacket. His hands were stuffed in his pockets.

Kester's smile faded. Clare turned to see what held his attention. Lloyd smiled and waved. Kester nodded, but his eyes narrowed.

"Hi, doc," Lloyd said. He turned his head and leered at Clare. "How's it goin', Clare?"

Kester and Clare didn't respond.

Lloyd perched on the edge of the picnic table and propped his foot on the bench. "I saw you over here and thought I'd see if you'd heard anything more about the murder on the ward." He stared down at Clare, who quickly sat up.

"Um—nothing so far, Lloyd," she said. She looked at Kester. His eyes remained locked on the younger man.

Lloyd slapped his forehead. "Holy fuck! What a way to go, huh? A nail right through the brain!"

"How did you know?" Kester asked. His voice came out calm but menacing.

Lloyd spread his arms. "What's the matter, doc? Do you think maybe you're the only one who hears stuff? The whole fuckin' hospital knows about it." He smiled. "By the way, sorry about that deal with the union. I was out of line." His voice oozed insincerity.

He looked back at Clare as she slid off the table and stood by Kester. Lloyd's gaze moved up and down her body.

"How do you like those bike pants, Clare? Are those pretty comfortable?"

She didn't answer.

"We're going now," Kester said.

Lloyd lifted his other foot onto the bench. His right pant leg rode up, exposing a black nylon sheath. Kester glanced at it. Lloyd pulled his pant leg higher.

"I wear it when I'm away from the hospital," he said. He pulled his pant leg down again, hiding the knife. "Just a little protection." He patted his leg. "You never know when you'll run into some shitbag who needs cutting." He laughed and waved his hand. "Well, you two have a nice bike ride. See you at work."

Clare and Kester picked up their bikes. Kester turned back. His eyes didn't blink as he walked over to stand next to Lloyd. He brought his face in close, keeping his voice low and menacing.

"If I find that on you at the hospital, I'll take it away from you."

Lloyd stepped back.

Kester turned and straddled his bike. He and Clare pedaled away.

"Try it, motherfucker," Lloyd whispered. Kester didn't look back.

Lloyd reached around, patted the gun nestled in its holster beneath his jacket, and then walked to his car.

They'd ridden home from the park in silence. Clare checked over her shoulder whenever a car approached. Each time, her eyes squinted with worry. At home, she hurried to change out of her biking clothes. Kester came out of the kitchen and found her huddled on the couch in the living room.

"Come on, hon. Don't let that idiot ruin our day," Kester said.

Clare pulled her legs up onto the couch. "It's hard to be cheery right now." She turned and looked out the window. "He is one scary little creep."

Kester sat and hugged her. "Well, if he gets froggy, I'll kick his ass for you," he said.

She smiled at his joke and then grew serious again. "Really, Kes. That guy scares the hell out of me. He wants to undress me. And he wants to hurt you."

Kester turned and gazed out the window.

On Monday, Kester called Carly Martinez and asked if she'd interviewed the rest of the ward staff.

"Yes, we've worked through the list from the ward, and we're starting on people from other areas of the hospital who have access to C Ward. The family members have all been interviewed. No leads so far."

Kester hesitated. "How about an aide named Lloyd Simpson?"

The sound of papers rustling came through the phone. "Yes, we interviewed him over the weekend. Nothing suspicious. He wasn't on duty at the time of the murder. Why do you ask?"

"It's probably nothing," he said.

"I'll be at the hospital this afternoon," she said. "Can we talk then?"

"Sure," Kester said. "See you then."

Kester found Clare sitting in the conference room. Her forehead rested on her hand as she wrote in a chart. The door scraped open, and footsteps clicked along the tiled floor. She turned quickly, fear in her eyes. Her body relaxed when Kes entered.

"God, Kes, you scared me." She stood and hugged him.

"I'm sorry," he said. "Everyone's on edge here. Nothing like a murder to get the adrenaline pumping."

Clare sat. "I haven't worried about the murderer for some reason."

Kester stroked her hair. "You're worried about him, aren't you? I know he's at work today."

She nodded. "But I've managed to avoid him all morning," she said.

"I saw him at the end of the hall after rounds," Kester said, "but we ignored each other." Kester patted her shoulder. "Let me know if he tries to bother you."

He walked to the door. "I don't think he has the knife with him. I don't see any bulge on his ankle, and I doubt he's stupid enough to bring it here after telling us about it."

"Still, be careful—please," Clare said. "I've never felt this way, even with some of our worst patients."

Kester opened the door. He smiled. "Don't worry, hon."

The room was barely big enough to hold the small, gray metal desk, two chairs, and an institutional-tan metal bookcase. Carly knocked on the open door. "Come in," Kester said. She entered. "This is your office, huh?" She looked at the scratched and dented desk. "If this is one of your perks, you should renegotiate your contract, doctor."

Kester smiled and gestured around the room. "Plush, isn't it? All this and a salary to match. Was it hard to find me?" Visitors often needed help finding his office tucked away in the basement of the therapy building. He motioned her to the chair next to the door.

"No, I had good directions. But it is out of the way."

"I like the quiet," he said, "and I get by on simple things."

Carly opened her notepad. Kester rocked back in his chair, his eyes studying her. "Would you mind if this was off the record?"

She closed the notepad and leaned toward him. "Doctor Grayson, they only say that in television shows. In a real-life murder investigation, there's no such thing."

He waved his hand in dismissal. "Yeah, I thought it sounded a bit dramatic myself." He wrinkled his forehead. "It's just that I'm not sure if any of this is even pertinent or of any value to you."

Carly laughed and opened the notepad again. "Don't worry, doc. This isn't off the record, but it is confidential." Her voice softened. "Just tell me what's bothering you."

Kester told her about Lloyd and Dennis and the death of Pastor McNair. He related the incident in the park.

"Did he threaten you or Clare?"

"Not directly. It was just his whole attitude. And the knife."

Carly scribbled some last notes and stood. "If he's found with the knife strapped to his ankle, we can get him for carrying a concealed weapon. He can be fired and prosecuted if he's found with the knife on hospital property—concealed or not. But we can't do anything to him based on what happened in the park."

Kester's phone rang. He answered it and listened for a few seconds. "Okay, on my way." He turned back to Carly. "I have to get back to the ward. Sorry."

"No problem." Carly stood. "Thanks for letting me know about this."

He hesitated at the door. "What about the connection to Dennis Enger?"

"That's a very slim lead," Carly said.

Kester looked at the floor and stuck his hands in his pockets. "I feel a little foolish about

this, you know."

Carly patted his arm. "No worries. Don't you doctors make a diagnosis on slim information occasionally?"

Kester looked at her. "Sure."

"So do we," she said. "I'll have another talk with Mr. Simpson."

Chapter Thirty-Two

Reggie jammed the accelerator to the floor. The Ford Taurus gradually picked up speed as they merged onto the interstate. He turned to Kester. "These damn state cars are a testament to the wisdom of committee decision-making." He scowled.

Kester smiled at his friend. He turned his head and looked west to where the deep-blue peaks of the Front Range stretched southward. The twin points of Long's Peak and Meeker Peak towered above the other mountains, still white in places with late snow.

"You know," Kester said, "When I was seventeen, I made it from Fort Collins to Denver in less than forty-seven minutes in my mom's Chrysler Newport."

The line of cars in the left lane flashed by. "I believe some of these boys may beat your record."

The air conditioner struggled to cool the interior of the car. As the morning heat rose, both men opened their windows.

The rushing air made conversation impossible. Near the turn for Northglenn, traffic slowed to a crawl.

"I'm not looking forward to this," Reggie said.

"The meeting?"

"Yeah. I think even the governor may be there." "You've met him before, haven't you?"

"Sure," Reggie said. "But that was social. Not for an ass-chewing."

"Who says this will be that kind of meeting?"

Reggie hunched forward in the driver's seat. He swept his eyes from side to side, watching the traffic. "This is a meeting at CDHS Headquarters. Ass chewing is sort of their specialty."

Kester swallowed the lump in his throat. He reached over and punched Reggie lightly on the shoulder. "Cheer up, boss. If we get canned, we'll open a little storefront clinic and write marijuana prescriptions."

Reggie smiled. "Sounds like a great plan."

The meeting room held a conference table even larger than the one in the administration building at Foothills. Business-suited state employees filled most of the seats. All of the people in the room talked at the same time.

Reggie hesitated at the door. He turned to Kester. "It's even worse than I imagined," he whispered.

A thin, balding man at the head of the table glanced up at them in the doorway. He smiled and motioned them over. Kester followed Reggie. The bald man shook Reggie's hand. "Thanks for coming, Doctor Wilson." The man's smile showed an even row of white teeth.

Reggie turned to Kester and placed his hand on his shoulder. "Mr. Cranston, this is Doctor Grayson."

The balding man leaned forward and shook Kester's hand. "A pleasure, Doctor. I'm Bill Cranston, Director of CDHS." His smile beamed. He motioned them to the two empty seats.

The murmur of conversation around the room continued until Cranston struck a small wooden gavel on the tabletop. "Let's get started," he said.

A four-inch stack of papers rested in front of each chair. Kester turned and whispered to Reggie. "I didn't know there'd be homework."

Reggie frowned, his forehead wrinkling into deep furrows. He looked at Kester and made a faint shushing sound.

Cranston looked around the table. He sat up slightly straighter in his chair and lifted his chin to a forty-five-degree angle as if the extra height might help cast his words to those at the far end. His eyebrows arched. "We have quite a few items on the agenda this morning, but I wanted to start with one that will probably put us under the microscope in the coming days."

He turned to Reggie. "Some of you may be acquainted with Doctor Wilson, the medical director at our Foothills facility in Fort Collins." He turned to Kester and gave a slight nod. "He and Doctor Grayson are here today because of an incident at their facility late last week."

Cranston's face no longer held a friendly smile. Kester mused that a man like Bill Cranston probably practiced a mug for every occasion. At the moment, he looked calm and severe.

The director cleared his throat and began. "On Friday night, one of the patients at Foothills was murdered—in the facility."

Conversation erupted around the room. Cranston raised his voice. "It will be announced in a press conference later this afternoon." The buzz increased. Cranston struck the tabletop once with the gavel. The islands of noise gradually subsided until the room was silent. "I've asked Doctor Wilson and Doctor Grayson to be present today in case you have any questions regarding the hospital or the specific incident."

He held up a thin sheaf of papers from the pile on the desk. "You each have a copy of the news release from the Larimer County Sheriff's Office and our department's official response." He fluttered the papers.

Several people around the table shuffled their stack of paper to find the statement. Kester found his four-page copy. He turned to Reggie. "Well, that's not so bad," he whispered. Reggie looked even gloomier than before.

Cranston turned to Reggie. "Doctor Wilson, would you care to make any general remarks before I open the discussion up for questions?"

Reggie fussed with his papers and cleared his throat. "Thank you, Director Cranston." He paused and studied the documents in his hand. "The report from the Sheriff's Office will give you some of the details, and Doctor Grayson and I are certainly at your disposal for any questions you may have."

He looked around at the crowd of bureaucrats. "Frankly, this is a situation I've not experienced before during my tenure at Foothills. So I don't really know what to tell you." He turned to Kester. "Doctor Grayson will probably tell you the same thing."

Some people around the table looked on with polite interest. A few read their handouts. One man raised his hand. His salt and pepper hair swept back full and perfectly groomed above his forehead. His thick eyebrows arched up as he looked at the department director for recognition.

Cranston pointed at him. "Yes, Martin, you have a question?"

The man leaned forward and planted his pen upright on his stack of documents. His mouth remained in a frown even while he talked. "Bill, I'm sure the gentlemen from Fort Collins—" He shot a quick glance toward Kester and Reggie—can provide us with valuable information about the details of the murder." He forced the corners of his mouth into a brief, dispassionate smile. It faded quickly. "But this is probably going to be the kiss of death for quite a few of our staff and clients, not just one patient at one of our facilities."

Cranston and the speaker exchanged practiced, somber looks. The director fidgeted and flashed his toothy smile.

He turned to Reggie. "I'm not sure you know Senator Bridges," he said, nodding toward Martin. "The Senator is

Chairman of the Health Services Committee in the State Legislature.

The attention of all those around the table shifted to the senator. He leaned back in his chair and rested his chin on his left hand. His index finger pointed upwards along the side of his face. "I'm sure most of you are aware of the dismal history of our state mental institutions." He tapped his pen against the tabletop. "And this latest incident will only add to that unfortunate record."

The director leaned forward. "Senator, it certainly isn't fair to say this patient's murder is anything more than a random incident."

Bridges raised his pen in the air. "I'm talking about how this will be perceived, Bill." He pointed the pen at the director. "I don't have to remind you of the budgetary and social pressures brought to bear on our system of institutions over the past few years."

He beamed his quick smile over at Reggie and Kester. "And I'm also aware that great improvements in care have been made over the years, thanks to people like Doctor Wilson and Doctor Grayson." He turned to address the entire room. "But I can assure you all that after the press and various interest groups get through with this, the public will once again be clamoring for a change in how we care for our mentally ill." He looked back at Reggie. "And an incident like this, with all the sensationalism it will bring on, could be used as the catalyst for certain people to close facilities like Foothills for good." He slashed the pen through the air.

"Senator Bridges, with all due respect, that's not going to happen, in my opinion," Reggie said.

The senator's lips settled into a thin, tight line, and he glared at Reggie. "And why is that, doctor?"

"Because there's no other place to put patients like ours. We're the final stop."

Reggie's voice softened. He raised his arm. "A show of hands. How many of you have ever been to Foothills or a similar facility?" Several people raised their hands. "And I don't mean a regular nursing home," he added. Almost all of the hands dropped.

Reggie turned back to Senator Bridges. "We house one hundred and fifty individuals who, for various reasons, have ceased to be the people they were. They've drained the resources—and in many cases, the compassion—of their families, friends, and communities. Their behavior has overwhelmed the expertise of even the most skilled nursing homes."

Senator Bridges leaned forward. "We don't need"...

Reggie raised his hand. "Let me finish, Senator."

Kester's mouth hung open. He'd never seen his boss so commanding.

Reggie spread his hands and spoke softly, although his eyes blazed. "We have a staff of around three hundred dedicated individuals who spend every day trying to make truly dreadful situations a little less horrifying for our patients and their families."

He turned and gestured toward Kester. "Even talented professionals like Doctor Grayson sometimes find the results of their efforts disappointing. Their motivation and dedication are tested daily because of what they're asked to do."

He turned back to the senator. "Oh, I know all about the efforts to close down our institutions." He leaned forward and tapped his index finger against the table. "But understand this. We get the lost of the lost in our facility—the people who should be long gone to a better world, but for whatever reason are still among us."

Reggie picked up the press release. "This will pass." He shook the papers. "This will be resolved. But when it's over, the citizens of Colorado will find that they can't do without a place like Foothills. If they close us down, the public will soon discover an uncomfortable dilemma. They'll find we're an indispensable balm for their guilt and unease. Places like Foothills."

Reggie dropped the papers onto the table and turned to Kester. "Doctor Grayson, do you have anything to add?"

Kester shook his head. The only sound was the slight rustling of papers.

Senator Bridges rested his arms on the table. His frown deepened. "Doctor Wilson, I may not fully understand the challenges you face in your chosen work, I'll admit." He leaned forward and pointed his pen at Reggie. "But let me assure you, I fully understand the challenges that I and Director Cranston face."

He pointed toward the head of the table, but his eyes stayed locked on Reggie. "Nobody needs to lecture me about a fickle public. 'Out of sight, out of mind' has always been their attitude toward places like Foothills."

He picked up the press release and waggled it at the two doctors. "This will place your facility—as well as Director Cranston's department—and ultimately my committee—very much in the public's mind." He paused and looked around the room. "In cases like this, the shit does not roll downhill, people. First, it rolls into my committee. And then I'm expected to act." He sat back in his chair. "And I promise I will roll it along to the rest of you."

Director Cranston pursed his lips and drummed his fingers nervously along the table's edge. The room fell uncomfortably silent. Finally, he smiled and looked down at the table. "Well, Doctor Wilson and Doctor Grayson are probably anxious to return to Fort Collins. Are there any questions before they go?"

The people around the table sat with indifferent stares. A few sorted through the rest of the agenda items in front of them. *Just another workday for most of them.* He and Reggie, and even the murder investigation, represented only a passing thrill—just one minor issue within the four inches of paperwork before them on the table.

The director's eyebrows shot skyward, and his smile broadened as if on cue. "No questions?"

He looked at Reggie. "I'd like to thank you for coming today, gentlemen. I'm sure you're anxious to be on your way." He tapped the gavel against the table. "As for the rest of us, let's take a fifteen-minute recess and then resume."

A drone of conversation erupted around the table. Chairs scraped across the floor as people stood and stretched. Bill Cranston shook Kester's hand. The director's smile appeared glued in place.

He slapped Reggie on the shoulder. "Thanks, Doc," he said. "I'll call you later today."

Kester shook his head in the hallway and looked around at the crowd pouring from the conference room. "That's it? We drove all this way for that?"

"Yeah, your government in action."

Senator Bridges strode through the conference room door. He spied the two doctors and hurried over, forcing a smile as he grasped Reggie's hand and gave two quick pumps. The gesture came as naturally to the politician as breathing.

"Doctor Wilson," the senator said. Two more rapid hand pumps. "I'm sorry you drove all this way for such a short meeting."

Reggie shrugged his shoulders and fixed the politician with a tight smile. "No problem, senator. We understand, what with the full agenda and all."

Bridges sighed and shook his head. "Let's just hope this murder investigation doesn't put us all in the middle of a firestorm," he said.

Kester offered to drive. Reggie slouched in the passenger seat as the Denver traffic inched toward the interstate on-ramp.

"That was an incredible exchange between you and the senator," Kester said. "I was about ready to tell them all to go screw themselves. Especially that Bridges guy."

Reggie drummed his fingers absently on the dashboard and checked the surrounding traffic. "Yeah, being in the state bureaucracy, I've learned a few things." He smiled. "I've always thought of this give-and-take as a skill, like being a great hooker. You might be damn good at it, but it's not something you brag about."

Kester laughed. The mountains came into view, stretching north toward Fort Collins. "Do you think he's right? About the firestorm coming?" Kester said. He hit the gas, accelerating into the flow of traffic.

Reggie snorted. "If all the firestorms predicted by the politicians came to pass, Colorado would be one crispy state by now." His mouth turned down in his usual scowl. "But sometimes they're right as right can be."

He reached over and slapped Kester's shoulder. "We may want to consider that little marijuana clinic," he said.

Chapter Thirty-Three

The firestorm hit two hours after they returned from Denver.

The Larimer County Sheriff Wayne Nesbitt stood before a microphone in the County Building and announced the murder investigation to a small crowd of local journalists. That evening, the national press picked up the story on the logical assumption that a lurid tale of murder in a mental institution would be irresistible to the general public.

Kester parked his ancient Toyota in the hospital's covered lot the following day. It meant a longer walk to the administration building, but he hoped to avoid the reporters and television crews crowding the main parking lot in front of the hospital.

He turned to Clare. "You ready?"

She closed her eyes and nodded. He reached over and rubbed her neck, and her shoulders relaxed. She smiled and looked around the parking lot. "It was a brilliant move, buying this car. None of those news people would ever expect to find a doctor hiding in a junker like this."

Kester laughed. He unlatched the driver-side door and hit it with his shoulder. It squealed open. "Let's go," he said.

They walked quickly across the parking lot and along the sidewalk. Halfway to the administration building, a reporter intercepted them. The man glanced toward the front of the building to see if any other news people had followed him and then turned back to Kester and Clare.

"You're Doctor Grayson, right?"

Kester put his palm on Clare's back and walked forward. The reporter backpedaled beside them. Kester smiled at the young man. "Am I famous already?"

The reporter grinned back. "Well, today you are."

Kester and Clare kept walking. The young man stuck a small recorder in front of Kester's face. "How's it feel to know there's a murderer loose in the institution?"

They walked faster. The reporter galloped alongside, the recorder bobbing close to Kester's face.

Near the administration building's back door, Kester stopped. He turned and faced the young man. "I don't know how it feels." He shrugged. "How does it feel to run around asking people how it feels?"

He hurried Clare up the steps and through the door, leaving the report outside.

"I've always wanted to do that," Kester said.

Clare hugged him and left for the ward. The reporter was back with the rest of the milling crowd at the front of the building. Several hospital security guards stood on the front steps, keeping the crowd clear of the entrance.

In the conference room, Reggie sat in his usual place. The five staff psychiatrists, including Nathan Mallory, occupied one side of the table. Mike Flores and several other non-psychiatric physicians sat along the other side. Carly Martinez and another woman stood along the wall.

Kester nodded to Carly and settled into the chair next to Mike Flores.

Reggie scanned the room. "Okay, I think this is everybody except for Doctor Rahm, who is on vacation."

"Lucky her," Mike whispered.

Reggie raised his voice. "I'm sure you all noticed our visitors outside this morning. I hope you all were asked how it feels to have a murderer running around the loony bin." He smiled. The doctors around the table laughed nervously.

Mike turned to Kester and whispered. "If that hot babe from the Morning Show in Denver is here, I'll give her an exclusive interview."

Reggie frowned at Mike and turned to address the room. "There will be no—I repeat, no— interviews by staff members."

He motioned to the woman standing next to Carly. "Crystal Preston is here from the department's public relations office."

The young woman stepped forward and nodded. Her dark, two-piece suit and impeccable white blouse stood out in sharp contrast to the slouching, disheveled doctors.

"She'll be handling all interactions with the press." Reggie glared at Doctor Flores and kept his voice low. "All of them, Mikey."

Mike frowned. Crystal Preston smiled, winked at Mike, and stepped back against the wall.

Reggie pointed at Carly. "You've all met Inspector Martinez from the Sheriff's Office."

Carly walked over and stood next to Reggie. Even seated, the Medical Director matched the investigator in height. "She's asked to speak with the staff about new developments in the case."

He nodded to Carly. "They're all yours."

Carly stuck her hands in her jacket pockets and studied the floor for several seconds, then raised her head and looked out at the doctors around the table.

"The investigation into the murder of Frank Gustafson continues. We interviewed all staff, visitors, the victim's family, and friends. Our forensics investigation has yet to be completed, but we have no major suspects. I know you're all anxious for this to be over." She glanced at Kester. "We've still got some leads, and we'll check those out over the next few days."

She turned toward Reggie. "I'm afraid there's more bad news today. Early this morning, a body was found east of town.

We don't have confirmation, but it appears to be your missing hospital employee."

Carly smiled. *Doctors have such terrible poker faces.* Nathan Mallory slumped low in his chair. His half glasses slipped even farther down his nose. Reggie shook his head slowly from side to side. His jowls hung even lower than usual.

Mike turned to Kester. "Jesus. This just gets better and better." His friend didn't respond.

Carly continued. "I'd appreciate it if you didn't discuss this with the rest of the hospital staff just yet. I'm giving the medical staff a heads-up because the press activity you witnessed this morning will seem quiet compared to the frenzy you'll have around here once this information gets out."

Her mouth turned up in a faint smile. "I'm not sure you ladies and gentlemen have ever experienced such a media frenzy. The medical staff will be prime targets for the reporters." She gestured toward the public relations officer. "Ms. Preston will prove invaluable over the next few days and weeks."

Reggie winced when Carly mentioned weeks. He looked around the table and stood. "Well, we still have a hospital full of people to care for," he said. "Like Ms. Martinez said, keep all this under your hat for now."

After the meeting, Kester found Janet, the administrative secretary, in her office near the lobby.

She rose from her chair when he hurried in, then sat down again when she recognized him. "Oh, Doctor Kester!

I thought you were another reporter trying to sneak past."
She glanced out the window at the crowd in the parking lot.
"They're a persistent bunch."

A grin spread across his face. "Against you, Janet? They
don't stand a chance." He grew serious. "I need to get into the
medical records room this afternoon. Do you suppose that will
be okay?"

"I'm sure it will be," she said. "The investigators have already
done their work down there."

"Okay." He started out the door. "I'll be back later."

The staff on C Ward stood in small, animated groups in
the halls, nervous and distracted. It was clear that patient care
would suffer today, thanks to all the excitement. The news of
Dennis Enger's death would only compound the problem.

Clare walked out of the dayroom. "Did you run into any
more reporters?"

Kester put a hand on her shoulder and led her to a quiet
stretch of hallway. "No, but I keep thinking one of them will
pop out of a ventilation duct or something."

She squeezed his arm. "Everyone is pretty jumpy today.
We're having trouble keeping our people focused on work.
They're even getting some of the patients riled up."

"Well," he said, looking around at the jittery workers, "it's
not going to get any better."

"Why do you say that?" Clare frowned.

Kester turned and faced her. He kept his voice low. "Is
Simpson here?"

"No," she said. "At report, they told us he called in and said he had an appointment today. Something that came up suddenly."

He nodded. Maybe Carly had scheduled a second interview with the aide. "Can you meet me in medical records after lunch?"

"I guess," Clare said. "Why?"

"I'll tell you when you get there."

After lunch, Kester hurried back to the administration building. News vans and trucks filled the parking lot, with reporters and gawkers clustered around several sheriff's deputies and security guards.

The medical records department took up most of the basement. After morning rounds, he'd used the ward computer to make a list of all the patients who had died at Foothills over the past six months. By the time Clare joined him, he'd piled a large stack of charts on a table at the front of the room.

"What are you doing?" Clare asked.

Kester disappeared down one of the long aisles. He walked back and placed two more charts on the table. "That's all of them," he said. "I'm going over our recent deaths to see if I can find any patterns." He gave Clare a quick peck on the cheek.

"Didn't the sheriff's department already do that?" she said.

"Yeah, but I thought I'd do it again to see if they missed anything. Besides, you and I have seen a lot of deaths in this place. We probably have a better feel than they do for what's ordinary and what's not."

He sat at the table and opened the top chart. Clare sat next to him. *Should I tell her about the discovery of Dennis Enger's body?* In the end, he kept the information to himself. No sense in alarming her at this point. He was finding it hard to keep an open mind about the identity of the murderer—or murderers. The image of Lloyd Simpson hovered in his mind, vivid and undeniable.

"Okay, we've got Lawrence Verstig, eighty-seven, died on B Ward on May 3. Pneumonia. No autopsy." He handed the chart to Clare.

"What exactly are we looking for?" she asked.

Kester was already lifting the next chart from the stack. "I don't know." He smiled. "I suppose we could look for any references to chewing gum."

Clare flashed a wry smile. "Quit it." She closed the first chart and set it aside.

He opened the second chart. "This is Marion Pettigrew's record." He read the morbidity and mortality report clipped to the inside cover. "I remember this one. She had some rib bruising found on autopsy. " He set the chart to the side by itself. "It wasn't the usual pneumonia or sepsis, so we'll look that one over a little closer."

Clare nodded toward the chart. "I remember that one too."

"Maybe just a coincidence again," he said.

They worked their way through the rest of the charts. Most of them recorded similar stories of lives ended by disease and age. After an hour of work, they were left with a small pile of charts listing causes of death that were not fully explainable.

Clare sorted through the pile. She looked puzzled. "All from C Ward." She set one chart apart from the others. "Frank Gustafson. I guess we both agree a spike in the brain is out of the ordinary." She picked up a second chart. "Mr. Garza. I suppose that one makes sense, at least as to being an unusual way to die."

She picked up the third chart. "Ivan Tyler. I still don't see why you want him in the 'suspicious' pile."

He shrugged. "I'm not sure yet. Just a hunch."

She read off the rest of the names. "Danny Toth, Mary Denton, Samuel McNair." She turned to Kester. "I don't see any other connection, other than all of them died on C Ward—our ward."

Kester sat back in his chair and crossed his arms. He looked at the charts briefly, deciding what to tell her.

"Clare, they found Dennis Enger's body this morning. Carly told us about it at the meeting."

Clare sat silent for several seconds, considering this new information. Her eyebrows shot up. "Lloyd."

Kester picked up the small stack of charts. "I'll take these and go over them again later. Let's not jump to conclusions on this."

They walked to the door, where he flipped the light switch. "All we have right now is a couple of murders and some other suspicious deaths, all connected to one ward." He stopped for a second and thought. "Well, when I say it out loud, it does sound worse, doesn't it?"

Chapter Thirty-Four

His dream was terrifying and exhilarating, vivid and rich in detail. Once again, he stood before the abandoned farmhouse. A lone figure cowered on the crumbling sidewalk. Lightning lit the scene, followed by a clap of thunder. This time, the figure was not Dennis Enger but Kester Grayson.

He fired, and Grayson spun and fell. Another figure appeared in the dark. Lightning flashed to reveal Hector Lopez. The gun bucked, and Hector whirled away into the darkness. More figures followed. Each time he fired, his tension eased. Bodies littered the weed-filled yard.

The rain came with a blast of wind. The rush of cool air blew the bodies like leaves. He laughed as they disappeared into the black basement window.

Clare Williams clutched his arm, smiling.

Lloyd opened his eyes and looked at the clock beside his bed. He found his cell phone on the nightstand. The dream images faded as he punched in the numbers and brought the phone to his ear.

"Foothills Hospital," said a voice on the other end.

"Yeah. Give me C Ward."

"Just a moment."

Lloyd rolled onto his back while the operator rang the ward. When the ward secretary answered, he told her he wouldn't be coming in.

"I've got an appointment I can't get out of."

He set the phone down and stared at the ceiling. The image of Clare blurred and disappeared.

After a few minutes, he got out of bed and walked to the bathroom. The power he'd felt over the past few days was fading away. Last night's call from the Sheriff's Office rattled him.

The investigator's voice was pleasant and friendly. "We just have some more questions about the hospital and the staff, Mr. Simpson. Would you mind coming down for one more interview?"

He'd hesitated before answering. "Sure."

He showered and put on the slacks and shirt he'd worn at the union hearing. Upstairs, his grandmother sat at the kitchen table, reading the newspaper. She squinted through the cigarette smoke rising from the Camel between her lips. "What're you all fixed up for?"

He ignored her and pawed through the refrigerator. She turned back to her paper. "Did you know this boy they found? This Dennis Enger?"

Lloyd closed the refrigerator door and turned. "What?"

She pointed at the paper. "It says they found a boy named Dennis Enger dead out east of town. They think he was murdered. He worked at that place you work at."

Lloyd strode to the table and ripped the paper from her hand.

"God damn it!" Nora pinched the cigarette from her mouth and jabbed it into the ashtray next to her coffee cup. Smoke leaked from her lips with each word. Her eyes narrowed. She pushed up from the table, clawing at him. "Give me back my paper!" Her fingernails raked Lloyd's arm, leaving red furrows.

"Shit!" He pushed her back down onto the chair with one hand. His other hand gripped the nape of her neck. The newspaper fluttered to the kitchen floor. Nora winced with pain.

Lloyd's lips stretched thin across his teeth. His words came out soft, almost in a whisper. "Don't you ever fuckin' touch me again." His grip tightened on her neck. He twisted her to face him. Her eyes popped wide. Smoke huffed from her mouth.

He raised his other hand to rub the welts she'd raised along his forearm. Nora whimpered. His grip relaxed, and he let go. The marks on his arm burned like fire. He grunted in disgust and turned away.

When he bent to pick up the newspaper, his grandmother cowered in her chair. He leaned against the kitchen counter and read the article about Dennis. The farmer who leased the land where the abandoned farmhouse sat discovered the body. There were no leads in the case, no suspects.

He studied his grandmother with expressionless eyes. Nora's hand trembled as she reached for her cigarette. Lloyd tossed the newspaper onto the table and walked out the back door.

"Thanks, Doctor Grayson." Carly hung up the phone and closed her notebook, and walked to Ed Ralston's office. She knocked on the door frame. "Got a minute?"

Ed motioned her in. "What's up?"

"This thing at Foothills is bogged down."

Ed motioned to a chair.

Carly sat and took out her notebook. "We've interviewed everybody in the place. It doesn't make sense."

Ed picked up a paper and scanned it. "I read the coroner's report. The metal they dug out of Frank Gustafson's ear was pretty nondescript. They're still not sure where it came from."

Carly hesitated. "Well, there's one thing." She referred to her notes. "I just got off the phone with Dr. Grayson.

"The doc from the hospital."

"Yeah. He's been tracking some recent deaths on the ward where Gustafson was killed."

"Patients or staff?"

"Patients. Except Grayson said one of the aides—Lloyd Simpson—was friends with the kid they found out east of town in the farmhouse—Dennis Enger."

Ed shrugged. "Mighty thin lead."

Carly nodded. "Yeah, I know. But Grayson said this Simpson threatened him and his girlfriend at the park. Said he had a knife."

Ed sat forward. "Okay, that's interesting. You want to bring him back in?"

"Yeah. Let's see what he has to say."

At ten o'clock, she walked to the lobby. Lloyd Simpson sat in a chair along the wall.

"Mr. Simpson?" Carly said.

He rose and walked to meet her.

"Thanks for coming this morning," she said. "How about some coffee?"

"I don't drink coffee," he said.

She led him to her office. "Have a seat."

He sat and folded his hands in his lap. Carly leaned against her desk and flipped open a yellow legal pad. "Have you heard about Dennis Enger?"

Lloyd nodded. "Yeah. I read about it in the paper this morning."

"You two were friends, weren't you? I'm so sorry."

Lloyd stared at his hands. "We hung out at work sometimes." He shrugged. "He wasn't, like, a buddy or anything."

"But you hung out together?"

"Sometimes."

"Just at work or away from work too?"

Lloyd fidgeted on the chair. "Work, mostly."

Carly scribbled notes on the pad.

"I ran into him downtown a couple times." He coughed. "I was never at his house or anything." He rested his fingertips on the desk. "Not even sure where he lives—lived."

Carly crossed her arms. "You didn't see him last Friday?"

"Just at work." He sat up straighter. "After work, I gassed up, bought a sandwich, and drove around for a while, but I was home by about eight. Watched some TV and went to bed."

Carly studied his face. "I didn't ask you where you were after work."

Lloyd laughed nervously. "Sorry. Too many cop shows, I guess. All that stuff about alibis and—and stuff."

Carly picked up the notepad. "Well, as long as we're talking alibis, can anyone confirm that you were home most of Friday night?"

Lloyd nodded. "Yeah, my grandma. She'll tell you."

He leaned forward and looked across the desk. "You know, I understand you have to talk to a lot of people, and I don't mind coming in today. I hope you find out who killed Dennis. He wasn't my best friend, but I liked the guy." He paused and studied Carly's face. "But, am I—like—a suspect here?"

"No," Carly said. "We're trying to talk to anyone who knew him—who might give us information that could lead to his killer. It could tie in with the deaths at Foothills." She wrote on her notepad for a few seconds and then looked up at Lloyd.

"Do you own any guns, Mr. Simpson?"

Lloyd concentrated on his breathing. "A gun? No."

Carly continued. "But you do own a hunting knife, I understand. I wondered if you were a hunter or maybe collected weapons."

"A knife? Yeah, I bought one for protection." He quickly continued. "I live with my grandma. She gets scared someone will break in and hurt her."

"It's not here with you today, is it? The knife?" She smiled. "You're not allowed to bring weapons into the building."

Lloyd forced a tiny, tight smile. "No, ma'am. I leave it at home, mostly."

She asked him more questions about his work on the ward and some of the patients who died, but he showed no nervousness about those deaths.

Finally, Carly stood and moved around the table. "Well, thanks for coming in again, Lloyd."

Lloyd stood. "No problem."

Carly shook his hand and escorted him to the lobby. "I can't guarantee we won't be talking again, but I appreciate your cooperation. These things can get a bit drawn out sometimes. Anyway, thanks again." She reached up and placed her hand on his shoulder. "It must be hard, with the deaths on the ward and now Dennis's death. Don't worry. They'll find your friend's murderer."

Lloyd nodded and turned away.

Outside, he forced himself to saunter to his car. His heart beat in his chest like blows from a fist. He waited for a shout or the shrill blast of a police whistle behind him.

In the car, he sat quietly for several minutes, acutely aware of the revolver in its paper bag in the trunk and the knife in the glove compartment. He took a deep breath, started the car, and drove slowly out of the parking lot.

The kitchen was silent and empty. The creak of bedsprings drifted down the hall from his grandmother's room. He called out to her, but she didn't answer. In the basement, he collapsed on the bed. The fear eased, although his gut still knotted and burned.

The interview played in his mind. His answers and movements came across as relaxed and sincere, but maybe Carly Martinez could dig beneath that and see the terror he'd kept bottled up. Perhaps they'd found something at the farmhouse that would inevitably lead to him. Maybe tire tracks or the empty beer can. Had he touched it? He couldn't remember. Maybe fingerprints on the bucket. Or footprints in the dust of the basement. There was no way to know.

Carly's comments about the knife had almost thrown him into a panic. It was easy to figure out who gave her that information.

Chapter Thirty-Five

"C'mon, Virgil, time to get out."

He's told me that three times now, but I want to stay under the warm water longer. The
spray smacks at the back of my head with pleasant pressure. The stream splits and waterfalls past my ears. It's loud, almost like standing under an actual waterfall. It's been a long time since I enjoyed anything quite this much. If I shut my eyes and listen to the water, it blocks out everything else.

The spray cools, and the helper reaches in and cranks the faucet handle to stop the flow. The water cascades out across my belly and swirls down the drain between my feet.

The helper hands me a towel and uses another to rub my head. I slap his hand away, but he clucks at me and keeps rubbing. Water drips off my legs onto the cold tile.

"You could help here," he says. I ignore him. I'm listening to the racket of the ward outside the door. It's never bothered me, but lately, it's been as annoying as a car alarm.

He hunkers down and holds my underwear. When I step into them, the helper shimmies them up my legs so hard I have to reach out and steady myself on his shoulder. He looks up and smiles at me. I try to smile back, but I don't know if my lips make a smile anymore.

In the dayroom, the clamor is even louder than usual. Ten or eleven conversations are going on at once. Are there more people here than usual, or is it just my imagination? My clean sweatpants rub against my thighs with a soft, swishing sound. When I sweep my tongue across my teeth, it releases the sweet taste of toothpaste.

It all crushes down on me—like a physical blow- the voices, the movement, and the din.

My eyes squeeze shut for a few seconds. When I open them, I'm standing by the big picture windows. Grass stretches down to a lake that backs up against brown ridges that break like waves against the blue mountains. In the distance, I see a few snowy peaks. More than anything, I want to break the glass, cross the green lawn, swim the lake, run up those hills, and disappear over the horizon.

I could've done that in the past, but now my gut and my pale, flabby thighs would make it a hard go. The walk to my room is a little easier than that run up the mountain would be.

With the door closed, the noise from outside muffles down. Even lowering my butt onto the bed sends a jolt of pain down my back—another reminder of the Mexican. The piss smell and his hair tonic and watching his head bounce off the beige-colored floor come rushing back. My shoulders tremble when I conjure up the sound of bone against tile.

The door opens, and a helper comes in. "Let's go, Virgil. Party in the dayroom." He leads me down the hall. The television is off. Oh, blessed day. Red, white, and blue balloons rise up above the wheelchair people lining the walls of the room. A few look up at the balloons with perplexed expressions, but most are slumped forward or arched back in their chairs with their eyes closed.

The tables are set with paper plates and little flags. The table people cluster in silence, many with vacant smiles. A lady bangs out a song on the piano in the corner while helpers move among the table people, shoveling squares of cake onto plates. The piano lady sings about a flag, and some of the helpers sing along. Their smiles are as set as concrete while their eyes watch the table people to see if anyone is singing along.

Doctor K and the cute nurse come in from the nursing station. A helper pours them some juice and hands them each a plate of cake. They stand by the piano and scan the crowd. Doctor K catches me watching him and smiles and nods like we're two colleagues meeting at a convention.

I turn away and find a chair near an empty table by the window. Heat rises from my chest and into my face, and I flush with shame. The smiles of the helpers mock the table people, who don't seem to be aware of their own bewilderment. The wheelchair people doze on beneath the bright balloons. It's all so sad.

The skinny girl brings me a piece of cake and a plastic cup of apple juice. The juice is the same color as the piss under the Mexican's head. I leave the food and the juice sitting on the table.

The melted lady sits to my right. I concentrate on her to block out the singing and the horror around me. She sprawls in her wheelchair like a fat, half-burned candle. Her hair hangs down to her wattled jaw. Someone has slashed a straight line of crimson lipstick across her thin mouth. Her body slumps like it's melted and flowed down into the chair. Only her arms, perched on top of the armrests, keep her from dripping down out of the seat into a puddle on the floor.

She's none too pleased with what's going on here, either. Even over here, I see the sparks of anguish in her black, disapproving eyes. A helper sets a cake plate on the tray for the melted lady, who bypasses the plastic spoon, scoops up the whole piece, and shoves it in her mouth. A hand reaches out to stop her, but the melted lady moves her red mouth around a couple of times, and the whole wad is gone in one gulp. She coughs some and then glares at the helper.

I disregard the piss color, drink my cup of juice, and pick up the cake with my fingers. The icing is a dark blue, like the mountains outside. It's layered thick over the white cake. I try a nibble, but the sweetness clings to my tongue and the roof of my mouth like a waxy coating. The rest of the cake goes into my empty cup. Two more plates sit untouched on the table. I slide the paper plates over, dump their cake into my cup, and squish it all with my fingers.

The singing finally winds down. The piano lady does a final solo and then gets up to help clean frosting off faces and hands. Doctor K and the cute nurse, and a couple of the other doctors wander around the room for a few minutes, talking to some of the table people, and then leave. Someone turns on the television and starts lining up the wheelchair people in neat windrows.

Some of the table people sit for a while; others drift off to their rooms. Helpers clear away the plates and cups and the little flags.

The skinny girl flicks the brake levers on the melted lady's wheelchair and starts to push her out of the dayroom. The melted lady glares at the girl and then gives me one more sharp stare for good measure. While she passes, I get a better look down into her eyes and find the fire I thought I'd seen before.

Nobody notices me carry the cup out the door. The skinny girl emerges from the melted lady's room and returns to the dayroom.

The melted lady sits in the middle of the tile floor in her room. The skinny girl has plunked her down on a little plastic toilet they sometimes use. It has a metal frame and a big white pot hanging underneath. She's belted in with a strap across her belly, and her pants pooled around her ankles like they melted off and ran down her thick, blue-veined legs. Her fat thighs spill over the sides of the toilet seat.

She spots me and drills in with those flinty eyes. Heat pours out of them. No wonder she's melting. When I get near, she squirms in the chair, but the seatbelt holds her in. Her eyes follow me, and her gash of a mouth opens. No sound comes out.

The cake comes out of the cup as a solid wad. I crook my arm around her head and use my hand to pull her jaw down. My other hand pushes the lump of cake and frosting into her mouth. Her gums slide smooth and toothless along my thumb. I use my fingers to cram the cake in further. It fills her mouth clear up until her cheeks puff out.

She works to swallow, moving her jaw and neck around the wad. Her chest heaves, and she bends forward and tries to cough it up. I hold the cake until it's clear it won't fall out. Her eyes water, but she manages to look up at me with one more stare of contempt.

She claws at the mass of cake with her hand. Some of the wet, blue frosting falls out onto her blouse. She gives one big, convulsive cough, and the wad plops out and rolls into her naked lap.

I back up to the door and watch her take deep breaths. Her eyes bore into me, hateful and accusing. The skinny girl appears behind me in the doorway. She looks at the melted lady and then at me.

"Virgil! What are you doing?"

She runs over and slaps the melted lady on the back, but there's no more cake to cough up. She turns and yells, "Staff!"

The sound of running fills the hall, and several helpers and Doctor K come through the door. Somebody pushes me out into the hall, but not before Doctor K sees the cup and the blue frosting on my hands.

I go back to my room and wash the cake off. A nap in my chair by the nursing station would be better than anything, but I can't make myself go back down the hall. Doctor K knows, and probably the rest of them know too. Better to lie on my bed and let whatever is going to happen just go ahead and happen.

My whole body shakes, even when I turn on my side and draw my legs against my belly. Right now, I feel like Mia's old goldfish. A good whack with an axe doesn't sound bad at all. My life is so strange. So sad.

Doctor K comes in and sits on the edge of the bed. He pats my hip and asks if I was trying to feed Betty the cake. I know he means the melted lady. I didn't know her name is Betty. When I close my eyes, tears roll across my face. I'm sure I've never cried before—in this place. The tears burn like they were cooked way down deep inside my head.

Chapter Thirty-Six

Kester stood next to Clare, watching the crowd. Attendance at ward parties wasn't mandatory, but if he showed up, he got fewer accusatory stares from the Recreational Therapy staff.

Nell Rogers looked over from the piano bench and smiled when he and Clare entered the dayroom. Nell turned and checked to see who showed up. Her hands hit the keys with gusto. Kester leaned against the wall, his arms crossed and an insincere, rictus grin on his face. Most of the patients sat unheeding or stared at the walls. A few sat with smiles and closed eyes, maybe remembering other places and other music.

Kester gritted his teeth and smiled. *God, how I hate this.*

Somebody handed him a piece of cake and some juice. "Happy Almost-Fourth of July, Doc," the aide said.

Virgil Washington stood across the room, watching him. Kester nodded. Virgil bent his head a fraction of an inch downward in acknowledgment. His face flushed crimson.

Clare's touch interrupted Kester's thoughts. He turned back to her.

"Having your usual wonderful time?" she said.

His tight smile relaxed, and he leaned and whispered in her ear. "These parties always make me want to find something else to do with my life."

Clare punched him lightly on the shoulder and grinned. "Quit it, Kes. Eat your cake."

He mingled with the staff and patients for a few minutes and then returned to the nursing station as soon as he could.

Mikayla's call for help echoed across the ward.

Kester sprinted down the hall and into Betty Woodrow's room. Mikayla wiped at Betty's face with a towel, smearing blue frosting and red lipstick across the old woman's mouth and chin. Betty pushed the towel away with her blue-tinged hand and coughed. More blue frosting sprayed out of her mouth and onto her blouse.

The aide who'd entered the room in front of Kester turned Virgil Washington toward the door and pushed on his back to move him along. A plastic cup dangled from Virgil's frosting-smeared fingers.

Kester stood next to Mikayla. "What the hell?"

Mikayla wiped cake and frosting from Betty's lap. "She was choking on a big lump of cake."

Betty coughed again and squinted her watering eyes at Kester.

Mikayla bent and wiped one last crumb from Betty's lip. "She seems okay now,"

Kester put his stethoscope against Betty's chest. "Clear breath sounds. I don't think she aspirated any of it," he said. Betty grunted with disgust.

Kester picked up the wad of cake. "Holy shit, Mikayla, no wonder she was choking."

Mikayla looked toward the door. "I don't know if Betty snuck it out of the dayroom or Virgil brought it to her." She used the towel to pluck the cake from Kester's hand.

Kester finished his examination while Betty glowered and coughed. "Well, she seems fine now. Let me know if she has any fever or trouble breathing."

"Okay, Doc," Mikayla said.

Kester walked to Virgil's room and peeked through the doorway. Bare walls, no pictures. No mementos sat atop the dark, veneered dresser. Personal items tended to disappear, carried off by other patients or mislaid by staff until the rooms wore down to the bare essentials.

Virgil filled the single bed, crying silently.

Kester sat on the edge of the mattress and patted Virgil's hip. "You okay, buddy?" He ran his hand along Virgil's massive thigh. "If you're worried about Betty, she's fine. No harm done."

Virgil opened his eyes and turned his head toward the doctor. He sniffed and wiped at the corner of his eye. An overwhelming sadness washed over Kester until his own eyes blurred with tears. He looked around the bleak room.

Kester wiped his eyes. "Pretty goddamn pathetic, isn't it, buddy?"

The men sat silently, like two old friends about to part after a final visit.

Kester gave Virgil's leg one last pat and tried to stand The mattress sat low to the floor, and he had to reach down and grab the bed frame to push himself upright. His fingers closed against a sharp, rough edge of metal.

"Damn!" He jerked his hand away and checked to see if he'd sliced his fingers.

Virgil closed his eyes and turned toward the wall.

That evening, Kester sat on his patio as Clare moved the sprinkler in the backyard. She dodged the spray and skipped back across the grass. Back on the patio, she picked up Kester's wineglass and drank.

"There." She plopped onto his lap and shook her head. "You don't have a green thumb at all, do you?" She looked out across the shadowed yard. "I think you might need a gardener for this place."

Kester brushed a wisp of blonde hair away from her eyes. "You looking for a permanent position, ma'am?"

She sipped the wine and arched her eyebrows in mock seriousness. "Maybe. Any fringe benefits go with the position?"

"Well, you get all the wine you can drink. Plus, you get to sleep with the homeowner."

Clare laughed. "Deal."

The evening sky darkened. Only a faint light glowed across the top of the mountains to the west.

She leaned back against his shoulder and nuzzled her head into the hollow of his neck. "You're kind of distracted tonight," she said. "Is the wine getting you all maudlin?" Her voice grew serious. "Or are you worried about Lloyd?"

He kissed the top of her head. "No, we've done everything we can about him for now. The Sheriff's Office said they're looking into it."

Clare shivered against his chest. He stroked her hair. "And if that little worm ever tries to back up his tough words, it'll give me an excuse to break my Hippocratic Oath about doing no harm."

Clare laughed. "Okay, my noble protector, what horrible thing has you staring out at the yard like you're a million miles away?"

Kester's smile disappeared. The muscles across his shoulders tense. She pivoted from his lap onto the seat of the chair beside him.

"I'm thinking about how difficult it's turning out to be—figuring out the murders." He stood and paced the flagstone patio, his hands buried in the pockets of his cargo shorts.

"What I mean is, did we waste our time trying to tie all this stuff together?" He spread his hands apart. "Hell, we know Lloyd Simpson is a monumental jerk, but is he a killer? Probably not. We're sort of jumping to a lot of conclusions here."

Clare tucked her legs onto the chair as he walked back and forth. "You know," she said, "one of the things I keep coming back to—he wasn't even at work when some of those deaths happened." She hugged her arms to her chest. The evening light faded.

Now Kester was only a silhouette moving against the sky. "The deaths all happened at different times—even different shifts sometimes. Who's on the ward all the time like that?"

The dim light hid Kester's troubled face.

Chapter Thirty-Seven

Maybe the pain that hit my head knocked out all my doubt. Doubt must be the curse of a stable mind, and my mind got scrambled. Now it feels like it's unscrambling.

The melted lady must've been what started it. I was so sure about her. I saw the fire right there in her eyes. Maybe doubt wouldn't be gnawing at me if the cake had stayed put and the light in her eyes had dimmed and finally faded out. But she clawed that cake out and sucked in air as if living was still the best thing in the universe. That was a surprise.

The skinny girl and another helper snap the blanket and settle it on the grass. The skinny girl kneels and smooths the blanket, and pats the ground. "Sit down, Virgil."

I squat and fall back cross-legged along one edge of the blanket. The vet limps over and uses his left arm to steady himself as he lowers his butt onto the other end of the blanket. His right sleeve flaps empty in the breeze off the lake. He wheezes and coughs after the walk from the dayroom.

The skinny girl pours lemonade into a cup and passes it to me. It's a lovely day out here, but I'd rather be inside. The last thing I need right now is a bunch of distractions. My memory gets better every day as if I'm finally dialing in the right frequency on a radio.

I used to smoke back before the pain. One time I quit for a while, and when I took that next drag six months later, it hit the back of my throat like scalding soup. That's how I feel right now, with all the confusion and uncertainty.

The skinny girl hands me a little plate of potato chips, but I'm not hungry. I set it on the blanket and ponder the vet. He's still wheezing away, swaying a bit as if the breeze might knock him over. I don't know why his right arm is gone. He wears a cap with USS something-or-other sewed on the front, so I guess he was in the Navy and maybe lost his arm in a war. So I call him the vet.

One of his eyes is gone too, but the one that's left flits around twice as fast to make up the difference. He never screams or moans or does much of anything except what the helpers tell him to do. But he's one of the horses, for sure. Maybe even the head stallion among the herd on the ward. I looked down into his one good eye earlier, and the fire almost seared my vision away.   Maybe I should help him. Or perhaps he's like the melted lady and dead set on staying around until the bitter end, come hell or high water.

"C'mon, Virgil." The skinny girl grabs my hand and helps me up. She laughs and pulls me down the hill toward the lake.

Anger brakes me to a stop. I pull away and run, veering off to the side. The slope speeds me up until my breath grunts out every time my foot hits the grass.

The skinny girl heads me off, grabbing at my waistband. I turn and slash at her arm with the side of my hand, breaking her grip. Two other helpers bound down the hill and slam into me, sending us sprawling down the slope.

The two helpers stand, but one bends down and pushes his hand into my back. His breath huffs out. "Lay still, Virgil."

But I'm too winded to fight them and too ashamed. The skinny girl stands to the side, rubbing her arm where I hit it. The fear in her eyes makes my face burn with self-loathing. She hangs back when they hustle me inside.

I sit by the nursing station while the skinny girl tells the chubby nurse about my run. They both peek over and frown their disapproval at me. The skinny girl rubs her arm again, and the shame climbs up in my brain and spins like crazy.

Dickweed slithers down the hall and slaps me on the shoulder. "Shower time, Running Deer." He chortles and pulls me up and across to the washroom. "Let's get that grass stain off your face."

He sets the water slightly on the cold side, but I don't care. The washcloth stings against my cheek, but I ignore that too. Dickweed tosses the washcloth onto the tiled floor and crosses his arms. He gets an evil grin on his face and leans in close.

"Too bad they don't let me bring my gun to work. I could've popped a couple of slugs into you and ended your troubles, you poor, dumb motherfucker." His eyes flick to the door, and he edges in even closer. "Just like I did that dumb shit, Dennis."

I let the water cascade around my ears to block out his voice, but I hear him anyway. He twists the handles shut and throws me a towel. "Dry off, Marathon Man." The clean sweat suit sticks to my skin.

I know who Dennis is. They have a big poster on the wall in the day room, with a picture of the mountain man. It says, "Have you seen Dennis Enger?" I call him the mountain man because of his bushy beard, which makes him look like he's been living up in the hills for too long. And now dickweed says he popped a couple of slugs into him.

The helpers edge around me in the hall, keeping their distance. I guess they've heard about my run. The entire thing still puzzles me, too. The skinny girl's always been nice to me, but for some reason, I needed to run down that grassy slope, climb the hills, and disappear.

The whole situation has me frazzled. And now this thing with dickweed and the mountain man. I shuffle into the dayroom and sit at the table where I first looked down inside gray guy and discovered the flames. There was no hesitation in my mind that day or with any of the others. At least not until the melted lady.

The run was exhilarating for a few seconds before the helpers tackled me. It started a lot of possibilities churning around in my head. Oh, but the world looks a million miles away, down that slope and across to those hills. I could've run for days and never even made it close to my old life.

I walk down the hall and switch on the bathroom light. Up close to the mirror, my face still shows some raw spots from dickweed's washcloth. I try to see down inside, but the dark, round dots at the center of each eye soak up the light and stay as black as ink. They should be blazing like torches, considering how I feel right now.

The vet hangs out on a couch about halfway down one of the halls. Most of the helpers and patients are in the dayroom, getting ready for lunch. But the vet still sits ramrod stiff in his usual place. His palsied arm twitches up to his lip every few seconds as if he's still having a smoke on the bridge of some battleship. He sweeps his one good eye around to survey the passing ocean. Like I said, he's not one to scream, moan, or make a fuss, but his flame burns beyond anything I've seen before.

I sidle up on his blind side and get an arm around his head under his chin. He scrunches his neck and brings that good eye to bear. His shaking hand steadies and grips my wrist to break the hold. A conflagration roars deep down in him, but he ignores it and pries at my wrist even harder.

A helper rounds the corner. His eyes bulge, and he turns to yell. "Staff!" People converge from both directions and move toward me. But I've already relaxed my arm and swung around, away from the vet. He gives out a wet cough and sucks in air.

Doctor K appears and looks on as one of the helpers pulls me away from the couch.

They put me in the seclusion room overnight—a place I'd never been before. Someone looks through a little window in the door every few minutes. I lose track of time, but at some point, Doctor K comes in and squats down next to my mat. He watches me for quite a while. I want to tell him about the fire and the horses and rocks and about my doubt and the guilt that feels like it might kill me.

Chapter Thirty-Eight

"So." Clare pulled the brush through her hair. The mirror reflected the anger on her face. Kester leaned against the bathroom door, his arms crossed.

"Uncle Nick calls and offers to sell you his cabin, and just like that—" she waved the brush in a tight circle—" you decide to leave Fort Collins and the hospital and move to Steamboat?" She turned, her eyes flashing. "What about this?" She swept the brush around in a half-circle at the clutter of his possessions intermingled with hers. "What about us?"

Kester glanced around the bathroom. "It's just stuff, Clare." He stepped closer and caressed her shoulder. "Come with me."

She put the brush on the counter and looked up at him. A tear filled the corner of her eye. Her hand rose to wipe it away as she returned to the mirror.

"Come with me," he said again. His arm encircled her shoulders, but she pulled away.

Anger flashed once more in her eyes. She pointed to the hairbrush. "What is it with you, Kes? Why can't you be happy?"

He cocked his head back, looked at the ceiling, and then back at Clare. His hand gripped hers. "Because I don't want to be there anymore."

"Where? The hospital? Why?" "Just because." She sniffed "That's not a reason."

He thrust his hands into his pockets and lowered his head. "Screw this." He turned and started out the door.

"Kes, where are you going?"

"To work. I'll drive myself."

Kester slumped low in his chair during morning rounds, only half aware of the discussion. His stomach clenched. He wanted to stand and walk out of the conference room, through the ward door, and away from the hospital. Nathan and the others cast furtive glances his way and directed their conversations away from his end of the table.

After report, Kester retreated to his office. He shuffled through the papers on his desk but then spent two hours swiveling from side to side in his chair, staring at the wall.

Jen called late in the morning and asked him to come check on a patient.

He'd finished his examination when the urgent call of the aide echoed down the hall.

When Kester rounded the corner, Ernie Benito was still sprawled on the couch, coughing and sputtering. Virgil

Washington stood alongside. Virgil spied the doctor and shuffled from foot to foot.

Later, Virgil lay on a mat in the seclusion room, his legs curled under him and his head cradled on his arm.

Kester squatted beside the mat, resting his elbows on his thighs. He frowned, tight-lipped. His chin rested in the notch between his thumb and index finger as he studied his patient. Virgil cleared his throat. His lips moved as if he might suddenly offer an explanation for his behavior.

Only a moan, soft and plaintive, came from his throat. His eyes, wide and white, flicked back and forth from Kester to the red plastic mat beneath his head.

Kester stood and walked out of the room.

Lloyd Simpson and two other aides stood outside the door. They stepped aside for him, then one of them closed the door, locked it, and then looked through the tiny window at Virgil.

Lloyd sneered at Kester. "Too bad that big, fat fucker couldn't run faster this morning, huh?" He grinned at the other aides. "He could've been halfway home by now." He shook his head, and his lips curled up in contempt. "What a moron."

Kester stopped and turned. The other two aides shuffled their feet and looked away.

"What did you say?" Kester moved toward Lloyd until they stood toe to toe.

Lloyd's eyes drifted to the side toward his co-workers. Their frowns wiped the grin from his lips. He started to back away.

Kester rested his hands on his hips and studied Lloyd's face briefly. His voice came out measured and low. "Why are you here, Lloyd?"

"Huh?"

"I mean, why do you work here—at the hospital?"

Lloyd swiveled his head to the side and then looked forward again. His lips struggled to

form words.

"It's obvious you hate these people." Kester pointed down the hall. "You treat 'em like shit." He shook his head. "I don't get it." He stuck his face even closer to Lloyd's. "Why would you do that?"

Lloyd's face flushed. His puffy lips compressed into a thin line. He started to say something, then looked at the floor.

Kester poked his index finger against the younger man's chest. "You're an ignorant, evil, malignant little dick, Simpson."

Lloyd's face burned red. His hands formed into fists.

Kester moved in until their noses almost touched. "You don't like that, Simpson? Kester whispered. " Well, do something about it, you worthless piece of shit." He turned away but swung back to mutter in Lloyd's ear. "But if you do, you'd better bring more than your fucking knife, boy."

Kester turned and stomped down the hall.

Chapter Thirty-Nine

Clare pressed the phone closer to her ear, struggling to hear through the music in the background. "Kes, where are you?"

His response came through slurred and jumbled. After a few seconds, his voice trailed off in a clatter of noise, and another voice came on the line.

"Is this Clare?

"Yes. Who's this?"

"This is Tim Fredricks. I'm a bouncer at the College Inn. Kes asked me to call you."

"What happened? Is he all right?"

"Yeah, but he really needs a ride."

"I'll be right there."

Kester slumped on the barstool. A huge, blond young man stood beside him, his arms crossed.

Clare hurried across the crowded bar.

The young man nodded. "You must be Clare." He turned and steadied the wobbling body. "I'm Tim."

Clare pressed her hands along both sides of Kester's face. "Are you okay, hon?"

Tim helped Kester stand. "He's pretty shit-faced." He laughed. "Old Kes here tried to start a fight with about half a fraternity, but we broke it up."

Kester's head hung, swaying. He looked up. "Oh, hi, sweetie."

Clare nodded to Tim. "I'll get him home. I appreciate your help." She ducked under Kester's right arm and steadied him through the late-afternoon crowd and out the door.

As she settled him into the car, Kester's head smacked against the backrest with a loose thud. She belted him in and hurried around to the driver's side. His head rolled to the side, staring at her with unfocused eyes. "Thanks a bunch, babe."

She yanked the wheel and spun out of the busy parking lot, driving in tight-lipped silence.

Kester's head rolled to the right as his eyes stared out at the passing scenery.

"They called me from work looking for you," Clare said. "They said you just took off."

Kester shrugged. "Yeah, pretty much."

Clare bit her lip and glanced over. Her forehead wrinkled. "What happened? What's going on with you, Kes?"

"Oh, you know," he said. His hand swayed above the dashboard. "Just wondering if I'll wind up trying to kill somebody again, and..."

Clare straightened, her knuckles white where she gripped the steering wheel.

"Oh yeah—I think I might've pissed off that Simpson guy, too." Kester shook his head from side to side. "Not a good idea. Probably get a knife stuck in me."

Clare turned into the driveway and helped him into the house. Kester wilted against her like a dead weight. She let him slip onto the couch as soon as they were inside. He muttered something incoherent and began to snore. An hour later, she found him curled into a ball, shivering. She covered him with a blanket, then sat and listened to his breathing.

The sound of the toilet flushing woke her. Kester shuffled out of the bathroom and sat at the kitchen table. His forehead fell against his open palms. She stood and moved into the circle of light.

He turned and squinted. "What time is it?"

Clare glanced at the clock above the stove. "Two thirty." She moved beside him and leaned his head on her hip.

He closed his eyes and groaned. "I'm so sorry."

Her hand moved to rub the hair above his ear. "It's okay."

The sound of crickets drifted through the open kitchen window. Kester's face drooped, pale, and swollen. Clare pulled out a chair and sat, studying his red-rimmed eyes. "You okay?"

He shook his head.

"What you said in the car," she murmured.

"I remember." He lifted his head and looked into her eyes. Finally, he patted her hand and stood. "Let me make some coffee, and I'll tell you a story."

Clare sat and listened to the crickets until Kester shuffled back and handed her a cup. He sat beside her and looked down at the table. At last, he cleared his throat and began. "Do you believe in that old saying— about a fate worse than death?"

She stopped with the cup halfway to her lips. "I—I don't know." She looked into his eyes. "Why?"

Kester smiled. "It's something my dad used to say." He sipped the coffee. "He always said life is the most fatal disease—nobody survives it."

Clare moved closer. She reached for his hand. "Was he afraid of a bad death—there at the end?"

"Yeah. He was one gutsy son of a bitch about most stuff"... Kester rocked the cup from side to side. "but it wore him away, there at the end."

He wiped a fist across his eyes and sniffed. "Anyway, he asked me for the pills when we were alone in the house one night." The curtains rustled above the sink in the cool morning air. "I'd never seen that kind of panic in the man—never in my whole life." More tears trickled down Kester's face. "So I got the pills. I know I got enough—I made sure it would do the job."

He rubbed his hands along his thighs, his gaze still locked on the wind-blown curtains.

Clare bent forward and wrapped her arms around her chest.

"But something went wrong. He took the pills and went to bed but threw them up. Mom just thought he was sick, but it was the pills."

Kester shuddered and closed his eyes tight. "Mom called me to come over and check on him. He was crying, and I'd never seen him do that."

Clare reached to stroke his arm. Kester took a deep breath. His hands rested motionless on his legs. "He never told Mom about the pills. Three days later, he shot himself."

Kester wiped the back of his hand under his nose and sipped the coffee. He smiled. "When I'd lose a wrestling match in high school or get less than a perfect score on a test, or something like that, he'd say, 'For Christ's sake, Kes, you'd think you'd suffered a fate worse than death. Get over it, son.'"

Kester stared into the dark living room. "You want to know what a fate worse than death is?" He sniffed. "It's when you want death, and something cheats you out of it."

He turned and grabbed Clare's hand, looking deep into her eyes. "On the ward—with all those broken, played-out people—I feel like I'm that something."

She stood and wrapped her arms around his head, pulling him against her chest.

Later, in bed, she leaned up on her elbow and whispered. "I'll go with you, Kes—to Steamboat—if that's where you need to be."

Chapter Forty

The left side of the narrow road across Spring Canyon Dam dropped off to the waters of Horsetooth Reservoir. To the right, jumbled rock sloped to the canyon below. It would be so easy. A quick steering wheel jerk to one side or the other would send the car sailing off into the lake's deep waters or rolling into the tangled brush and trees at the bottom of the canyon. Either—or.

Lloyd hesitated, then drove north across the dam. Dennis' murder weighed on him like a stone. He missed Dennis's friendship even though his friend's betrayal still cut like a knife.

The gun and the Buck knife possessed a power that flowed through his body as real as his blood. All of his senses told him it was true. So how could it have led to his utter humiliation at the hands of that son of a bitch Grayson? How could his reward be cowardice and shame? How had he been so betrayed?

North of the dam, he spotted a small picnic area. He parked, walked to where the hillside dropped away, and gazed out over the plains stretching to the east. Fort Collins and Foothills Hospital lay before him.

An occasional car passed by on the road, but the secluded picnic grounds were quiet and empty. He opened the car trunk, pulled out the paper bag, and sat on one of the picnic tables with his feet on the bench.

The heavy revolver still smelled of spent gunpowder. He pointed the muzzle at his face, careful to keep his index finger away from the trigger.

He remembered Dennis staring into the gun barrel the same way that night in the car. *Do you want to blow your fuckin' head off?* Lloyd edged his finger around the trigger guard and pushed the muzzle against his forehead.

The sound of tires on gravel forced its way through the rush of blood in Lloyd's head. He lowered the gun and looked up. A truck with a camper top pulled in next to his car, and a young man got out of the driver's side. He carried a backpack and a large thermos. A woman and a young girl walked around from the passenger side. The girl found a fallen pine log and walked along it, holding her arms out for balance.

The man smiled at Lloyd. He was halfway to the picnic tables when he spied the gun. His smile faded. He stopped and looked over at the woman and child.

The gun hung loose in Lloyd's right hand, and the barrel pointed toward the ground. He brought it up level and jerked it to the side. "Get the fuck out of here," Lloyd said.

The man nodded, his eyes wide as they tracked the barrel. "Yes, sir."

He backed up a couple of steps and turned toward the truck. "Come on," he called. The child glanced up, puzzled. The woman looked over at Lloyd. Her smile drew down into a tight, straight line across her face. She gathered up the girl and headed to the truck.

The truck spun in a cloud of dust and shot north down the road. The gun grew heavier in Lloyd's hand, like a pail filling with water. He laughed and jumped down off the picnic table.

At home, he worked with the waistband holster until he could tuck the gun low into the small of his back. It didn't bulge too much, and with a coat on, it wasn't noticeable. He strapped the Buck knife to his ankle, stood before the mirror in his room, and smiled at his reflection.

It struck him that his confrontation with the doctor was a test. The weapons strapped to his body had not betrayed him. They only waited to see if he deserved them. Dennis Enger was the first test. Now the gun and the knife called to him again, urging him to strike back against those who tried to make him weak with shame and self-loathing.

Rusty opened the door to the length of the security chain. He looked past Lloyd's head. "You alone?"

"Yeah."

"Where's your car?"

"It's a nice day. I walked."

Rusty unlatched the chain and opened the door. Lloyd moved inside and slid the backpack off his shoulder.

"That's the stuff?" Rusty asked, nodding at the pack.

"That's it."

"How'd you get so much?"

"I hit a drug store the other night."

"Fuck."

"Yeah. You call Hector?"

"He's on his way."

Rusty lit a cigarette and paced the squalid living room. "Shit, man, I can't believe it. This is going to make us some serious coin." He turned to Lloyd. "You're not going to try to screw me over this time, are you, man?"

"No." Lloyd moved close and put his hand on Rusty's shoulder. "Sorry about last time." He grinned. "This time, I'll give you what you deserve."

His hand darted forward with the knife, burying it in Rusty's stomach below the ribs. The force pushed Rusty back across the coffee table and onto the living room floor. He grunted and dropped his cigarette and rolled to his knees. Newspapers and trash rustled under him. He crawled toward the kitchen.

Lloyd cut him off. He grabbed Rusty's long ponytail, jerked his head backward, and whipped the blade beneath the narrow, frightened face and across the neck. Blood spurted onto the filthy carpet. A sound like percolating coffee started along the wound. Rusty struggled forward onto the scarred linoleum and collapsed.

Lloyd knelt beside the blood trail, breathing hard. Smoke drifted over from the scatter of papers around the coffee table. He crawled over, located the smoldering cigarette, and then tamped it out in an empty dish.

The body slid easily across the kitchen floor and down the basement stairs. The red trail on the carpet disappeared beneath the litter of newspapers and old clothes. He washed the blood from his arms in the kitchen sink and returned to the living room.

By the time the doorbell rang, his breathing had settled. Hector stood on the porch. He squinted at Lloyd and chuckled. "Well, if it isn't the fuckin' drug lord." He peered into the dark doorway. "Where's that tall vato?"

Lloyd looked out at the street and held the screen door open. "Come on in. Rusty's in the basement." He grinned. "I'll show you what I've got."

Clare squirmed when his hand slid along her hip. "Quit that." She slapped his arm. "Your brother will see."

Kester leaned against her and ruffled her hair. "But you're so sexy when you're sweating." She laughed and unwrapped another dish and set it on the counter. "Uh-huh."

He picked up the crumpled newspaper and tossed it into a large pile on the floor. "Is this the last of the kitchen stuff?"

"Yeah." She stood with her hands on her hips and looked at the stack of moving boxes. "Just the big stuff now."

Paddy came in from the patio and set another box on the counter. "I found this in the car. I think it's the last one." He sat at the table while Clare wrapped paper around a plate and place it on the stack on the counter.

"I don't know why you want to live in squalor with my little brother when you could be shacking up with me in my palatial digs at Ma's."

Kester picked up a ring of keys. "Yup, that's one palatial room you have." He turned to Clare. "We'll go gas up the truck and meet you at your apartment, okay?"

She nodded. Kester and Paddy left through the front door. Clare leaned against the counter and surveyed the dishes and other kitchenware stacks. So much to combine. But she'd have plenty of time to pare it down before the move to Steamboat later in the year.

Kester had already approached a small group practice in Craig, a town near Steamboat, about joining them. She could always find employment with her nursing skills. Kes dreaded his talk with Reggie about leaving, but that would come in time.

She picked up her keys and entered the bedroom to find her purse. The small slider door to a private balcony off the master bedroom stood open. She crossed the room to close it.

Movement at the corner of her vision made her hesitate, but the shadow had already swung around behind her. A blow to her back sent her forward onto the bed. A hand gripped her neck, forcing her face deep into the mattress. Hard, deep breathing huffed next to her ear.

She kicked out, connecting with rough fabric. Her foot slid off to the side, bringing a grunt of pain from her assailant. The pressure built against her neck, but she fought it, twisting her head to the side long enough to snatch a breath of air.

The sound of the front door opening and footsteps in the living room came down the hall. The hand on her neck loosened and froze for a moment.

"Forgot my wallet," Paddy's voice called out.

The hand lifted from her neck, and the mattress jostled as her assailant stood. Clare turned her head further to the side and screamed. A small table lamp on the dresser crashed to the floor. She raised her head in time to see her attacker jump over the railing and disappear. She screamed again.

Paddy appeared in the bedroom doorway as she rolled to her side. "What the hell?"

He started for the bed, but she pointed to the balcony. Paddy raced across the room, leaned over the railing, and scanned the backyard.

Kester appeared in the doorway. "What's the matter?"

Clare sat up on the edge of the bed and tried to stand. Her legs wobbled, forcing her to sit back down. "Someone—someone in the room."

Kester stooped, pulled her against him, and cupped his hand around her head. "Someone was in the room?"

She leaned forward and put her hands on her face. "Yeah." She sat back up. "I came in to get my keys, and someone pushed me from behind."

Kester held her at arm's length and checked her face. "You okay? Did he hurt you?"

"No, he just threw me down on the bed."

Paddy came in from the balcony. "No sign of him. I'll call the police." He rubbed Clare's head. "You okay, kiddo? Do you need an ambulance or anything?"

Clare shook her head. "No, I'm fine. Just let me catch my breath." Her cheeks flush, and sweat trickled down her forehead.

When the police officer arrived, she wasn't able to give him a description. He took a report and made a cursory survey of the room and the yard. "Probably a botched burglary," he said. "They'll do that—watch for situations where someone is moving, and then wait for the people to leave." He stood with his thumbs in his belt, sure of his appraisal. "He probably didn't expect to find the lady here." He nodded at Clare. "We'll keep an eye on the neighborhood and let you know if we hear anything."

The officer left, and Paddy took off soon afterward. "Call me if you need anything, you two. I'll just be a few blocks away,"

Kester brought a glass of wine and sat beside her on the porch swing, his arm around her waist. "You sure you're okay?" he said.

She nodded. "Fine." She sipped the wine. "He didn't really hurt me. Maybe it was just some guy looking to rob us." She shivered.

"You're thinking it might've been him, right?"

"I don't know. It's such a strange thing—feeling like someone might be hunting you. Not like in the movies" She leaned against him.

Kester took out his cell phone and looked up Simpson's Fort Collins phone listings. He remembered hearing that Lloyd lived with his grandmother somewhere nearby. He found a listing for Nora Simpson and dialed the number.

A smoke-harsh voice answered. "Hello?"

"Is this Ms. Simpson?"

"Yeah. What do you want?"

"Is Lloyd there?"

"He's still sleeping. What do you want?" Kester hung up.

Nora hung up the phone as her grandson climbed the stairs from the basement. "Who was that?"

"They didn't say." Lloyd limped to the kitchen table. Nora's hand trembled as she raised the cigarette to her lips. "He asked for you. I told him you were sleeping—like you said." Her husky voice wavered and cracked.

"Good," he said. "Thanks."

She scuttled down the hall and into her bedroom, closing the door.

Lloyd rubbed his thigh. The kick hadn't connected with much force, but it still throbbed.

He limped back to the basement. The gun and the knife hummed against his skin.

From the moment he'd pulled the gun away from his forehead at Horsetooth, he'd known his path lay in one narrow direction. Looking back, he remembered only years of helpless drift. If that were to end, it would end at a time of his choosing and at that place where he'd suffered his most recent and agonizing humiliation.

Chapter Forty-One

On Monday morning, Lloyd pulled into the covered parking lot at work. He was half an hour late for his shift, but he took his time adjusting the waistband holster and the revolver under his nylon jacket.

His eyes swiveled and checked the quiet parking lot before he propped his foot on the rear bumper and pulled his pant leg up above the knife sheath to adjust the Velcro straps.

Mike Flores appeared from behind a nearby car. He looked surprised when he spied Lloyd but smiled and waved. "Hey, buddy, did you oversleep too? His eyes locked on the exposed knife.

Lloyd yanked his pant leg down and slid his foot off the bumper as Mike walked toward him.

Mike stopped beside Lloyd's car and put his briefcase on the ground. "You carrying a knife to work?" He looked around the parking lot. "Man, don't be doing that. Why do you need that?" He smiled. "Especially with all the shit going down lately."

Lloyd stood silent and impassive.

Mike moved a step closer and held out his hand. "Don't be stupid, amigo. Give me the blade, and we'll avoid a lot of trouble." His voice was soft but commanding.

Lloyd leaned down and slid his pant leg up over the sheath. He stood with the knife in his right hand. Mike reached around and patted him on the back. The doctor smiled. "That's okay, buddy. We'll just keep this between us".

He touched the bulge in Lloyd's lower back and froze.

Lloyd pushed him away, opened the blade, and lunged forward, forcing Mike to backpedal. The briefcase tangled in Mike's feet, sending him sprawling to the concrete floor. He rolled to his stomach and pushed up to stand.

Lloyd kicked Mike's right knee. Mike somehow kept his footing and ran limping toward the exit. Blood ran down his dark hair. He looked back. Lloyd thrust the knife into Mike's right shoulder.

The blow sent Mike skidding along the rough concrete on his hands and knees, but he reached the retaining wall along the parking lot's perimeter and pulled himself upright. Lloyd crashed into his chest, forcing both men up and over the wall and into the shrubbery beyond.

Lloyd straddled Mike and buried the blade into the right side of his ribcage. Blood welled along the hilt and spread in a rapidly expanding circle. Mike grunted and flailed his arms.

Lloyd knelt and drew in great, rasping gulps of air.

Mike's eyes squinted closed, and his breathing grew labored. The circle of blood grew larger, bubbling and hissing and soaking the right side of his shirt.

Lloyd stood, panting. Mike's chest heaved with each breath. He glanced into the deserted parking lot, then vaulted back across the retaining wall and brushed the dirt and twigs from his pants. No sound came from the other side of the wall.

He wiped the blade clean on a piece of litter near his car. He slowed his breathing, slipped the knife back into the sheath, and tossed Mike's briefcase over the wall. The revolver still hung securely in the small of his back as he walked to C Ward.

Lloyd disappeared into the break room and emerged wearing his white coat. Clare steeled herself to confront him for being late, but his silent indifference stopped her. He didn't leer at her, smile, or even acknowledge her presence for once. His mouth hung open, and his cheeks were flushed as though he'd finished a run.

Lloyd walked into the dayroom and stopped to talk to Mikayla. She gestured out the window to where two aides led three patients down to the lake. Lloyd strode to the door and out to join them.

Kester opened the half-door to the nursing station and found Clare gazing out at the retreating fishing party. He picked up a stack of lab reports and gestured toward the window.

"He still giving you the creeps?"

She nodded. "Something's changed." She shook her head. "I don't know what, but something."

He squeezed her arm. "Don't worry, babe. It wasn't him. He was home, asleep at the time. I think he's all talk and no action."

"I hope so," she said. "You going to your office now?"

"Yeah. I'm checking something."

She turned away from the window and smiled at him. "Hey, give me your car keys. I left my lunch on the front seat."

He reached into his coat pocket and pulled out the keys. "Here." He touched her shoulder. It trembled beneath his hand. "You okay?"

Clare nodded. "Still a little jumpy after yesterday." She gripped his hand and smiled. "I'll be fine."

Kester squeezed her shoulder and turned toward the door. "Okay, babe." See you at lunch."

The shade in the covered parking lot felt good after the heat of the morning sun. Something struggled to come clear in her mind—something about Lloyd. His walk. He'd walked down the slope to the lake with an almost imperceptible limp.

Clare opened the car door and winced when it squealed. It echoed through the quiet parking lot.

A weak moan rose from the bushes along the retaining wall. She ran to the wall and stood on tiptoe to look over.

Mike Flores lay in a crush of evergreen bushes. Dried blood ringed his mouth. He rolled his head to the side and opened one eye.

Clare ran back to the parking lot and yelled. "Staff!" She jumped up, leveraged her body over the wall, and knelt beside Mike. His right hand held a plaster of bloody leaves and a scrap of paper against the right side of his chest.

He lifted his head and looked at the wad of leaves and paper. "Sucking chest wound," The cough that followed rattled in his chest, wet and deep. He grabbed Clare's arm with his left hand. His eyes squeezed shut with pain, but he forced them open and looked up. His jaw worked back and forth. "Lloyd. Knife. Gun, too."

Footsteps echoed across the concrete. She looked up. Gerry Walters and another nurse peered over the wall. Mike shook her arm. She turned back to him. He smiled, showing white teeth stained with blood. "Don't worry," he whispered. "The dumb bastard forgot to finish the job."

Clare checked his pulse. It beat strong along the side of his neck.

"Hang in there, Mikey," she said, keeping her voice quiet. She turned to the nurses, who were still climbing awkwardly over the wall. "Call 911 and get an ambulance rolling," she said. She stood and handed Gerry her cell phone. "Stay with him. I have to get Security."

She ran along the wall until she found a break in the shrubbery and sprinted toward the administration building.

Halfway there, she glanced to her left toward the lake. Abruptly, she turned down the hill and ran to the water.

Chapter Forty-Two

All night, he'd stared at the ceiling while Clare slept beside him. By morning rounds, his mind buzzed from lack of sleep. He listened to Nathan drone on about treatment plans and drug doses.

The ward had settled into its old routine as the excitement surrounding the murders drifted away with the departing journalists. Crystal Preston lived up to her billing as a public relations expert and managed to shelter most of the employees from the press. Most of the television vans rushed off to new stories, and the hospital staff stopped clustering in excited groups to talk about the latest developments. Martin Bridges appeared to have hunkered down in his committee and allowed the firestorm to pass. No other suspicious deaths came to light, or at least none that could be called a homicide.

"You okay with that?"

Kester looked up. Nathan squinted at him over his reading glasses.

"Huh?" Kester said.

"The med changes on Fred Waring. You okay with that?"

Kester nodded. The conversation around the conference room table returned to a background hum in his head until Nathan said, "Virgil Washington seems more animated lately. Finally making some progress, I think."

Kester sat up in his chair.

"How about it, Kes? We might be able to transfer him to a skilled nursing facility pretty soon?" Nathan said.

Katie Lattimer cleared her throat. "He does seem more attentive lately." She smiled. "I think there might be more of that big boy in there than we realized."

"Let me think about it," Kester said.

Later, he sorted through the stack of lab results in his office until he found the paperwork from the coroner's office. The autopsy results on Frank Gustafson listed the cause of death as traumatic penetrating brain injury with massive cerebral hemorrhage. A picture of the metal fragment recorded its length as eleven centimeters.

Kester took a ruler from his desk and returned to C Ward. In Virgil Washington's room, he knelt by the bed, pushed the mattress up, and propped it against the wall. The gray metal side rail ran smooth and straight along its length, except for one thin, jagged section. He held the ruler up along the jagged portion. Eleven centimeters.

He sat back on his heels and tapped the ruler against his knee while mentally reviewing the death charts he'd collected in Medical Records. Finally, he rose and strode from the room.

At the end of the dock, Virgil cast a line far out into the lake and slowly reeled it in. Two aides led a couple of the patients farther along the bank, looking for a new fishing spot. Lloyd leaned with his butt perched atop the dock railing. He looked out of place in his white lab coat.

Kester slowed as he got closer. Virgil turned and stopped reeling in the fishing line. Lloyd slid his butt off the railing and glared at the doctor. Kester ignored him. He stopped a few paces onto the dock and studied Virgil's face. Virgil hunched his shoulders and turned away, fidgeting with the fishing rod.

"Virgil?" Kester said. He kept his voice soft, afraid of what he might discover. "Did you do it? Did you kill Mr. Gustafson?"

The reel clicked as Virgil cranked the line in faster and faster.

Kester took a step forward. "And the others—did you kill them too?"

Virgil glanced at Kester with wild, frightened eyes and looked back at the lake.

Lloyd snickered.

Kester turned. "Shut up, Simpson."

The smile on Lloyd's face disappeared. He pushed off of the railing and stood. His hand glided along his hip as his cheeks flamed red with anger.

Someone called Kester's name, and he turned. Clare sprinted down the hill, waving her arms as she raced toward them. She opened her mouth and shouted something, but all he heard was "gun."

Kester turned back. Lloyd strained to reach something behind his back. His hand caught in the flapping coat, slowing him. He finally managed to get his arm under the hem.

Kester sprang forward when Lloyd's hand reappeared from under the coat. The gun barrel swung around to point forward as the two men collided.

Lloyd smashed the barrel against the side of Kester's head, but the force of their collision loosened his grip. The gun arched through the air and came to rest in the grass next to the dock.

Clare skidded to a halt, bent almost double and gasping for air. She knelt and picked up the revolver, clutching the grip with both hands.

Kester and Lloyd rolled together on the dock. Kester caught a glimpse of Clare, standing with her arms extended, pointing the gun toward the two men.

"Stop it!" she screamed.

Lloyd kicked his legs into Kester's stomach, forcing their bodies apart. His hand went to his right ankle. He snapped the blade open and rolled to face Kester.

"No!" Clare screamed. She leveled the gun at Lloyd and pulled the trigger. The barrel jerked skyward, sending the shot toward the distant foothills.

Lloyd rose into a crouch and scuttled backward a couple of feet. Kester knelt on the dock, shaking his head from side to side to clear it. His eyes concentrated on the blade.

Lloyd raised his arm and moved forward. A shadow blocked the sun. Lloyd turned his face upward to where Virgil loomed over him. The big man scooped him up like an infant and lumbered down the dock.

Chapter Forty-Three

Dickweed squirms in my arms. I can't see his eyes, but I imagine they are wide with surprise. I hoist him up and across my shoulder and settle him there like a bale of hay, steadying him with my arm.

He's poking me with the knife, jabbing it into the muscle in my back. It hurts, but it doesn't matter. The end of the dock is coming up fast, so I look up at the mountains and the blue sky one last time.

We bellyflop into the water, and dickweed almost squirts away from me. The water closes over our heads. The knife blade flashes as it twirls down and out of the sunlight. I curl my arm around dickweed's waist and kick for the bottom.

Calling him dickweed strikes me as a little cruel under the circumstances. I know his name is Lloyd. Lloyd Simpson. He's probably about the same age as my Josh. Just a kid.

One more kick, and I find the bottom. The light's dim here, but I root around in the mud until I find a tangle of old cable.

I hold Lloyd with one arm and wrap the other around some of the wire, anchoring us there.

Lloyd thrashes and squirms, but the strength has gone out of him. Soon, he's settled in my arms, like Mia used to do. It's sad, him being so young. But it's time for both of us to leave. There's nothing for either of us here anymore.

He shudders and goes limp. His face is a ghostly white mask in the murky water. I can't see deep down into his eyes, but I know he's done suffering.

A splash, muffled and distant, sounds through the water. A desperate attempt to save us, no doubt. But, of course, there will be no salvation.

My own vision dims. I open my mouth and suck in the cooling waters. Tiny glitters of light swirl around us like a windstorm until we're both spinning in a shower of sparks up to the sunlight on the water's surface. We spin—faster and faster—whirling up out of the lake, and above the foothills, and across the mountains.

Chapter Forty-Four

Kester pulled the plastic bag containing his uncle's ashes from the heavy decorative urn and undid the twist tie. Clair stood nearby, her hands in the pockets of her heavy coat. The wind along the river stirred her hair as she watched Kester lift the bag and shake the ashes onto the snow along the bank.

Clair sniffed in the cold air, pulled one hand from its warm pocket, and wiped it across her nose. "He would've liked the spot you chose, Kes," she said.

Mike Flores watched the ashes whirl away in the wind and settle onto the river's surface. He nodded. "Yeah, it's not a bad place to wind up."

Kester shook the last ashes onto the snow and stuffed the empty bag into the urn. His head bent forward, and he closed his eyes, his lips moving in a brief prayer. Then he stepped back, stood beside Clair, and put his arm around her. His eyes scanned the clouds moving in from the west. "More snow coming tonight." He looked down at the scattered ashes on the snow. "By morning, you won't even be able to see them."

Back at the cabin, Huck ambled from the porch and nuzzled against Clair's leg.

Mike smiled and reached down to pet the dog's head. "Well, he sure seems to have found a new master."

Clair laughed and scratched Huck behind the ear. "Since we moved in, he's decided he has to sleep on my feet every night."

After dinner, the three friends sat by the fireplace and shared a bottle of wine. Kester watched the snow swirl outside, then turned to Mike. "You think you're ready for the slopes tomorrow?"

Mike patted his ribs where Lloyd had stabbed him. "It still gives me a little jolt now and then, but I think I can keep up." He smiled. "If Liz weren't at her sister's, she'd be here telling me to stay on the bunny slope."

Clair laughed. "If you're expecting my husband to show you any mercy out on the mountain tomorrow, you don't know him as well as you think you do, Mikey."

Mike rolled his eyes and frowned. "That old guy? I'll probably have to stop and wait for him every few minutes."

Kester picked up a pillow from the couch and threw it at his friend. "Hell, Mikey, you couldn't keep up with me back in high school."

They all laughed, then Clair grew serious. "You sure you're okay, Mike?"

Mike touched his ribs again. "Yeah. But it's a good thing that maniac didn't know his anatomy. A couple of inches to the right, and you'd be throwing *my* ashes out on the snow."

The mood turned serious as the three thought back to the events at the hospital on the day Virgil Washington dragged Lloyd to the bottom of the lake and saved Kester's life. They sat in silence, sipping their wine and staring into the fire.

Finally, Kester broke the tension. "So, how are things at the hospital now? Is Reggie still fighting off the bureaucrats in Denver?"

"Naw," Mike said. "But I think that bottle of tequila he keeps in his desk is about due for a refill." He set his wine glass on the coffee table, poured it half full, and then sat back in his chair. "Old Reg hates to admit it, but he's damn good at unsnarling a mess."

Kester nodded. "Yeah. I know he hates the red tape, but he does have a knack for working things out."

"True," Mike said, "but he might be going to depositions for the next ten years. The lawyers for some of the victims' families are still circling like sharks."

Clair sipped her wine. "And how is Virgil's family doing?"

Mike shrugged. "I don't know. How do you wrap your head around your husband or father being both a hero and a villain?"

Clair shivered. "Those poor kids. Of course, they have to know that their father wasn't competent. He wasn't responsible like a normal person would be."

Kester sat and rocked in his chair, his wine glass twirling slowly in front of him. He stared into the fire, lost in thought. Finally, he looked up at Clair. "That may be true, dear, but I don't know."

Clair started to say something, but Kester continued. "I've made peace with the whole incident, but then look at how I did that. I just ran away to the mountains and left the problem for someone else to deal with." He looked over at Mike. "And I still wish you'd consider coming up and joining the practice, buddy. We need a guy with your skills."

Mike nodded. "I've been talking it over with Liz, and we may have an answer for you soon." He looked around the cabin. "Of course, I kind of like coming up and taking advantage of your hospitality."

They laughed, and then silence descended.

"Kes, why did you say you don't know? About Virgil and the competence thing Clair mentioned?"

Kester flushed red, then looked down at his wine glass. He stole a glance at Clair and smiled. "I promised my wife I wouldn't brood about all that stuff that happened, so I hope this doesn't sound like I'm doing that again."

Clair reached over and patted his knee. "No, you've been very good about it since we moved here, dear." She studied his face for a moment. "But I'm curious too. What did you mean?"

"Well, look," Kester said. "I know Virgil wasn't normal. But think about what strokes do. Extraordinary things sometimes.

I mean, Lloyd was just an evil guy, although we could probably get into a discussion about why he was the way he was. But Virgil wasn't a bad man. And I'm not sure you can just assume his stroke tore away all his humanity and exposed a bad man underneath."

Mike nodded. "Okay, I suppose that's a fair assessment. But you're saying Virgil's damaged brain somehow convinced him that he was doing something good when he killed all those people?"

Kester shook his head. "I don't know. But I keep thinking about something my brother told me last year—about people yearning for a second death, and there's nobody around who is willing to help them. I mean, really help them when they're suffering."

"Why isn't there anyone to help them?" Mike said. "Isn't that what we were trying to do there at the hospital?"

Kester smiled. "It depends on semantics, I suppose." He looked over at Mike. "Remember that talk we had at the College Inn when you told me all that stuff about euthanasia and all the different ideas people have about it?"

"Yeah. But that was after a few beers."

"Well, I thought you presented a damn good explanation of all the different ways folks try to come to grips with the problem."

"Okay, dear, but what are you getting at?" Clair said.

Kester swirled the wine in his glass, the light from the fireplace turning the liquid red as blood. "What if Virgil's stroke tore away all the doubt—all the uncertainty—all the hesitation and moralizing and—and the bullshit, and showed him only unadorned, true mercy?"

Clair looked on, frowning. Kester reached over and grabbed her hand, and smiled. "Never fear, my dear. It's just an academic topic for me now."

The light from the nursing station on C ward held back the darkness along the hallway. The night nurse lifted her head and listened to the wailing. The new patient they'd brought in earlier that day was at it again.

"Harold? Where are you, Harold?" the thin, quavering voice called into the darkness.

The nurse made a mental note to leave a message for the ward physician to check the patient's meds in the morning, then returned to her charting.

Afterword

In the early stages of my medical career, I held the belief that the paramount duty of a medical provider was to heal. Medicine is often said to deal with "the healing arts". When one begins the study of medicine, the healing part is about all the practitioner can get their head around. There is simply too much to learn and to practice. Too many skills to hone. It is an important first step in the journey toward competency in the profession. But it is only the first step, and only half of the world we have stepped into.

Later, usually after entirely too much exposure to it in all its terrible forms, we discover that suffering is the other half of that world. Even when healing is underway, the patient may experience profound suffering. Worse still, there may be no healing to be had. Then what is to be done?

As a society, we have wrestled with this question forever. It is a proper topic for discussion. But it is in the end an abstract discussion. Here is a less abstract situation.

When I was a child, my barber, George, was also my father's hunting buddy, and like a second father to me. George was a large, boisterous man, and loved life. After my medical training, I returned to my hometown and briefly took over the clinical practice of one of my childhood heroes—the physician who first ignited my interest in medicine.

One of my first patients in that clinic was my old friend George, who had developed a rhabdomyosarcoma, a rare and usually fatal tumor. After a couple of years of various treatments by the specialists, George had come to the end of the road as far as his tumor was concerned. He was dying, and suffering almost unendurable pain in his back. He was a tough man, but the pain could bring him to his knees unless hit with potent opioid pain medicine. There at the end, George was finally hospitalized for pain control and what would now be called hospice care.

The days passed and he required more and more pain medicine. The nurses on the ward grew alarmed and vocal about the dosages required, and they all but refused to give George the injections ordered in his chart. Every time I made rounds, I could see the sweat popping out on my friend's forehead as a visible sign of his suffering. He was within days of dying from his tumor, but the nurses would stop me in the hall and express their fear that the large doses of pain medicine might kill the patient, or worse, "get him addicted".

At first, I tried reasoning with the nurses. They were not bad people or unprofessional. They were for the most part very skilled and caring. In most cases, they'd be quite right to question my orders. But they weren't addressing George's suffering.

Finally, I decided to give George his pain shots myself. Every few hours I would return to the hospital and give him his next dose, under the watchful eye of his wife of fifty-seven years. Ellen had known me for most of my life, so maybe that is why she trusted me when I went rogue on her husband's treatment. I wrote an order in George's chart to "titrate pain meds to comfort", which meant giving George enough to make him quit writhing on the bed and sweating through the sheets when the waves of pain washed over him. By the end, he was receiving some truly impressive doses.

At no time was I actively trying to kill my friend. After the last dose I administered to him, he relaxed and slept through the night and finally died early the next morning. I don't remember any guilt or worry when he died. I was just glad he was no longer suffering. Only later did I start to think about the issue in a more abstract manner. Did I "do no harm" as the Hippocratic Oath says? I don't know. Maybe I gave him enough to ease him out a little ahead of schedule.

Later in my career, I spent several years on the medical staff of a large state hospital with several very active dementia wards. That experience and the questions it raised in my mind inspired me to begin working on the manuscript for *The Thief of Moments*. (Except I never had a patient who killed other patients.) As one would expect, such an environment lends itself to both a philosophical discussion of death and euthanasia and what is to be done with people at the end of life. There is plenty of actual physical and psychological suffering to be observed in such a setting too. I should also mention that the character Lloyd is hardly representative of the dedicated people who care for these very challenging patients.

I wish I possessed the wisdom to figure it all out, but even after pondering it for many years, I don't have the answer. It is my hope that in writing about Virgil and Kester and the rest of the characters in the story, I can stimulate a few readers to examine the issues more thoroughly.

TR Hull

About the Author

TR Hull grew up in northern Colorado and attended Colorado State University and the University of Colorado School of Medicine. He and his wife, Linda, live in Idaho. TR Hull is also the author of *Glad Tidings*, as well as *Elixir Six*. His fourth novel, *The Galileo Moon*, will be published in spring 2024.